A Day Like Any Other

Isla Dewar

First published in Great Britain in 2020 by Polygon,
an imprint of Birlinn Ltd.

Birlinn Ltd
West Newington House
10 Newington Road
Edinburgh
EH9 1QS

www.polygonbooks.co.uk

1

ISBN 978 1 84697 495 8

British Library Cataloguing in Publication Data
A catalogue record for this book is available on request
from the British Library

'A reali...   ...ery funny'
The Times

West Coast Review

ABOUT THE AUTHOR

Isla Dewar's first book, *Keeping Up with Magda*, was published in 1995. Dewar found success with her second novel, *Women Talking Dirty*, the film of which starred Helena Bonham Carter. She contributed to the collection *Scottish Girls about Town* and has also written for children. Isla's most recent novel, *It Takes One to Know One*, was published by Polygon in 2018. Born in Edinburgh, Isla lives in the Fife countryside with her husband, cartoonist Bob Dewar, and a bunch of pheasants outside her kitchen window.

To Ida, who is perfect and deserves a book.
But then, everyone deserves a book.

Two Ladies, One with a Stick

There they go, Anna and George. Two old ladies walking down the street. Nattering. Anna uses a stick, places it carefully to support her arthritic left hip. She wears black jeans, a blue T-shirt under an ankle-length black cardigan and a green silk scarf that hangs down past her waist. She has high-top trainers on her feet. Silver earrings dangle at her neck. She is serious.

George is in black velvet. Her boots are red, a dazzling shiny red. But sensibly flat (a sad thing for her: she has said goodbye to silly footwear and could weep to slip her feet into something strappy and sexy just one more time). Her lips are softly pink and she smiles a lot. A small pearl hangs on a silver chain round her neck.

Nobody looks at them. Nobody would guess at the lives they've had. Between them they've clocked up one hundred and thirty years, three abortions, one miscarriage, four children, ten lovers, four husbands (one gay), a hysterectomy, nine cats, six cars, too many winter coats to mention, wild nights, quiet television evenings, and enough wine to float a battleship. Anna has published three poetry pamphlets. George has held the hands of people slipping from life. They have both mopped up many tears, not always their own. They have known abandoned laughter. They have wept for dead parents and lovers and lost dreams. They have regrets and still nurture a few longings. George has a child gone from her. She weeps for him daily. Yet nobody gives them a second glance. They are just two old ladies walking down the street. One with a stick.

Tonto Was a Woman

They'd met, George and Anna, when they were nine years old. George's family had not long moved to a house four doors down from Anna's family home. Two days after arriving George took her beloved yellow bicycle out of the garage while her mother, a social worker, and father, a maths teacher, unpacked. She cycled to the end of the road, turned and cycled back. Three times she did this and on the third return journey she met Anna riding an identical yellow bike. They stopped. Stared at one another. For a sliver of a moment it could have gone either way – friends or enemies. They chose friends. Yellow bikes were all it took. In days they'd formed a gang. They called it the Two Yellows (it was a small gang) and it was dedicated to helping the poor and needy, world peace and the downfall of Dorothy Pringle, who lived in the next street, had blonde curly hair, pink socks, always did her homework and always got ten out of ten for the arithmetic.

Over fifty years later the Two Yellows were still talking, reminiscing, laughing, opining on the ways of the world and squirming with embarrassment at their youthful stupidity.

Anna envied George one thing – her name. It wasn't just that George was called George. She'd been named after a specific George – one of Enid Blyton's Famous Five. 'I want to be called after someone from a book,' Anna had said to her parents. They'd looked bewildered and shrugged. They weren't readers.

'Breck from *Kidnapped*. That would have been excellent.

Breck after Alan Breck, you know.' They didn't. 'Or Scout from *To Kill a Mockingbird*. You could have called me that.'

Well, they might have if they'd heard of the book, but they hadn't. Besides, they associated the word 'scout' with a boy's organisation and Baden-Powell and campfires and woggles. It didn't seem like an odd name for a girl, it seemed like an odd name for anybody. But then Anna was a difficult child. She questioned everything – the way her mother made soup, why she had to go to Sunday School, indeed why she had to go to school at all, the clothes they bought her, the food they ate. Sometimes they wondered if they'd been handed the wrong baby.

George envied Anna one thing – her fearlessness.

It was always Anna who led the pair in adventures and mischief. She organised their apple scrumping afternoons, encouraged their shoplifting trips to Woolworths, where they took pencils and sweets from the pick'n'mix. She brought cigarettes to their secret place behind her dad's garden shed. George was the one who smoothed troubled waters when they got into trouble. She stopped Anna eating too many stolen apples. 'Diarrhoea,' she warned. In time, she pointed out the dangers of smoking. She curtailed her cider intake so she could keep Anna upright and onto a night bus home. But sometimes she couldn't stop Anna overdoing things.

Anna wanted to be a poet, a vet, a nun (it wasn't a God thing, she briefly fancied she'd look cool in the outfit) or an actress. By the time she was fourteen the poet ambition was winning. She favoured rhyming verse. Her favourite words were 'whisper', 'chrysanthemum', 'joyous' and 'verdant'. She hadn't managed to put any of these in a poem. Her masterpiece to date was 'The Tonto Syndrome'. Tonto was her hero, a gentle misunderstood man. She felt the Lone Ranger was mean to him. He had the shiny white horse and the silver bullets and never shared. And at the end of every episode someone always asked, 'Who was that masked man?' Nobody wondered, 'Who was that mild-mannered trustworthy Indian fellow?' It just wasn't fair.

There was a poetry revival going on at the time. A few pubs hosted poetry happenings. Angry young poets would stand and shout their work to a drunken audience. Anna wanted to join in. 'Poetry should be shouted,' she said. 'People need to hear it.' She planned to go to a wild extravagant poetry pub night. George said they were fifteen, they wouldn't get in. Anna said they would, and 'We're not going to drink' (they were at their cider consumption peak and planned to indulge in serious swigging afterwards). 'We're just going to do a bit of poeming. Well, I am. You're my roadie. You carry the notebook.'

On the night, a Thursday, they plastered on Anna's mother's lipstick and mascara, slipped from the house and ran to the bus stop. Forty minutes later they were in the pub, a small one in the Grassmarket, feeling out of their depth. The thick smell of booze, the noise, the laughter, the people staring at them, the barman pointing to the door telling them to get out, it was all over-whelming. They were asked how old they were.

'Eighteen,' said Anna.

The barman snorted.

'We're not here to drink. I've come to read my poems,' Anna said.

The barman said, 'Out.'

'My poem,' said Anna, 'is about Tonto. It is about the sorrow of the Indians and women. Tonto, though you may not know it, was a woman.'

And the barman said, 'Out.'

'I am going to read my poem. I won't touch alcohol.'

The barman said, 'Out.'

George cringed. She wanted this to be over. She wanted to go home. It was early, six-thirty, the pub was fairly empty, but the few people who were there stared.

Anna had perused every person present and decided there wasn't a single poet among them. She imagined poets to have long hair and beards (if male) and to wear tight jeans or baggy corduroy pants. Old poets would be bald and have rimless glasses. She decided that if there were no poets here, the people watching must be poetry lovers. They would hear her poem.

'My work is about Tonto, a man who suffered as women suffer. He was servile. The Lone Ranger wasn't very nice to him.'

The barman said, 'Out.'

It occurred to George that she and Anna did not look like eighteen-year-olds. They looked like fifteen-year-olds who had slapped on too much make-up so they'd look older. Suspecting the thick make-up made them look like clowns, she backed towards the door.

The barman came out from behind the counter, strode across the room, opened the door and pointed to the street. 'Out.'

Anna took the notebook from George and waved it in the air. 'You will be sorry. One day you will blush to recall you denied the world the first hearing of my poem, "The Tonto Syndrome".'

The students in the corner cheered. The old man at the bar supped his beer and stared.

And the barman said, 'Out.'

Back in the street, heading for the bus stop, Anna said, 'Philistine. The man is a philistine.'

George wasn't so sure. She felt overly made up and foolish. In fact she wasn't keen on poetry. She'd spent too many wearisome hours learning 'View from Westminster Bridge' by heart. She worried Anna would become a famous poet and children in generations to come would have to labour over 'The Tonto Syndrome'. But probably not.

They went upstairs on the bus hoping their favourite seats at the front would be available. They were. The bus was quite crowded. The two battered up the aisle and sat down.

'I should have been allowed to read my poem. I'm a poet,' said Anna.

George agreed. 'Poetry belongs to the people.'

Anna gripped her arm. 'You're right. It does. People deserve to hear poetry. All sorts of people.'

'Yeah,' said George. 'Rich people, poor people, professors and that, authors, plumbers and ordinary people like the people on this bus. Poetry needs an audience.'

Anna turned and considered her fellow passengers. They were mostly silent, gazing ahead or staring out of the window at the passing world. 'These people here could do with a poem. They are here and they look bored. A captive audience for me to entertain.' She took the notebook from George and turned to face the crowd.

'Good evening. I am Anna MacLean and I'm a poet. Thank you for coming this evening. I'm going to read you my latest work. "The Tonto Syndrome".'

Silence. Passengers exchanged looks. The atmosphere was of bewilderment. Someone said, 'Huh?'

'I believe Tonto was mistreated by the Lone Ranger. He was used in the way women are often used and mistreated by men. In other words, Tonto was a woman.'

A man leaned forward, clutching the back of the seat in front. 'When you grow up a bit, darlin', you'll find he wasn't.'

People laughed. A woman called out, 'Will you sit down? I did not get on this bus to listen to poetry.'

Anna ignored her. '"How did Tonto get his jollies? Please pause and consider that. No late nights in caffs. Cold beer and laughs. He slept rough on a celibate mat."'

She took a breath and looked round. The faces looking back at her were blank. She didn't care. She was especially proud of her 'celibate mat' reference. 'Celibate' was a new word to her. She'd been introduced to it by Arthur Watt, who sat next to her in French. He'd also told her two other words she needed to know – lesbian and nymphomaniac. She'd asked what these words meant. Arthur had winked and said, 'You know.' Anna then knew that he didn't. She'd looked them up in the family dictionary when she got home. 'I didn't know there were words for these things,' she'd said.

She started on her second verse and chose not to meet the eye of anybody who was looking at her. The puzzled, slightly irritated expressions put her off. '"Were you filled with lust and greed? I want a shot on the shiny white steed."'

A woman a few rows from the front shouted, 'Will you be quiet! I'm trying to have a conversation here.'

Anna ignored her. '"Did you cry, 'Lone Ranger, cool it'? Gimme gimme a silver bullet."'

George looked at her best friend; saw the notebook was held in trembling hands, heard the nervous trill in Anna's voice and the eyes brimming tears and marvelled. That's what fearlessness looked like – a person stepping through their dread to do something extraordinary. Reading a poem to passengers on the top deck of a bus, for example. For the rest of her life George would know that this was the moment she started to love Anna. Anna would be her best pal for ever and ever.

The woman stood, stepped into the aisle and said she was going to fetch the conductor. 'You are disrupting the peace.'

She returned with him a few seconds later. 'This child is making a menace of herself, disturbing us all by reading *poetry*.' She spat out the last word. 'Poetry, for heaven's sake, on a bus. What have I done to deserve this?'

The conductor assured her, 'You have done nothing, madam. You have a right to an untroubled bus ride. No poetry.' He turned to Anna. 'Please sit down.'

'I'll sit when I'm finished. I have twelve more verses to go.'

'You'll sit now or you'll get off the bus.'

'I'll read my poem. You can't tell me what to do. It's a free country.'

'It may be a free country but it's not a free bus. It's my bus and you'll get off.'

'I've paid my fare. I refuse to get off.' Anna was vehement.

'Off.' So was the conductor.

George got up and made her way to the platform. Anna followed. She thought she heard someone clap. Back on the pavement Anna asked George if she had any money to pay their fare on the next bus. She hadn't.

'We'll have to walk then,' said Anna.

'I'll be ages late home. I'll get hell. I hate walking.'

'I know. But that's a poet's lot. We're misunderstood. You'll see when you write poems.'

'God, Anna, I'm not going to be a poet. To hell with that. I'm going to be a nurse.'

*

Walking towards her car, a yellow Mini, George said, 'I've been remembering you and your first reading. The bus especially.'

Anna said, 'Ah yes. A splendid failure. My first, not my most spectacular. But a very fine failure, I have to say. Actually, I was shocked when I found you didn't want to be a poet. I'd thought everyone wanted to be a poet.'

'How foolish you were. But on that bus I loved you. I thought you were fantastic. I was jealous but at the same time wanted to be your best friend for ever.'

'And you were. You are,' said Anna. 'The Two Yellows live.'

'Prepare to die, Dorothy Pringle.'

'The things we were going to put her through. The torture. Drowning her in a vat of school semolina, for example. Where were we going to get the vat?'

'Where were we to get the semolina?'

'Indeed,' said Anna. 'I always thought she looked pale and unfinished.'

'She was quite the sports queen. A star of the hundred-yards hurdles,' George said.

Anna scorned. 'Belting down the track she looked like a wet scone in knickers.'

'I see you haven't lost your poetic touch.'

'Never,' said Anna. 'Truthful and succinct always.'

The day was cloudy, not cold enough for a coat, and not

warm enough for bare arms. Cardigan weather, Anna called it. She moved along the pavement, measuring her steps, watching the ground beneath her feet. 'Damn, this talk of Dorothy Pringle has made me lose my walking rhythm. It's one step with good leg followed by step with wonky leg and stick. I just did good leg and stick, meaning that wonky leg has to go it alone without back-up.'

'Calamity,' said George.

Anna lifted her stick and pointed to George's car. 'Ah, the yellowmobile. I'll get a seat at last.'

'You should walk more. It's a fact. Walking is good for you.'

'Well, I almost enjoyed the small trek from the coffee shop to here. But now I will sit and I'll absolutely enjoy that. How old is that car anyway?'

'Fifteen, I think.'

'It's ancient. No sat-nav. You play cassettes, for God's sake. The seats are worn with years of bums landing on them. It's a dilapidated wreck.'

'Like us. It's on the road legally. It gets me where I want to go. The thing about it being old and not glamorous is nobody looks at it. It slips through life unnoticed.'

George zapped the car unlocked. Anna opened the door, sat and sighed. 'Like us. Unnoticed is good, I have come to believe.'

George slipped into the driver's seat, wiggled the gear stick, started the car and said, 'Why?'

Anna said, 'You can do stuff. Be outrageous and nobody really thinks to stop you. They don't see you. We should resurrect the Two Yellows.'

'Wear our pants over our tights? Punch the air and hope to fly? Perhaps not.'

'Enjoy our new invisibility. Have fun.'

George said, 'Ah yes, fun. I remember it well.'

3

Not a Bird . . . Not a Plane . . .
Not Even Lois Lane

Anna's poem about waiting for Superman appeared in a
pamphlet called *Stand Aside, Untrousered, Ragged Woman
Coming Through Shouting Out Loud* that she produced herself.
She'd written all of the twelve poems it featured. She had it
photocopied in a small print shop and piled the thin booklets on
the bar of the Black Lion, the pub she frequented. There were a
hundred copies and she sold twenty. She was so thrilled at this
success she forgot to collect her takings.

The pamphlet's first poem was 'Not a Bird . . . Not a Plane . . .
Not Even Lois Lane'. It was about her stupidity when it came to
men. '*Sixty floors up and dangling/God, my wrists are sore/My
life scuds by every two minutes/Down there the crowd's beginning
to bore.*' This, Anna explained to the other five members at a
meeting of her writing group, was about her dismay at women
who, finding themselves in a bit of a pickle, do nothing but
complain about their wrists being sore rather than find a solution
to their situation. The group agreed heartily.

'See,' said Anna, 'that's the trouble with us women. Instead
of hauling ourselves to safety, clambering onto the balcony or in
through a window, we just dangle waiting for a man to come
along and save us.'

At that she sat down and said no more. She'd read and re-read
her poem 'Not a Bird . . . Not a Plane . . . Not Even Lois Lane'
and was beginning to doubt herself. Every time she set about

writing a poem she'd raise her right arm, pen in hand, and say out loud, 'This is it. This is the one.' And every time the poem was finished she'd look at it, feel the disappointment and say, 'No, it isn't.' Her writing was trivial. She was no Byron or Keats or Allen Ginsberg or Sylvia Plath or Dylan Thomas. She was simply a rhymester. She longed to be deep, complex and misunderstood. She was at university in Dundee at the time and felt she should be starving in Paris.

She confessed this to Colin, her flatmate and boyfriend. 'You may not have the depth you long for but you make people smile. You have what they call reach – people will buy your stuff,' he told her. She was almost grateful. It wasn't what she wanted to hear, though.

Their flat was on the third floor of a tenement, had two rooms, a small toilet and tiny kitchen. The living room Anna had painted white with one wall a striking midnight blue. The carpet was the colour of overused Plasticine. There was a bashed grey sofa which was badly sprung and, once sat upon, difficult to get out of, one armchair and three dining chairs round a small table. Here the writers – female, thin, prone to feel the cold except for one middle-aged man who'd bring biscuits – would gather to drink tea and passionately discuss their work. Colin went to the pub.

At least that was where Anna assumed he was going. She didn't know and didn't ask. She was obsessed with her poetry. Every night that wasn't a writing group meeting she sat at the small table and worked at her Olivetti Lettera 22 portable type-writer. She drank mugs of tea, listened to Joan Baez and Bob Dylan and stared into space muttering rhymes. All the while her dreams of being profound and insightful slipped away from her.

Colin would come home from wherever he'd been and find her sleeping slumped over her typewriter. He'd wake her, manoeuvre her into bed then undress and slip under the sheets beside her.

Lying next to him on a cruel January night Anna worked up the courage to ask why he never made love to her. 'You hardly even kiss me these days. You used to. You don't touch me. Don't you even fancy me?' She was wearing a flimsy black silk, extremely short, nightdress that she'd removed ('liberated', she called it) from Marks & Spencer without paying and was hoping this garment would arouse his passion. For a while, before she noticed the lack of bodily contact, bedtime had been her favourite part of the day. They'd huddle under the blankets, tell stories, sing silly songs, make one another laugh and exchange dreams and ambitions. The realisation that other people did a lot more than this, that they hugged, touched and made love, had come slowly to Anna.

'I'm sorry,' he said. 'You're beautiful. I love you. But not like that. I'm gay.' His voice was flat, matter-of-fact. He lay on his back looking at the ceiling.

'You're gay?'

'Yes.'

'You're homosexual? You prefer men?'

'Yes.'

'Why?'

'It's just how I am.'

She couldn't believe it. 'What about me? I thought you were my boyfriend.'

'I am your friend who is a boy.'

She threw back the covers, got out of bed, picked up her pillow and whacked him with it. Confused and furious she stormed out of the room, slamming the door. Shivering in the hallway between the bedroom and living room she was covered with goosebumps and crying. She was howling, stamping her foot, yelling, 'Bastard.' She shouted till her throat turned raw. Hands covering her face, she crumpled to the floor. She had been used, duped. The only one who had not known the truth about the man she loved.

It was cold out there. A fierce draught scudded under the front door and froze her bare feet. She wrapped her arms round her body, swamped by misery and chilled to the bone. She had a full five minutes of agony – she was useless, unlovable. She deserved to be alone. She deserved to be numb with cold. She was ugly. Nobody liked her. She wallowed in grief and self-loathing. But slowly, slowly it came to her that she was in *her* flat. She should be in *her* bed. Colin should be out here weeping. Instead he was comfortable, cosy as toast and probably sound asleep under the blankets. She charged back into the bedroom.

'So what are you doing in my bed? In my life?' She threw back the blankets and yanked him onto the floor. 'My bed. My life. Get out.'

He lay, arms spread, looking thin and pale and helpless. The sudden furious removal from mattress to linoleum had hurt. He rubbed the back of his head and swore. He wore black silk boxers. She thought, *Oh God, he's beautiful. He's the most beautiful person I've ever seen. What the hell is he doing with me?*

'Why me?' she said.

'I like you. You make me laugh.'

'Why don't you live with a bloke? What are you doing in my bed?'

'There's only one bed in this flat and there's room for two. It's cosier with two. I mean, this is a really cold flat. And I don't live with a bloke because I can't tell my family about me. My mum likes you.'

She said, 'Jesus.'

He smiled a weak smile. He had thick dark hair, huge brown eyes, long lashes and cheekbones. *Unfair*, she thought. *I want cheekbones.* She pulled off her stolen sexy nightdress and pulled on an old T-shirt. It was warmer. 'No point in trying to seduce you.' He agreed.

She climbed back into bed and hauled the covers over her. 'You can sod off. I'm sleeping here.' She punched her pillow, settled into her sleeping position and shut her eyes, pretending to sleep. But couldn't. She knew Colin was standing thin and pale and hopeless in his sexy underpants and felt guilty. He'd be cold. It was a cold room. The coldest room in the flat. The window didn't fit and rattled on windy nights. The fierce draught that swept under the front door swept on under the bedroom door. The room was plagued by gales front and back. And it was an ugly place – strange floral wallpaper – a mix of ivy and sunflowers, brown suspiciously sticky lino, fraying yellow curtains, bed with ancient blankets and thin fraying sheets and small wardrobe with green plastic door handles. Anna hated it in here. But she consoled herself by thinking poets always lived in shabby poverty.

Pretending to sleep, she momentarily saw the scene she was living through as an outsider might. There was a selfish, swollen-eyed woman lying in bed, covers hauled round her, and standing shivering pained with chill was the beautiful pale homosexual who'd promised to make the selfish lump famous. A tiny flash of guilt slid through her. 'Oh, get in,' she said, 'but keep your effing freezin' feet off me.'

He clambered back into bed, tugged at the blankets and mumbled thanks. Anna wondered what her mother might think of this situation. She was in bed with a homosexual. Actually, she supposed her mother wouldn't know what a homosexual was. Such things were never discussed at home. This made her feel suddenly sophisticated and worldly. Though she knew she wasn't. For surely if she was sophisticated and worldly, there wouldn't be hot fat tears running down her face and onto the pillow.

The next morning she finished her poem.

Sixty floors up and dangling,
God my wrists are sore.
My life scuds by every two minutes,
Down there the crowd's beginning to bore.

Oh, save me, Mr Superman, please.
Sorry I can't get down on my knees.
But I'm hanging here, I'm on the brink,
I've been here most of my life, I think.

Superman, if you judge me,
How I've behaved,
Why, you'll wonder should I be saved.
I've howled and screamed, I've cussed and raved,
And you'll see my armpits haven't been shaved.

But I'm a lady and I did mean
To be serene,
And lithe and delicate, shy and sweet.
I drink whisky, slug it neat.

Oh, I've been naughty, I'll confess,
I've said yes when I meant YES.
I've ruined my ears with rock 'n' roll.
Too much bass has taken its toll.

The music's gone, the music's gone.
The roar in my ears goes on, goes on.
I've smoked weed, sent daydreams creeping
Into night folds. In my living room I am weeping.
In upstairs darkness my babes are sleeping.

I've stooped to fashion, grovelled to fads,
Please let me be one of the lads.
Decisions bring me out in a sweat.
If I take this what won't I get.

I snivel and moan, complain and whine,
I want bread and I want wine.
Gimme gimme, mine mine mine.
Can't you hear it in my wailing?
I drag behind me, childhood trailing.

I'm up here struggling with my truth.
Are you down there in a telephone booth?
In a crumpled head your old Clark Kent's
No longer a man, but a supergent,
Apollo bronzed, strong, clean, astute,
Cute in your salvation suit.

Oh, save me, Mr Superman, please.
Sorry, I can't get down on my knees,
But I'm hanging here, I'm on the brink,
I've been here most of my life, I think.

Sweet Superman, you've come at last
Sailing through sky, sailing right past.
You won't make me cry, won't get the better of me.
Mama said men are plenty, fish in the sea.
This is my life, hold tight I can win it.
There'll be another superhero along in a minute.

It didn't voice her anger. It wasn't going to make the world tremble. But it made her smile. And that helped.

*

'Did you know Colin was gay?' she asked George, as the yellow car rattled and bumped down the road where Anna lived.

'Yes. Everyone knew.'

'I loved him. I was besotted.'

George stopped outside an old tenement. 'So you married him.'

'I know. Sometimes my foolishness takes my breath away. What was I thinking?'

'Did you and Colin ever, you know? Do it?'

'No. Of course we didn't. He was gay and I was obsessed with writing poetry.'

'Poetry is no excuse for celibacy. I was obsessed with sex when I was twenty. I could think of little else. It was like I was permanently in heat.'

'Really? I never knew that about you.' Anna opened the car door and heaved herself onto the pavement. She turned. 'That's probably too much information.'

George said, 'No. Too much information is if I told you what I got up to.'

'Sounds like my kind of information. Subject for discussion at our next meeting.'

'Probably not. Too shameful.'

Anna started down the path to her building's main door. Slow progress, but she was getting more expert with her stick every day. Good leg followed by stick and sore leg and then good leg again. She figured by the time she mastered it she'd no longer need the stick. 'Would your children blush?' she shouted.

'Yes. They'd be very surprised.'

'Then be proud. No doubt they've done a lot that would shock you.'

She reached the door. Looked approvingly at the areas of scrubby grass and weeds either side of the path and smiled. The neglect reminded her that her neighbours were as poor as she was. 'I do not embrace wealth,' she said. She moved painfully down the hallway and tackled the stairs, cursing with every step. 'Bloody stairs, bloody stick, bloody new hip, bloody me.'

Once inside her flat she went to the living-room window and gave George a small flicker of her fingers. 'I'm here,' she said. 'Safe and well and you really don't have to bother about me.'

George tooted her horn and drove off. This was their routine. Anna found it a little patronising. But it was good to know there was one person in the world who cared. In the kitchen she made a cup of tea and took it back to her sofa. It was four-thirty in the afternoon. Time to wonder if she should do something about the books. There were so many of them. They lined five bookshelves. There were books on the kitchen table, books on this sofa and books in the spare bedroom. Sometimes she filled bags and took some books to the local charity shops. Home again, she'd think about them. She missed them. What if nobody bought them and they stayed unread, unloved, in that shop for ever? She'd then go back to each shop, find her books and buy them back along with a few new ones.

She sipped her tea and hoped there'd be no phone calls. She wanted to think. She wanted to sink into golden memories. But she thought instead about Colin, and her stupidity at marrying him and denying herself proper love. And when she thought about that absurdity, more absurdities followed.

> Superman, if you judge me,
> How I've behaved,
> Why, you'll wonder should I be saved.
> I've howled and screamed, I've cussed and raved,
> And you'll see my armpits haven't been shaved.

That was what she'd written in her guiltiest moments. It hadn't expressed the hollowness, the loneliness she'd felt. Sometimes she'd be standing in the supermarket queue holding a basket filled with digestive biscuits, firelighters and potatoes, and these stupidities would come to her and tears would flood down her cheeks. Well, what else was there to do?

4

Don't Be Daft

George put her handbag at the foot of the stairs and draped her coat on one of the hooks by the front door. 'I'm home.' She went into the kitchen where her husband, Matthew, was sitting at the table reading a newspaper. She kissed the top of his head. Not a lot of hair there.

'I know,' he said, 'I heard you coming. You're noisy.'

'It's a gift, my noisiness. What did you do today?'

'I worked in the garden. Pulled out some things that may or may not be weeds. Then I came in and heated a tin of soup for lunch. After that I went into the living room and stood looking vacant, wondering why I'd gone in there. So I came back in here and here I still am. What did you do?'

'Walked with Anna. Couple of trips along Princes Street Gardens exercising her new hip. Then coffee and a sandwich. Then drove her home and spoke about her daft marriage to Colin. He told her he'd make her a famous poet and she believed him.' She sat down across from Matthew, made a face. 'Can you credit that? She wasted her young life pursuing a poet's existence. If she'd been wild and stupid like me she'd have had a lot more to write poetry about.'

Matthew gave her his famous look. *Oh God*, it said, *I am jealous of your past. It hurts to hear it.* And yet, he couldn't stop loving hearing it. He wished he'd known her back then, in her silly days.

'Oh yes,' said George. 'I did it all. I sulked. I drank. I smoked. I bellowed teenage angst.'

'You were obnoxious.'

'Oh yes. I couldn't forgive my mum and dad for calling me George. I yelled that I wanted to be Mary. I stormed out of the house and didn't go back for six years. I'm ashamed of myself.'

'You? Ashamed? That's a first.'

'I'm mellowing. But you have to admit I was a teenage queen. Five foot three inches of raging hormones and vile pink lipstick.'

*

Standing in her parents' living room – a pleasant bookish place – she'd allowed her blistering anger to flow. 'I hate you! I hate you, I hate you. Boys laugh at me, do you know that? They chant when I walk past. "Georgie, Georgie," they call.'

Her mother, Judith, a gentle socialist soul who marched to ban the bomb, looked up from her knitting, smiled and said, 'Ignore them, dear.' She looked back at the cardigan she was making and added, 'It's perfectly normal to hate your mother at your age.'

The dismissive words, the nonchalant attitude, enraged George further. 'How could you? You're nasty. You don't care about me. You called me George. You have no idea the pain this has brought me.' She thumped a dramatic hand on her heart. 'People say "George? You mean Georgina?". And I say I mean George. And they look at me as if I'm insane.'

Judith smiled. 'We thought you'd love it. We thought we'd named you after a character in a book you'd love.'

'I don't. I hate it and I hate you.'

Recognising a teenage tantrum when she saw one, Judith said, 'I know you do. But I don't hate you. And you can always change your name.'

'What to?' George's voice was raw with rage. Her throat burned. Wild tears blurred her vision. Snot oozed from her nose. She was not at her best.

'Fred,' said Judith. She grinned and popped the ball of green wool on the end of her needles. Stood up. 'Time for tea.'

She probably hadn't meant to be flippant. She was used to her daughter's tantrums and thought this one would pass like the others before it. George knew her mother understood her, in a way.

'The girl has appetites beyond the understanding of mankind,' she'd heard her say to her father once. 'She can watch a soap on TV while eating several chocolate bars and at the same time listening to her music at full volume. How does she do that? God help us when she discovers sex.'

'What makes you think she hasn't already?' her father replied.

'Don't say that.'

'She's sixteen thundering towards seventeen. Do you really think she's still innocent? You weren't at that age.'

But now George was packing. In her bedroom she shoved five pairs of knickers, five pairs of socks, a packet of digestive biscuits, two bars of chocolate, her favourite Frank Zappa T-shirt, jeans and her battered copy of *On the Road* into her school bag. She couldn't think of anything else she might need. Besides her school bag, a tattered haversack bought from the Army and Navy Store was full. She was ready to strike out into the world, change her name to Karen Nightingale and shine.

At eleven o'clock she slipped out of the house, strode down the garden path and headed for the heart of the city. She hadn't a clue where she was going or what she would do when she got there, wherever it was.

*

'I just stepped out,' she said to Matthew. 'The night air was so cold on my face. It smelled of coal fires. A dog was barking and it was very dark. I don't remember being afraid, though. I just thought I'd show my mother and father how I didn't need them and they'd be sorry they called me George.' She reached over and touched his arm. 'How stupid was that? I can't bear to think what might have happened to me.'

'Very stupid,' he agreed. He'd heard this story many times

and yet never seemed to tire of it. George suspected he'd stopped really listening and was just watching the expressions that flitted across her face as she related her tale of teenage rebellion. Even she could feel her eyes light up as she enthusiastically moved from one stupid thing she'd done to another even more stupid. 'When I think about it, I could have been murdered and raped. Well, raped and murdered, other way round. If I'd been raped after I was murdered, I wouldn't have known about it. I'd have been dead.' At that, she covered her face with her hands and cursed herself. 'Such a silly idiotic little madam, me.'

'No, you're not.' He touched her arm. 'I love you.' He always said that.

She made a face, flapped a dismissive hand at him. 'Don't be daft.' She always said that. She took a breath and continued with her story.

'Anyway, I got to the High Street. By now it was about midnight. Me alone in the city at midnight, can you imagine? I was so excited and so scared. It was getting quieter now. Less traffic, fewer people; everybody had gone home probably. But there were all-night cafés. Can you think of anything more alluring for a teenage girl running away from home? I went to one down a narrow wynd. You had to climb rickety stairs. There were pine tables. Not polished pine you get now. Sort of like newly cut wood. And they served Coke with actual ice cubes – sophisticated or what? Also frothy coffee. Out of this world. It was more froth than coffee but when you were as young as I was froth is what you wanted.'

She crossed the kitchen, filled the kettle and put it on to boil. Back at the table she smiled and said, 'Right, where was I? Oh yes, in the all-night café. I was at the end of my frothy coffee, scraping the sugary bits from the bottom of the cup and licking them off my fingers. This man came up to me and asked my name. I told him Karen because this was the start of me being Karen Nightingale. He told me he'd drive me home because I couldn't sit in the café all night. I could tell he wasn't safe.

He was creepy. Big huge paunch, shaggy eyebrows, his suit was a bit greasy. He wasn't someone you'd go home with. I didn't know what to do. I shrank away from him and he took me by the shoulder and said, "Come on." And then from nowhere my rescuer – Alistair. Who'd have thought it, a knight in shining armour called Alistair? He picked up my school bag, took my hand and said, "Thanks for waiting for me. Let's go." I knew he was safe. I went. I'd never seen him before.'

The kettle boiled. She made tea and jokingly asked Matthew if he wanted a cup. He shook his head. She made dreadful tea. She didn't know how she did it. Boiling water, tea bag, leave for a small while and add milk. Easy. But then she made dreadful coffee, dreadful everything. She was a terrible cook. Odd that, because she loved chefs – three husbands and two of them professional cooks.

She sat back at the table, sipped her tea, looked surprised at how awful it was and continued her tale. 'He had a ponytail. He smelled lovely. He was the cleanest man I ever met. His flat was filthy, though. He hustled me through the streets to get to it. He was furious with me. "What the hell were you doing in a place like that? Some very nasty people hang out there. Don't ever go there again. And why are you out alone at this time of night?"' she imitated him.

'He was a bit of a hero,' said Matthew.

George nodded. 'I told him I'd run away from home and he told me he'd see about that.'

Matthew asked, 'What did you make of that?'

'Not a lot really. He said it softly, like he was intending to sort it all out. I was a kid. I'd run away, I wasn't thinking straight. Actually, I didn't start thinking straight till I was thirty-five.'

He leaned back, looked at her. 'Oh really? I thought it was later than that. Last week.'

She shrugged. 'His flat wasn't far, one floor up in a crumbling building. He shoved me into the living room, brought me sheets and a couple of blankets and told me to sleep on the sofa. I could tell the place wasn't hygienic. But I was so tired I just zonked out. I worried a bit and thought about Mum and Dad. But sleep took me. Maybe six o'clock I woke. I needed a pee, as you do. So I got up to look for the loo. I found it, peed, and lost my way going back to the living room. Of course, by now it was light. I could see my surroundings. The filth, the filth, oh my God, the filth. It was a teenage rebel's dream, that filth. I thought it proved you didn't need to wipe and polish like my mum. You could survive in filth.'

She leaned toward him. He leaned toward her. She knew he loved this part of her story. 'I opened the wrong door and suddenly I'd come to a magical place. The living room was a muckheap – thick dust, sticky floor, spills and stains – but this room was amazing. The kitchen of kitchens. Gleaming. Rows of copper pans hanging up. A huge range to cook on. It smelled of coffee and mystical things I'd never tasted. There were herbs and jars. I stood there, wide-eyed and astonished. I felt as if I'd entered a fairy king's secret palace. It was so amazing I could hardly breathe.'

Matthew nodded. 'I love thinking of you, so young, standing with your mouth open in a magical place and forgetting to breathe.'

'Of course,' said George, 'I'd woken him up and he found me standing looking frozen and amazed. He brought me a big woolly jumper and told me to stop poking about his flat. I said I'd opened the wrong door and that this kitchen was the most beautiful room I'd ever been in. Shiny copper pots and gleamy jars and so forth. So he made me a cup of hot chocolate and a warm croissant. I'd never had a croissant. It was all melty and buttery. I couldn't believe it. All the time we'd been eating sliced bread people had been eating croissants. It just wasn't fair. It was the start of my love affair with food. What are you making tonight?'

'Chicken Milanese with a slightly spicy tomato sauce and little bit of pasta.'

'Wine?'

'We've got a nice Chablis.'

'Why are you not cooking it now?'

'I want to hear the rest of the story.'

He knew she didn't want to tell this bit. That she'd race through it.

'Oh,' she said. 'Well, you know. I stayed with him. I cleaned the flat. It took days and days to get it right. He only cared about the kitchen. The other rooms meant nothing to him. I went back to school. Nobody said anything there. Years later I found he'd got in touch with Mum and Dad and told them where I was. They told the school I was staying with an aunt for a while. And that was that. I stayed. I cleaned. He cooked. My folks sometimes walked by the building and looked up at the flat.' She sniffed. Wiped her nose with the back of her hand. 'I got pregnant. Of course I did. Contraception never occurred to me.' She spoke quickly, almost slurring her words. She hated this bit of her past. 'I had Lola. We were a little family. Cosy. He got himself killed in a car crash. I couldn't pay the rent. I got chucked out of the flat. I went home. That was that.'

'No, it wasn't,' said Matthew.

Once again, she'd made no mention of what she'd gone through. She and Alistair had gone clubbing. He'd hung out at the bar, she'd danced till her feet bled. They'd married when she was twenty-one. Matthew had been told George's mother and father had watched the pair emerge from the Registry Office giggling. He'd love to know how she'd been evicted from the flat. Had she been locked out? She wouldn't talk about it. She kept all details of this part of her life a painful secret.

'My mother answered the door,' she said. 'She just looked at me and smiled. And she took the baby. "There you are," she said. "At last." She had all the stuff. All the baby things waiting for me. Just like that. So kind. So forgiving.' George wiped her nose again. 'I didn't deserve it. She was wonderful. I hate myself for what I did. The worry I caused. I was a horrible selfish brat. Arrogant little madam.'

'No, you weren't. You were a kid. You came through. You became a nurse. They loved you. Lola loves you. I love you.'

George, lacking a hankie, blew her nose on her sleeve and said, 'Don't be daft.'

She never told him of the shame and guilt she suffered and how she'd spent her life atoning for the pain she caused. As always, she hadn't told him everything. She and Alistair had lived a free and easy life. Though they didn't know it, they'd become faces about town. The days and nights she was moving through thrilled her. She'd step out in her six-inch silver stilettos, breathing in air filled with petrol fumes, coal fires and restaurant food, anticipating the time ahead – and the city was hers.

They drank late in locked-in bars, underground cellar clubs, and she'd help him home, limping on her boogied-out feet. He'd roam the city on his days off. They laughed too much, drank too much, loved too much. It ended badly as all exquisitely naughty things do. They married when she was twenty-one and they had Lola. Everything changed. Babies do that.

5

What's the Point of You?

It's enough to make a Jesus cry
That pickled people could pass by

A couple of lines Anna had written once, years ago, when she'd given her bus fare to a homeless man begging in the street. She'd been upset at being the only person who'd noticed him and the two lines had come to her on the plod home. It had been cold but she'd felt content. She'd done a good thing. She'd enjoyed the air and watched the pavement pass under her feet. *Moving is good*, she'd thought. When she was home she'd write about how helping someone had helped her.

She always wondered if she'd been punished for her smugness. A woman who gave away her bus fare was not expected to congratulate herself on her good deed every step of the half-hour walk home. She was punished. She lost her writing way. Words were not gone from her. They arrived in her head, but when she wrote them down they seemed shallow, clichéd, obvious. There was no point to them, no sting, no beauty. After writing those two lines, she wrote no more.

She had flashes of poems. Moments when a couple of lines would spring into her mind unannounced. These lines always seemed unconnected with anything she was doing or thinking at the time. She might be writing a shopping list – *marmalade, cheese, potatoes, beans* – then from nowhere: *I'm a diamond lady, hard and bright/Put my lipstick on at night*. She'd stare at it, rummage through her brain for more, try to alter it or at least make sense of it. When nothing came she'd continue: *milk, tea bags, digestive biscuits.*

She was in hell. This was a nightmare. She confided in George, her only friend.

'Oh,' said George, 'writer's block. It goes away in time. I've read about it. You should relax. Worrying will only make it worse.'

'I'm not blocked. I know I'm not. I think I've finished. Like I've emptied the well. It's over.'

'Don't be silly. You're a poet. It's what you are. Who you are. It's all of you.'

'No longer.'

'Get drunk. Let go. Let your thoughts flow. Don't care. Just write.'

'Tried that. I drank a bottle of Chianti then several gin and tonics. I was sick and passed out. Didn't write a thing. Stinker of a headache in the morning.'

'It'll come back. You just need to wait for it.'

But it didn't come back. Anna took a job editing a small poetry magazine. She earned a pittance and gained a reputation for being exacting. She never forgave a cliché. She nurtured talent but kept a distance from her writers. She didn't want them to know she'd longed to be one of them in the distant days before words left her.

She came and she went. She stamped out of her tiny flat, red beret wedged on her head on cold days. When it was warm her long hair flapped and flew round her. She wore boots. She'd walked everywhere till one day she bought an old black bike. Apart from George and conversations with printers and contributors, she hardly spoke to anyone. She certainly didn't know any of her neighbours, though she suspected they thought her weird anyway. That hurt. If she caught any of them looking at her in a way that suggested they considered her odd, she'd look away and stride past acting as if she didn't care. She'd told George, 'I am joining squirrels, rabbits, weasels and other wildlife. I am avoiding human beings. Scuttling away from them. They are too complicated. I can't cope.'

George said, 'Good plan.'

*

Today they were sitting on a bench in the Botanical Gardens. Lunch was on Anna. It was cheese and onion sandwiches and a thermos of tea made in her kitchen. She still lived frugally; food had never been important to her. It was a necessity, she supposed. George brought chocolates, which she considered another necessity. Anna was on about her neighbours again. 'They call me Mrs Stomper or Old Red Hat. They know nothing about me.'

'True. But there is something in the nicknames. You do stomp and you wear a red hat. It could be worse. You could be Granny Smelly or Greasy Fizzface.'

'What a lovely picture of me you paint.'

'The people who dish out nicknames don't care if they're true or not. They just like to smirk.'

Anna said, 'I was married to a beautiful man who became very famous.' She chewed her sandwich. 'This is surprisingly good, considering I made it with old cheese and a soft onion I found at the bottom of my vegetable basket.'

'You can cook. I can't. I always admire people who can make food taste good. Alistair was a master cook. He could do fabulous things with an egg. Other men looked up to him. He was an alpha male.'

Anna said, 'Colin became an alpha male of our times. He was the cool beautiful guy in the amazingly expensive jacket who had perfect hair. He didn't strut. Didn't have to. Every step he took he said, "Look at me. I can't beat the shit out of you but I've got a lot more money than you.

'He left me and went on to spectacular things. He became a businessman, a face in the media. I stayed behind with my dreams and my ordinary clothes. He never mentions me in any of his interviews. If I told my neighbours I'd been married to him they'd laugh. "Mrs Stomper married to Colin Saunders, ha ha ha." They don't speak to me. I don't speak to them. But they watch me go in my stomping boots and think me weird.' She lifted her feet and gazed at her boots. They'd been bought from a charity shop and were pink.

'They are flamboyant,' said George. 'Just what you need at your age. They stop you from disappearing.'

'Oh, I won't do that.' Anna was positive. 'In fact, there's a woman across the road from me who stares every time I see her. I fear one day she may strike up a conversation. She has purple hair and a snake tattoo slithering up her arm.'

'Goodness,' said George. 'You live among interesting people. Here – now we've managed to finish the sandwich, have a Belgian chocolate truffle. I thought we might need them to cheer us after your austerity food.'

Anna took one, then another, and continued staring at her boots. 'I feel I have old feet in young footwear. I am too old for my boots.'

*

Two days later the woman with purple hair and a tattooed snake slithering up her arm spoke to Anna.

'Are you Mrs MacLean?'

'Mrs no, MacLean yes.'

She was setting out on her morning walk. It was part of her recovery. Her doctor told her it helped her exercise her new hip. She'd be walking normally in no time. She leaned on her stick and considered this woman standing before her. The tattoo was impressive and now, as the woman wore torn denim shorts, she could see there was a further tattoo snaking down her left leg. Anna stared at it.

'Took hours,' said the tattooed one. 'Long time to lie still.'

Anna nodded. 'I expect it was. You are?'

'Marla Jones. I've been watching you.'

'I noticed.'

'You don't go out to work.'

'I have retired.'

'What from?'

'I edited a small poetry magazine and often on Saturdays I worked in an independent bookshop. The extra money helped.' Before she was asked about her present income, she said, 'I have a tiny pension from the magazine and the state pension. I get by. I manage if I hold in my stomach, don't eat much and go to bed early to keep warm.'

'Yeah, eight o'clock.'

'Twenty-five past, more like. I eat, watch a soap, do my dishes and then bed.'

Marla nodded. 'Do people read poetry magazines?'

'Yes.'

'Is it just poems in them?'

'We published lists of poetry events, readings and so on, and also profiles of poets as well as poems.'

'But you didn't write poems?'

'Yes. I did once.'

'You actually wrote poems? You had a bit of blank paper and wrote a poem on it?'

'Yes.'

'Why?'

This was a terrifying question. Anna shrank from it. 'I love words. They thrill me.'

'You could just speak. No need to be writing things down. I couldn't be doing with it. I'd have to sit still.'

'There's that,' said Anna. She gazed at Marla. The woman was small and frighteningly thin. The purple hair was shoulder length and gleamed. Anna wondered what she used. Marla's face was pale, colourless. Her lips painted pale brown and her eyebrows two fine plucked lines. She had a selection of studs in her ears and a further blue one in her nostril. She wore a thin vest.

Her default expression was cynical. Her boldness was impressive. Anna liked her, even if she was dismissive of poetry.

'Did you get your poems published?' Marla asked.

'I published them myself.'

'Why?'

Another difficult question.

'Because I wanted to. I thought the world would enjoy them. I was wrong.'

'What's the point of all that? What's the point of poems? What's the point of you?'

Anna had no answer. She supposed she had just been asked the question she'd dreaded all her life. She opened her mouth to speak and nothing came out. She gazed past Marla and noticed a boy standing behind her. His hair was cropped. He wore jeans and T-shirt. He too was thin. On his feet green canvas boots decorated with duck pictures. Though she knew nothing of children and their likes and dislikes, she knew this boy was too old for his boots. Her heart went out to him.

'What's the point of me? That's not a very nice question.'

Marla looked ashamed. 'I suppose it wasn't. I just wondered why you sat in a wee room and wrote when you could be out doing stuff.'

'I was doing stuff. Writing.' She turned, starting once more on her walk. Then she turned and confessed, 'I didn't go out. I stayed in my wee room. I felt safe. Tell me, what's the point of you? What's the point of anybody?'

Marla put her hand on the boy's shoulder and manoeuvred him towards her front door. 'We're all numpties. We make cups of tea, have babies, eat heated-up pizza and complain about life. Nobody's very good at being a person.'

'That may be true,' said Anna. 'Now tell me why you've accosted me like this.'

'I'm thinking you're strapped for cash at the end of the week. You probably live on baked potatoes and beans. You could do with some money.'

'Not always beans,' Anna told her. 'Tuna, cheese from time to time. I could do with some money. Who couldn't?'

'Nobody round here anyway. Everyone's the same, worrying because there are more days in the week than there is money to see them through. Nobody's middle class like you.'

Suddenly furious, Anna said, 'Are you accusing me of being middle class?' This was insulting. Didn't the woman know poets were classless? They wrote the truth, that's all.

'Nah. You're too messy.' Marla shook her head and continued. 'I'd like you to look after Marlon two or three times a week.'

'Marlon?'

'My boy.' Marla turned and pointed to the child behind her. He winced at the sudden attention. 'He's no trouble. He'll watch the television or draw things for a few hours. You just have to be there with him. I'll be at work.'

Anna could hardly speak. Had her life come to this? She looked like she was so in need of money someone had asked her to look after a child. She didn't like children. She was sure some of them were fine. But the very young were incontinent. They couldn't help it, of course. But she had no idea how to deal with it. Changing a nappy was beyond her. Older children made odd noises, ran about at top speed with no idea of where they were going and said rude things loudly.

'I'm afraid that's impossible,' she said. 'I know nothing about children.'

In a quiet and sweet voice Marlon said, 'Didn't you used to be one?'

The directness of the question shook her. 'I did. But I remember very little about the condition. It doesn't qualify me for looking after one.'

Marla said, 'You'll learn. It'll do you good. Get your mind off all that poetry. If you take him, I'll want none of that. No poems.'

Angered, Anna leaned on her stick. 'We have songs. We have dreams. We have poems. I think in the end it's all we have.'

She realised she was shouting. After years and years in this street, coming and going, speaking to nobody, she was yelling an opinion. People came to windows to see what was going on. People stopped to stare. Anna squirmed. She was the centre of attention, stared at by neighbours who were not lovers of songs and dreams and poems. She was a fool.

6

Love in a Time of Tiramisu

George could never explain her love of food. It wasn't as if she'd been starved as a child. Her plates had been almost overloaded. But the fare had been dull, repetitive and tasteless. Her mother considered cooking a chore. She had a food rota that saved her from planning menus. Monday was second-day roast beef, Tuesday stew, Wednesday second-day stew, Thursday fish, Friday was lamb chops and Sunday was first-day roast beef. Saturday, then, was George's favourite day of the week. Her mother would serve something quick. A ready meal, usually Vesta Beef Curry or beans on toast. Her friends at school loved Saturdays because they were a day away from school and home-work; George loved them because of the sudden new flavours, and anything from a tin was exotic.

George supposed her mother thought of food as fuel. Taste didn't come into it. Certainly they'd need a plate of hot stew to keep them going on the CND marches the family went on. 'It was a surprise to me when I discovered how good food could be. Same with sex. When I was told the facts of life nobody mentioned how much fun it was.' She was indignant.

Matthew said, 'They didn't want you to do it. Not before you were past seventy at least.'

'When I was late teens I was obsessed with sex. I couldn't understand why people were standing at bus queues or working in shops or just walking down the street when they could be at home, you know, doing it. Same with food, I was stunned it was so good. Alistair would put a plate in front of me and I couldn't believe it. I should have named my children after food. Why not? These days parents seem to just pluck a word out of the ether and that's what they call their baby – apple, pick-up truck, shoe. I should have called mine Vichyssoise, Bouillabaisse and Gazpacho.'

'Pea and Ham, Tomato and Cream of Chicken,' Matthew said. He grinned.

'Ha ha. I should've called Lola Peperonata. It would have suited her. James could have been Ratatouille. Emma is a Gnocchi. Down to earth, but definitely not ordinary.'

'No mention of Willy?'

She shook her head.

'It wasn't your fault.'

'I know that in my head. My heart isn't convinced.'

*

Willy was a late child, a surprise for George. She'd thought she was past conceiving. 'No, it isn't the menopause. You haven't got indigestion. You're pregnant,' her doctor told her.

'How come?'

'I think you know how come.'

'I'm on the pill.'

'Have you been ill? Diarrhoea?'

She stared at him, remembering. It had been sweaty and vile. The day after the night before, oh God. A woman, a nurse, a mother should not suffer so shamefully. She'd drunk too much wine and eaten a very dubious prawn curry. She should have known better. Twelve hours thundering back and forth to the lavatory had been punishment enough, surely? But no, now there was this. A fourth baby on the way.

She was thirty-eight at the time, married to Frank and couldn't bring herself to tell him. She knew he wouldn't be happy with the news. He'd often told her he was done with children. 'I love them,' he'd said. 'But three is more than enough. It's all new shoes and fights and rubbish programmes on TV and worrying and notes from school and . . .' She hadn't allowed him to finish. She knew well what he meant. James had asked recently for a toy she'd never heard of. She'd stared at him. She was too busy with fish fingers and homework she didn't understand and shopping and her working life to keep up with what was happening. She felt alone in the world.

Frank was a big man with a big voice. A businessman busy buying and selling property, making a lot of money, he was away from home a lot. He could work a room. A man always in a bespoke suit living a bespoke life, George was familiar with the sight of him running a comb through his hair. She thought this a teenage thing to do. Recently it seemed to her they had lost the knack of speaking. And, as she'd said to Anna when they were having lunch in a busy city centre café, it had been a lovely courtship.

'Nights out, restaurants, cinema and weekends in posh hotels. He'd take me dancing. I couldn't believe it. That's what film stars do. You know, sit at a beautiful table, chat wittily, sip Champagne and twirl round the floor from time to time. He called me his heroine. I suppose I thought we'd just keep dancing. He proposed at midnight on New Year's Eve as we lay on a sheepskin rug in front of a log fire in a Highland lodge he'd rented. Lola was with my mother as I played at being Jeanne Moreau.' She sighed. Her memories made her wince. 'He thought we should make love and come together at the stroke of midnight.'

'I love it. What a good plan. A New Year thrill,' Anna said. George had noticed that while the clamour and noise of the café continued, there was a certain sudden silence at the tables nearby after her last remark.

'Very hard to do,' she'd continued. 'You either come too early or too late. You are guaranteed to miss the vital bong on the clock. My sex skills had nothing to do with accurate timing.'

'No, it isn't what you're thinking about.'

The couple at the table next to them exchanged a long look.

'Anyway, he proposed. I accepted. He was wearing floral

underpants. I wasn't wearing anything. He didn't even have a ring. But it was only really about his asking. The proposal was all. Marriage didn't occur to him.'

'Oh well, that's romance. All frills and no reality.'

'He wasn't a chef,' said George. 'I love chefs. They understand the mixing of things. They know how to simmer.'

'Simmering is good. I ended up just wanting a man who wasn't gay. But if he could simmer too, that would be a benefit,' said Anna.

The couple next to them had turned to stare. The man especially. He obviously had no idea what they were talking about. Anna had said she admired George. How much she knew life's messiness intimately. She'd seen it all – sex, blood, birth and death – in hospital wards, operating theatres and treatment rooms. Anna said, not for the first time, that George ought to have been a poet. She had a lot more to be poetic about.

George ordered Earl Grey tea and a simple tomato sandwich. Anna, chin propped on cupped hand, elbow propped on table, had looked at the food in front of her foodie friend and said, 'You're pregnant, aren't you?'

George nodded.

Anna said, 'And you haven't told Frank.'

George nodded. 'I don't know how. The right words escape me.'

But Frank noticed the change in George. She wasn't drinking. She was moody. She was putting on weight.

'You expecting?' he said.

George said, 'Yes.'

'Is it mine?'

She hit him then. She'd never hit anyone before and was surprised at how long her hand hurt afterwards. He slept on the sofa downstairs that night. In the morning he'd come to her and apologised. He held her face in his hands. 'I'm sorry. That was so wrong. Sorry. Sorry.' He kissed her. But there was something in the air between them, a heaviness, a certain shiftiness. He wasn't really looking at her. She knew then that her marriage hadn't been what she thought it should have been. He'd been unfaithful on his long business trips. A string of one-night stands, she thought. But now it was obvious he'd assumed that she'd been unfaithful too. She hadn't. She'd had the inclination on occasion, but never the time.

They sat on the bed taking in one another in a new light. As if they were seeing the person they were married to for the first time. Two emotional catastrophes in a perfect room, she thought. Their bedroom was white, everything white – bed, bed linen, wardrobe, dresser, carpet. It was a trial for the eyes when the sun poured in. It was also absurd, George thought. Toss a pair of red knickers to the laundry bag (white), and miss, and the knickers lay on the carpet in flamboyant insolence. They had no right to be there. Same for Frank's floral underpants. Floral underpants – George could hardly believe it. Who wore floral underpants? Well, Frank did. It occurred to her that the perfect bedroom was a bit messy with a breeze whispering in through a slightly open window and a bed rumpled after a night's love and sleep. A place where abandoned knickers looked happy on the floor. Here, in this hushed and stainless room, sat two messy beings considering their messy lives. It was wrong.

They had never bonded over the small stuff. Standing side by side in the supermarket deciding which soup to buy, or sitting on the sofa watching rubbish on television and being too tired to notice, far less change the station. Considering soup in the supermarket had been too trivial for Frank. The tiny intimacy of it would have scared him out of his floral underpants.

The marriage had lasted fourteen years. It had been wonderful from time to time – fabulous meals, expensive holidays and quite a bit of dancing. Oh, it had produced two beautiful babies. Mixed-emotion Ratatouille James and down-to-earth but never ordinary Gnocchi Emma were both a joy. They were balanced, sane, generous and loving. Probably not hers, then. She'd been handed the wrong babies. But she didn't plan to hand them back and in return get the bad-tempered, howling, rude ones, her proper children, who'd taken after her.

Willy was no exception. After months of cursing and complaining, indigestion, placing her hand on the small of her back and exhaling discomfort George produced a beautiful baby. She wept. She told the nurse and the midwife that she didn't know why. When asked what it was, she didn't know. She said she didn't know.

It had to do with love. She thought that at last she'd done something right. She desperately loved the child. She needed him to love her back. She called him William. But he was Willy all his days.

He was a special child to George. She thought that here was a chance to get motherhood right. Her time with Willy would be about patience, understanding and love. A time of wonderment and chocolate cake. The cake was easy, wonderment not so much but she'd give it a go.

She worried that her other children would notice her obsession with the new child and be jealous. The other three didn't need her in any physical motherly way any more, but still a sighting of favourite-child behaviour might stir resentment. George was surprised, then, when walking past the living room carrying the much-cherished baby she'd overheard James talking to his father.

'What's got into Mum?' James said. 'She's obsessed with that baby. She doesn't want to put him down. Is that what women are like?'

'Some of them,' said Frank. 'But George was like that with all of you. I think she's got too much love. It's a burden for her. She was like that with all of you.'

'She was?'

'Don't get me started on magic carpets and worlds behind wardrobes. She wanted you to be more than happy. She wanted to give you wonderment.'

'I never really liked *Winnie the Pooh*,' said James.

'Never read it,' said Frank. 'Your ma did. She loves you. She loves you all. But you know what she's like. She overdoes everything.'

George stopped to eavesdrop some more.

'Does it always come from books, this wonderment thing?' James asked.

'Yes. Not films or anything else. She'd love it if you found a world behind your wardrobe and went there every night.'

'That'd make me too knackered for football,' James said.

George moved on up the hall, heading for the kitchen. *Men*, she thought. *Too practical. Wonderment is wasted on them.* But in that moment she understood why her parents had called her George. It had been a helping hand to wonderment. It hadn't occurred to them that she might not be a tomboy. They thought she'd love being different.

She could imagine them sitting in their living room going through names. Rejecting everything because this child would be special and imaginative and very bright. George grinned. She'd been the same. She could almost see the delight on her parents' faces when they'd decided on the name. How they must have clutched one another, filled with glee. They'd cracked it by calling their daughter after one of the heroes of *Five on a Treasure Island*. They'd given their girl the key to wonderment.

It didn't matter any more. Nobody raised an eyebrow or made a comment when she told them what she was called. Everyone assumed she was Georgina. It was all down to guilt anyway, wasn't it? It swept through you as soon as your child was born. A keening need to give your new, freshly scented infant a perfect life. It was overwhelming. And there was no relief. There ought to be, George thought. The guilt-ridden ought to be given a place in the Beatitudes. Blessed are the guilty, for theirs is the kingdom of wine and chocolate and extra-strength tissues to wipe away the tears.

When Willy was four George realised she had a warrior on her hands. The child spoke constantly, argued a lot. He disputed the use of a green bowl for his cereal when he preferred blue. He hated being dragged from morning play to change into outdoor clothes. He took issue with the clothes George selected for him. He disappeared in supermarkets, running top speed. He ran everywhere. He shouted a lot. Oh, how he loved shouting. Another warrior, George thought. James and Emma were schemers and dreamers. But Lola had been a warrior. Still was. She'd raged daily about something or other – usually boys, the unfairness of women's treatment and the price of shoes.

Still, Lola's rants had been delivered at a relatively tolerable volume. Willy's shouting wasn't. He let his voice soar because it made him feel powerful. He was, after all, only little. In fact he was the littlest in the family, so making himself heard was life affirming. The child got exquisite pleasure in moving as fast as he could. He'd run round the garden, arms spread, shouting his name. The family, home for Sunday lunch, would watch. Lola, enthralled, joined in. James and Emma followed. All four children tearing round the lawn barefooted. They stopped in front of her breathless, grinning and pink. 'You should try it,' said Lola. 'It's great.'

George shook her head. She was too old for such behaviour. But that night, at three o'clock, when the world was silent, when as always she couldn't sleep, she sank into her nocturnal bout of black guilt about the dreadful things she'd done. She'd stormed out of her childhood home furious at the name her parents had given her. She'd gone to an all-night café where anything could have happened to her. She'd been rescued by Alistair and had fallen, ridiculously, for his kitchen. Oh, what a kitchen. She was sure cooks were the best lovers. They were about sex and food. Was there anything else? And was she a dreadful person to believe that?

She'd married her rescuer. Had his baby. She'd discovered that her parents had funded her schooling, her clothes and her food from a distance. They'd followed her life by keeping in touch with Alistair. The guilt George suffered over that.

Alistair had bought a car, an ancient thing – an MG convertible. It rattled and shook and made worrying noises as it careened along. One evening he'd set off and hadn't come back. The car had hit a tree. Alistair died, and for a while George hated him for doing that. To this day she worried when someone went away from her that they wouldn't ever return. But she kept it to herself.

There was more. After Alistair's funeral George continued to live at the flat. She respected the kitchen and used it only to make toast and heat baby food. She didn't pay rent or any bills and knew the end would come sometime. One day two men came to the door looking for Alistair.

'Excuse me,' said one of the men. *The main man*, George thought. 'We're looking for the bloke who lives here.' He took a couple of steps towards her. He was small, stocky, wedged into a smart suit complete with waistcoat. His head shaved. He looked like a man with a temper. His friend was taller, in jeans and a T-shirt. He looked like he could help with the temper.

'He's out,' George said. 'I'm just staying for a couple of days. I don't really know him.' She was frightened. She was young. She was grieving. She feared for her child. She thought she might be responsible for the overdue rent.

She packed a bag, stood a moment in the fabulous kitchen, took Alistair's favourite little knife, and walked away. There was only one place to go. Back home to her parents. She was surprised to find they were expecting her. They knew about Alistair. They welcomed her; she was still their George.

Lying in bed now, next to Frank, too guilty to chase sleep, George told herself, 'They were daft to love me. I didn't deserve it.' She cursed herself for denying Alistair. My friend, my soul mate, my lover, my love – and I said I didn't know him. He deserved better.

She slipped out of bed and went downstairs and stopped by the window and gazed at the moonlit garden. So tempting out there. So soft, so quiet, so soothing. She opened the back door and stepped out. The air was fresh and clean, as if she was the only person in the world using it. She wore her favourite sleeping outfit – wide black pants and strappy top, sheer flimsy material. The grass was early-morning damp. The lawn was long and wide with a flower bed in the middle. It was perfect for moonlight running.

George took off slowly. She was hesitant, perhaps a little old for this. But it felt wonderful and soon she was flying; top flapping silky against her, arms spread. She thought it wrong to shout her name. She'd wake the neighbours. So she whispered it hoarsely as she went. 'George. George. George.' On her third trip round she felt her legs getting sore and her breath catching in her throat. Hadn't experienced this since she was a child. 'GEORGE,' she shouted as she turned and headed down towards the back door.

Frank was leaning against the wall, watching. He wore his red silk dressing gown, a cigarette between his lips. He looked bemused and a little ashamed of her. 'What the hell are you doing?'

'Running. Trying not to shout. It's wonderful. You should try it.'

'I don't think so.'

She was standing before him now. She was breathless, pink but definitely not grinning. 'Oh well,' she said, 'your loss.'

'Running about like that is infantile.'

She walked past him into the kitchen and put on the kettle. 'You have the house. I'll take the children.'

'You'll need the house, with kids to look after. We'll sort it out after they've left home.'

It was over. The end had started with the face slap a few years earlier but this was what finally broke them apart. Oh, they'd behaved like a married couple. Had friends round, watched their children grow, gone on trips, bickered and eaten family meals. They'd even had sex. That was what it had been, though – sex. They'd stopped making love a long time ago.

He moved out two days later to a friend's vacant flat and in time to his own city flat. He lived alone. George had supposed he'd install a beautiful long-legged woman to warm his bed. But no, he just wanted to be a bloke again. No woman running barefoot and wild-haired round a lawn for him. The children visited every second weekend for take-away food and trash television. George moved to the middle of her king-size bed and comforted herself that single life had some perks.

We are enduring, George would write to friends. It wasn't anything she'd actually say. Speaking to friends, she'd tell them her family was fine. They were. Lola was studying design at Manchester, James was star of the school football team, Emma was tinkering with the notion of becoming a chef. Willy got bigger and smiled and wanted to be a fireman when he grew up.

It was May. The world was softly green and warm. Frank decided to take his children on a weekend break. James refused to go. He was centre forward and wouldn't miss a big match. Emma was at a crucial point in her early teenage life when going away for a weekend meant not seeing her friends so she refused to go as well. 'You'll see them on Monday when you go back to school,' George had told her. She received a scornful look that said she was old and understood nothing. For once, she let it go. 'It's just you and me, big man,' said Frank, picking up Willy's bag and heading for the car.

The call came at eleven o'clock on Sunday morning. The family was at the kitchen table reading the papers, drinking coffee. The radio was on. It always was. Sun streamed through the window highlighting toast crumbs. George picked up the receiver and knew from the small silence that something awful had happened.

'It's Willy,' said Frank.

George said nothing. Nerves gripped her stomach.

'He went to the swimming pool on his own. I told him not to. I said to wait till I got up. But he wouldn't.'

'My Willy,' said George.

'He drowned.'

Her mouth went dry. She could no longer hold the telephone.

It was as if she forgot how to breathe. Face ashen, trembling, she turned to James and Emma. 'Willy's dead,' she said and ran from the room.

When James and Emma came to her she was sitting in the living room staring ahead. Remembering this, she thought her mouth was open, her face blank. She entered a tunnel. She couldn't speak. The days and months that followed were mostly blank. George remembered hitting Frank when he came later that day with Willy's case. She screamed at him, 'Why did you let him go to the pool alone?'

'I didn't. He just went. Soon as I saw he was gone, I ran after him.' And he stood, arms by his side, unflinching as she slapped him. Over and over she slapped him.

She howled as this pain, this unbearable pain raced through her. It filled her. She thought it the end of her.

When they went to choose a coffin, George raged. 'Not white. He was no Little Lord Fauntleroy. He was a warrior. Red, he loved red.'

She slept deep dreamless sleeps. She couldn't get up in the morning. Couldn't face showering. Hardly spoke. Anna moved in and cared for the others. She'd had little to do with children but she fed them and laundered their clothes. She took time off work to make their lives as normal as possible. Hard when their mother was sleeping most of the day and wandering the house at night, deranged with sorrow.

'That stupid stupid stupid little boy,' George shouted, furious. 'He never did as he was told.'

Walking along a busy city centre street, moving through crowds of people, some going the same way she was, some surging towards her, George felt lost, helpless. She could hardly breathe. She was numb. Something happened to her hearing. It wasn't working. Pins and needles prickled down the arms. What was happening? Why were people going on living, working, just being when her lovely Willy had died? When her world had ended? The unfairness of it, the insanity of it, made her throat tighten, her blood stop running through her veins. 'STOP,' she cried. 'Just all of you STOP.'

For a small moment it seemed as if everybody did stop. Then they started up again. Streaming along the street. George stood, not knowing what to do. Someone took her arm, led her to a seat outside a café and told her to sit. 'Just get your breath.' She was brought a cup of tea. She took a sip. Looked at her rescuer. An older woman, maybe in her late sixties, she was obviously used to taking charge, had no reserves about gripping a stranger's arm and leading them to the safety of a small café. She had a kindly face. A man, her husband George assumed, stood back looking on. He had the slightly embarrassed look partners of opinionated, bossy people often had. He gave her a weak smile.

'My son died,' George told them, 'and people are still walking about as if nothing happened. I can't cope with this.'

The woman said, 'I know. How cruel is that? Drink your tea, then maybe we'll get you a taxi.'

George never discovered who that woman was. Months later she thought to put a notice in the local paper thanking her. But she never got round to it. She took to her bed and to her dressing gown. It saved the business of selecting clothes to wear. She stared a lot. Said little. It must only have been for a couple of weeks but it felt like months and months.

One day Anna, sitting on the chair beside the bed, said, 'I've written you a poem.'

'I thought you'd given that up.'

'No, I think it gave up on me. Anyway, here it is. "We are here. Waiting. For you to come back to us."'

'It doesn't rhyme.'

'Not all poems do. It isn't the rule.' Anna got up. 'I'm going downstairs to rummage in your fridge. You have children in the kitchen who need to be fed.'

'I know,' George said. 'I heard them speaking and moving about.'

'They're there all right.'

'I'm scared. I don't want anyone I love in my life to leave, to go anywhere. I fear they won't come back.'

Anna said, 'We will, though. We always will.'

George heard her cross the room. 'It's a good poem.'

'It's a true one, anyway.'

Fifteen minutes later, the family sitting at the kitchen table looked up as George entered the room. She was pale, tired, wearing her jeans and a favourite baggy jumper. 'We probably ought to order pizza,' she said.

Of course, she didn't get better. She mastered the art of smothering her grief. It was always there. Sometimes at work, or at home, she'd think of Willy – imagining him alone and fighting in the water, struggling to surface. She'd cry out. Hold her stomach and find a quiet, empty place to lean on a wall and calm herself.

*

Two years later, she decided she needed a holiday.

'I'm going somewhere warmer than here and where I don't understand the language. I don't want to know what people are saying. I'm going alone. I need to think.'

She settled on Italy. Lucca. It was late October – warmer than Edinburgh but not uncomfortable. Her hotel was in the town centre and every day she walked. Along the city wall she went and through narrow streets. She drank espressos in small cafés. She gazed at shoes and bought a pair she knew she'd hardly ever wear, but they were too beautiful not to own. She discovered a restaurant where the ceiling was covered with vines and a pizza place that claimed to be the home of pizzas. She fell in love with tiramisu. Ordered it everywhere she went.

Matthew was staying at the same hotel and took to watching her come and go. 'You didn't see many women on their own back then,' he told her later. He didn't want to appear to be stalking her, but he'd seen her go to the restaurant with the vibrant growing vines and he was there one evening when she came in.

He asked if she minded him joining her. In fact she did mind but didn't like to say, so she flapped her hand at the empty seat opposite hers and said, 'Knock yourself out.' They ate pasta with spinach, drank white wine and she didn't bother to look at the menu for pudding. The waiter brought tiramisu. 'We know you like it.'

'Ah yes,' said Matthew, 'it's everywhere, is tiramisu.'

George slowly scraped the drizzled cocoa from the top and put the spoon in her mouth and shut her eyes. 'Italians have perfected the trifle. They have perfected everything. Food, wine, coffee, life.'

He agreed. He told her he was a chef. 'I had a small bistro place on the west coast, seafood mostly. Then I branched out, opened another and another. I should have mastered tiramisu. It didn't occur to me.'

Years later, in bed, she told him he had the perfect face. 'Everything a woman wants in that collection of features – kindness, humour, compassion, intelligence – and your eyebrows don't meet in the middle.'

They'd walked back to the hotel. He bought her a tiny bottle of orchid oil from a pharmacy. They stopped for a glass of grappa. She felt it burn her throat. He took her out for dinner the next night and then back at the hotel he put his arms round her and held her. She'd told him about Willy. He put his hands on her back and pulled her close. He kissed the top of her head and let her lean into him. He knew she needed that. And he needed someone to hold close.

Twenty years on she was still leaning, still eating his Italian food. It was love in a time of tiramisu.

7

Maya Angelou Swung It

'I miss punk. I really liked it. The music almost hurt. People were angry and shouty. The hair was wild and pretty horrible, to be honest. It was a bit of an ugly time. I really fitted in,' said Anna.

'Yes. I remember,' said George. 'You were very angry. But your hair told everybody that you had a sensible streak. It was purple but very tidy. Your Marla who asked you to babysit sounds like a punk.'

'She is shouty. But I'm not a babysitter.'

'You should definitely do it,' said George. 'It would be good for you.' She wiped the last of her bouillabaisse from her plate with a piece of bread and popped it into her mouth. This week's lunch meeting was on her, so they were eating out at a small bistro in Leith.

'What makes you say that?' said Anna. 'I don't need anything that's good for me. I'm fine.' She took a swig of her house red.

'No, you're not. You live on baked potatoes and you hardly ever talk to anybody except me. Solitude and a mono diet is no way of life. Besides, you could use the money.'

'I have little time for money,' said Anna.

'But you have bills, and from time to time you need new shoes, and then there is the business of eating. You have to buy potatoes. The money could go towards classy potatoes.' She leaned back to let the waitress take away her soup plate. She took a sip of her sparkling water. 'Keats would have done it.'

'Babysat? I don't think so.' She raised her wine glass to her friend and bill-payer. 'Here's to not driving.'

'Percy Bysshe Shelley would have babysat.'

'Percy Bysshe Shelley had children.'

'An NCN man, then?' said George.

'NCN?'

'A never-changed-a-nappy man.' George nodded and thanked the waitress for her sole Véronique. The waitress smiled and said, 'I've met a few of them.' She placed Anna's peppered steak in front of her. 'Enjoy.'

'I will,' said Anna. 'A protein-fest for me. You are probably right about Shelley and nappies. But I should imagine his wife left that to some maid or other. I don't know. Such details were not in any of the books I read.'

George said, 'If you took the job you could buy steak.'

'Hmm. Perhaps not.'

'Maya Angelou.' George punched the air. 'She'd definitely have done it. She'd have turned it into something wonderful. There would have been songs and cake and fabulous food and poems. Love – she'd have taught the boy about love.'

Anna put a forkful of steak into her mouth and then shut her eyes to properly savour the flood of wine and pepper and meat. She didn't speak. She took a sip from her glass and let it mix with her food. This was perfect. She loved this. And she wasn't going to let her suspicion that George was right spoil anything.

George noted her friend's pleasure and said nothing. She knew Anna was reconsidering her decision not to look after Marlon. She was taken with the notion of cake and song and love. Maya Angelou had swung it.

It was almost four o'clock when Anna got home. Marla's car was parked across the road. Time then, Anna decided, to go and discuss terms before she changed her mind. She wasn't used to discussing terms, but imagined it to be a civilised exchange between reasonable adults.

In fact, she'd only had one job and hadn't negotiated anything. She'd received a letter offering her the position as editor of her beloved low-circulation poetry magazine after a short interview where it was obvious she was the only applicant. In her working life she'd had six wage raises and had come to accept poverty as a way of life. Present-day prices shook her to the soles of her charity shop shoes. 'It costs *what* to have a mobile phone? I could eat for a month on that.' She'd stand staring, mouth open, into shoe shops amazed at the amount people would pay for a pair of flimsy, strappy high heels. 'Ridiculous,' she'd say. She'd cycled to work on an ancient ex-police bike she'd picked up at an auction sale till arthritis got the better of her.

She pressed her forehead against the windowpane of her living room and indulged in glimpses of her times past. Oh, what a bike that old police bike had been. She'd painted it red to match the Doc Martens of the day. It was heavy, had no gears and pedalling uphill was a sweat and a grunt. But downhill was a thrill. Hair flying and breathless, with legs splayed out either side, she'd whoosh through narrow streets shouting at people to get out of the way. She'd been forty-two and on the way to her poetry magazine. What could be better than that?

There had been parties in posh living rooms dominated by huge pianos and in whitewashed candle-lit cellars. She'd danced, swigged cheap red and argued passionately about books and films and poetry and politics. She'd swigged pints of beer in smoky pubs and kissed lovers in back rooms. *Oh my*, she thought, *happy times. And look at me now. Arthritic and old and needing money.* She sighed, took up her walking stick and set out for Marla's.

The living room was warm and seemed crowded, though there were only three people there. Marlon sat, legs curled, on a blue and white striped sofa watching a cop show on a large television. Voices boomed, 'Put the gun down, son.' Marla stood, hands on hips, taking this moment in before turning to Anna and waving her towards one of the bashed blue seats either side of the fireplace. 'You'll be wanting a cup of tea.'

In fact, she didn't. But Marla disappeared into the kitchen to put the kettle on. Alone with Marlon, Anna felt awkward, old and out of touch with youth, but here was a chance to break the ice with him.

'So what are you up to?'

'Watching television,' he replied. A monotone.

'Do you watch a lot of television?'

Marlon made a snorting grunting noise that Anna assumed meant he did.

'What are your favourite programmes? I like *University Challenge*. Sometimes I even get a question right.' She laughed a feeble laugh.

Marlon didn't answer. It amazed Anna that someone could express extreme irritation without moving, speaking or even registering any facial emotion. She shifted in her seat. She scolded herself for being patronising, sounding like an annoying grown-up. God, she was irritating.

Marla appeared carrying a tray containing three mugs and a plate of chocolate biscuits. She put it on the floor, handed mugs to Anna and Marlon, and took one for herself. She took the chair opposite Anna's, sipped her tea and smiled. 'You've changed your mind.'

'I have,' said Anna. 'I think it would be good to get to know this young man.'

'You could do with the money.'

'Yes.'

She saw Marlon slide from the sofa and over to the plate of biscuits, take two, work his way back and slip back to where he'd been sitting. He didn't spill a drop of tea. That was quite an art.

Marla turned and grinned at him. 'No need to sneak.'

'Biscuits are better when they're sneaked.' He grinned back. His face changed. It lit up and, bathed in his mother's smile, he was suddenly handsome. He was loved.

Anna warmed to him. She thought she might quite like him. She agreed about the sneaking. Sneaked goodies are always juicier.

'The job can't be hard,' she said. 'Just make sure he doesn't wander off and get run over sort of thing. He can come to my place. Read and do jigsaws.'

The boy flinched, as did Marla. But she recovered. 'Well, you can work out what you do. It would be three days a week. The other two he does after-school stuff and I pick him up.'

'After-school stuff?'

'A dance class and drama. Can you start next week? Monday, Tuesday and Thursday, half-past three to six. Seven sometimes.'

Anna said, 'That would be fine. No problem. What do you do?'

'I deliver things. Celebration things. Balloons, cards, cupcakes, Champagne, cheap fizz, chocolate, that sort of thing, to people who are celebrating. You know birthdays, passing exams, having a baby. I find it depressing.'

'Really? Why?'

'Driving about through traffic, finding happy people who are whooping it up and sometimes start to scream when I come in wearing my uniform. It's upsetting. And it's been a hell of a long time since I celebrated anything. And when I did, I never jumped up and down and whooped.'

'Quietly cheering,' said Anna. She stood. It was time to go.

Marla walked with her to the door. 'Monday, then. You'll meet him at the school gates.'

'At the school gates? I thought he'd come to me.'

'He's not walking home alone. Not these days. You don't know who's about. Bullies and perverts. You meet him.'

*

Monday afternoon, three-thirty, Anna was waiting at the school gates. She was nervous. Editing a poetry magazine? Yes, she could do that. Discussing the works of Yeats or Auden? No problem. Picking up a child after school? She'd never done that. This was a new and perturbing thing. Suddenly she was the stranger at the gates. She was getting worrying looks. There was a scattering of mums with pre-school infants, an in-crowd talking animatedly, laughing and looking fashionably superior. But most of the picker-uppers were sitting in cars patiently watching for the main doors to open.

When they did, children tumbled out and sped across the playground. They looked like wildly enthusiastic escapee puppies. The air rang with their cries of glee. For a panicky moment Anna couldn't remember what Marlon looked like. What if she took home the wrong child? How would she sort that one out?

Marlon was one of the last to come out. He was alone, had no pal chattering at his side. His day in the classroom had taken its toll. Half his shirt was hanging out, one shoe lace was undone, his hair was lank and his face pale. His school bag, which resembled one Anna used all those years ago, had slipped to waist level, the straps at his elbows. He looked pained and watched the ground as he walked. He stopped briefly in front of Anna, made a sort of greeting that was more of a grunt than an actual hello, and set off down the street ahead of her.

She followed but not at the child's furious pace.

'Will you stop and wait for me? I can't keep up.'

He slowed till she had overtaken him. Then he trailed behind, moving so slowly Anna seemed to steam at a pace in front of him. She stopped.

'Why don't you try walking beside me? We could chat.'

He looked horrified. 'No. Won't chat. I don't want to go home with you. I don't want to walk along the street with you. You're old.'

Anna sighed. 'I know. It happened one day when I wasn't looking.'

He stared at her, that look young people give old people they consider to be not just unreasonably old but also insane.

'I'd like you to walk at the same pace as me,' said Anna.

Marlon said, 'Okay.' And he crossed the road to oblige her by walking at the desired pace on the pavement over there.

Anna said, 'Thank you.' It was a start.

They walked in step, but silently. Marlon resented every moment. Old ladies were clearly embarrassing. Anna had imagined they'd stroll through the late afternoon chatting about school, her reminiscing about her own young life, the corridors she haunted, the teachers she'd loved and those she'd hated and the books she'd read. This was awful. Children were a mystery. She gazed down at her Doc Martens moving over the pavement and worried. What if the child ran back across the road, got run over by a car and ended up in A&E, or worse died? How to break this news to his mother? This was not going well. She thought she'd dressed appropriately for the occasion – jeans, baggy red jumper. But it seemed that some mothers dressed up for this. She sighed again and wished she was back in her old life – safe in her tiny office, desk covered with typescripts, telephone ringing from time to time and a cup of coffee at hand. She'd been happy then.

Marlon suddenly, and without checking the road was clear, bolted to the pavement she was on and disappeared down a narrow lane. Alarmed, Anna hobbled as fast as she could after him.

'Hoi. Where are you going?'

He stopped, turned and said, 'Home. This is a short cut.'

'Do you behave like this when you're with your mother? Not talking? Shooting down little narrow lanes on your own?'

'No.' He looked surprised at her suggestion. 'We're in the car, silly.'

'Oh.'

She'd passed this lane often, but had never in all her years living in the neighbourhood explored it. She'd assumed it led to more houses and gardens. It was almost too narrow for two people to walk side-by-side and was fenced. Anna thought that for a short cut, something that should offer some sort of danger or thrill, it was boring.

In fact, it led to a joiner's yard. Marlon lit up as he went through the gate. In painstakingly handwritten letters a sign on the fence read

RICHARD BARCLAY
JOINER • MASTER CRAFTSMAN

This place had been here for a long time, but Anna knew nothing about it.

A man was concentrating on sawing a long plank. He didn't look up. Anna stood with Marlon, watching. She felt awkward. It was obviously private here. He stopped and greeted the boy.

'Hey, Marlon. How're you doing?'

'Fine,' Marlon grinned.

'And who's this you've brought?'

'Anna.' There was a certain disapproval in Marlon's tone. 'She's looking after me when my mum's at work. I had to bring her.'

The man stood up straight and put down the saw. He nodded to her. He was tall, muscular and old. His hair was long. He wasn't quite ugly, just getting there. His nose was a bit big for his face, lips full and his eyebrows on the wild side. He looked to Anna like one of the interesting extras she'd seen in French movies. He was a Parisian gangster, a man of many opinions, some of which she'd find annoying. He looked like a man who knew himself and was content with that. Anna was transfixed. She was in love.

8

How Long Have You Been Old?

Was it love? Anna didn't know. *Probably a crush*, she thought. She'd had many crushes in her life, but not recently. She didn't think such a thing would happen to her now. Old people don't fall in love, or indulge in wild infatuation.

Trying not to stare at Richard, Anna remembered her first and longest-lasting crush. It had been in her distant days, when her fellow school pupils had swooned over John Lennon and Ringo Starr. The object of her adoration had been Lord Byron. One day, she sighed, he would be behind her in the queue in her local shop where, on messages for her mum, she'd come to buy bread or milk or sugar. He would see beyond the navy school blazer, white blouse with permanently askew tie and white ankle socks to the shy sensitive literary genius she was. He'd smile. 'But words are things,' he'd say, 'and a small drop of ink, falling like dew upon a thought produces that which makes thousands, perhaps millions, think.' 'True,' she'd reply, pocketing her change and tucking her pan loaf under her arm. Nights in bed she'd imagine he'd come to her, stroke her cheek and tell her there was no instinct like that of the heart. She knew he was long dead, but when she slipped into her imaginings this didn't matter.

Byron's kiss is but a trembling butterfly pressed a moment on my lips, she'd written on the inside cover of her Geography jotter. Her mother, who had left school at fourteen and had ambitions for her daughter's education, had come across this and asked about this Byron person. 'Are you seeing him? You're too young for all that nonsense.'

Anna had sighed dramatically and flounced from the room. 'He's a poet, mother.'

'A poet. You stop that. You're too young for boys and you're way way too young for a poet. I forbid you to see him.'

In the park next day Anna and George sat on a bench – two worldly girls sharing a Mars Bar and discussing parental relationships.

'My mother thinks I'm seeing a bloke called Byron,' Anna had said.

George snorted.

'She told me I'm too young to go out with a poet. God, she's embarrassing. She doesn't understand anything. I'm misunderstood. It's boring.'

'You have no idea what I have to suffer,' George said. Tears blurred her eyes. 'My mother is awful. I hate her. She understands me. She's kind and gentle and makes me hot chocolate when I come home. I tell you, if there's anything worse than being misunderstood it's being understood. You just can't rebel.'

Standing in Richard Barclay's messy yard remembering this, Anna smiled. There was no crush like a first crush. Richard noticed her grin and gave her a quizzical look.

'I like your yard,' Anna said. 'It's lovely, full of interesting things.'

It was indeed. There were a couple of unfinished doors awaiting locks and handles, planks of wood leaning against the wall, more wood in piles inside the workshop, a circular saw and a scattering of sawdust on the ground. Anna indicated the interesting things with a sweep of her arm, caught Richard's dismissive expression and gave him a watery smile.

'I've never been in a working yard,' she told him.

'They're full of interesting things,' he said and turned to speak to Marlon. 'You want to get on with your spice rack?'

Marlon was already in the workshop putting the half-finished spice rack onto a bench. His school bag and anorak were abandoned in a heap in a corner.

'You want to take a seat and wait?' Richard said. 'We'll be half an hour or more maybe.' He led her inside to a low leather seat beside an ancient woodburning stove. He stood back watching as Anna lowered herself into the seat. 'Came from out of a Jaguar.'

'A car seat, how clever,' said Anna. Getting into it had been a little bit tricky. She fancied her knees creaked. Getting up again was worrying her, but she nodded and praised the innovation. 'Very comfy.' Now, however, she was close to the ground and sitting looking up at him.

'How long have you been a child minder?' he asked.

'I'm not a child minder. I'm doing some light babysitting so Marla can go to work.'

'Ah,' he said. He went to join Marlon and his spice rack.

The heat from the stove was soft and soothing – a gentle enveloping warmth. Anna leaned back and let it soak in. The walk here had been a trial. She needed this. She stretched out her legs. Listened to Richard instruct Marlon on the business of sanding his wood. 'Just back and forth till it's like silk. Size do you want to make it?'

Marlon didn't know. 'Big enough for all the spices, I think.' His voice was thin and shrill. 'How many spices are there?'

Richard said, 'Not sure.' He came over to Anna. 'How many spices are there?'

'Probably hundreds,' she said. 'But I only know of a few. Cayenne, nutmeg, turmeric. If you allowed for about ten, that would do it.' There was sawdust under her feet and the smell of burning pine in the air. If it weren't for the embarrassment of falling in love with a man she was beginning to dislike, it would be pleasant here. 'Cumin,' she said, 'and paprika.'

'So what did you do before you took up light babysitting?'

'I'm retired.'

'Retired from what?'

'A poet.'

'You're a retired poet? I didn't think poets retired.'

'I edited a poetry magazine. I no longer do that.'

He returned to spice-rack duties.

Anna wished she'd never abandoned her crush on Byron. At least dead heroes didn't ask questions and make stupid remarks.

For half an hour she worried about getting up out of this car seat. But when the time came she heaved herself to her feet using her stick. 'Managed,' she said. Then she asked Marlon if he thought it time they headed home. 'It'll be dark soon and we should get back before your mum.'

The boy led the way. A short cut, he said. They left through a gap in the fence at the back of the yard. This took them into a dense weeded area that Anna was convinced was somebody's garden. 'I don't think we ought to be here.'

'Nah. It's fine. Nobody minds.' Marlon charged ahead. He climbed a low wall and stood waiting for Anna to follow. She sat on the bricks at the top, heaved her legs over and slid to the ground. Marlon stomped through long grass, dropped to his knees and crawled under a hedge.

Anna said, 'Enough. We're going back. No more short cuts.'

'I suppose you're too old for them.' Marlon's voice drifted over the hedge.

'Yes. I'm old. I no longer crawl under hedges.'

'I'm not old, though.'

'You're new. I've noticed. And as you're new, you can come back through that hedge and we'll go home the normal way.'

'Don't want to.'

'Fine,' said Anna. 'I'm going back. And when I'm home I'm having a mug of hot chocolate and toast. A new person who uses a short cut gets water.'

She started to walk back to Richard's yard and heard Marlon come after her. She'd heard about bribery. Friends who were parents had told her they'd vowed not to use it but had in the end done so. It hadn't taken her long to succumb. *An hour? Maybe two*, she thought. *I have failed at being a babysitter light.*

She could hear Marlon trudging behind her. He was panting. She admired that he could sound so resentful while breathing heavily. They renegotiated the wall, stamped through the weeds and squeezed back into the yard. Richard nodded as they walked past him.

'Wondered if you'd be coming back. It's a bit of a jungle going that way.'

Anna jerked her head at Marlon. 'He said it was a short cut.'

Marlon said, 'She's too old for short cuts.'

Richard nodded. 'Happens.'

Marlon looked up at Anna. 'How long have you been old?'

All my life, she thought. But she told him a fortnight.

'What were you before that?'

'Long before I was old I was young. Then I was getting older. This lasted quite a while, years and years. Then I was simply getting old. Now I am old. Those are the phases.'

Richard agreed. Anna moved away. 'Time to go home.'

After they reached the street, Marlon asked, 'So did you used to be a hippie when you were getting older?'

'No. I was a bit of a hippie when I was young. Though not as young as you. Older than that.'

'Did you smoke dope and sing songs about love and peace? I've seen it in films. Shaggy people with a lot of hair.'

'Not really,' she lied.

They walked in silence, Marlon looking at his feet and contemplating, Anna thought, his untied shoelace.

She drifted back to her hippie days. They hadn't lasted long. But they'd been happy, or happyish. When it came along, she preferred the rawness of punk. George had been a better, more committed hippie than she'd been. In fact, George had done a lot more in her life than she had. George should have been a poet. George lived. Anna had spent her life trying to write meaningful things about being alive.

She'd only smoked dope once. The memory still made her wince. It hadn't been her finest hour. It had been at a student dinner party in a grubby flat somewhere off the High Street. Her Afghan coat had been slung flamboyantly over a dull maroon sofa. She sighed. God, she'd loved that coat. She wondered what happened to it. She had no recollection of throwing it out. But she didn't have it now. It was gone. Gone like her golden hippie days.

She stamped along, hitting the pavement with her stick and sighing loudly. Marlon gave her a quizzical glance but said nothing.

There had been a lot of dope at that party. She remembered sitting at a table that was cluttered with bottles of wine, candles, plates of salad and ham and a large bowl of peas. Apart from an Aubrey Beardsley print on the wall, the bowl had been the most beautiful thing in the room. It was cream with a dusty blue pattern and a couple of very dark red flowers either side. The joint had been handed to her. She was a novice and not sure what to do, but owning up to that was not on. She was in the company of wild and free flower children; she wanted to be one of the gang. She inhaled deeply. Inhaled again and passed the joint along. She wasn't bogarting it. Conversation flowed. Vietnam. Nixon. Bob Dylan. Life. *Easy Rider*. Everything was discussed. She ate a slice of tomato. The joint came her way once more. She inhaled very deeply. Twice. Handed it over and noticed the peas. They were green. Not just any green, but a shimmering deep green. The green of the universe – the most wonderful, meaningful colour in the world. She had to tell everybody.

'How green are my peas,' she said.

The conversation stopped. Everyone looked at her.

'That green,' she pointed at the peas, 'is the colour of life. It is exquisite. It is everything. It is the green of the universe. We must believe it. We must try to be it. If we do, there will be no more wars.'

Walking home now, nearly there. She groaned. She'd never touched anything other than wine since then. If her fellow diners had been hostile, that might have been all right. But they'd smiled quietly, patronisingly. They'd known a novice hippie when they met one.

Marlon and Anna reached her building and climbed the stairs to her flat. Inside Marlon slid his school bag to the floor and looked round.

'You've got a lot of books. Have you read them all?'

'Most of them. Some are for dipping into.'

He went into the living room and surveyed the pictures on the walls, the odds and ends on shelves – a green wine flask, an ancient typewriter, a phrenology head, a ceramic hen and more. 'You've got a lot of stuff and hardly any television.'

'I don't watch much. The news.' She also followed several soaps but rarely admitted to it. 'Shall we have hot chocolate and toast?'

'Yeah.'

He followed her into the kitchen, still gazing round as he went. 'I like big TVs. Yours is small. Do you get Netflix?'

'No.'

She put a pan of milk on the cooker. Spooned chocolate into mugs. This child thing wasn't going to be as easy as she'd imagined. Jigsaws and books weren't going to do. 'What's your favourite thing?' she asked.

'Hot chocolate. Puppies. Cartoons. Drums. I'd like to play the drums.'

Tricky, she thought. *I'm out of my depth with the boy.* She was about to ask if he had any friends and decided not to. Of course he didn't have friends. He'd come out of school alone. He wished nobody goodbye. Didn't even look at his fellow pupils. A friendless skinny boy who liked puppies and wanted to play the drums. Her heart went out to him.

9

Not a Crush – An Awakening

'He made me doubt everything about myself,' said Anna. 'Children do that,' George told her.

'He said I had more stuff than television. He looked round at the books and I saw that he didn't understand why I had them. I realised I was a hermit who lived through reading. I absorbed other people's feelings and thoughts instead of giving out my own. I thought I appeared to others as fierce and unapproachable.'

'You don't.'

'I charge along the street, hair flying. Old coat buffeting out, glaring at people.'

George laughed. 'A child looks round your living room, gives a juvenile opinion of what he sees and you beat yourself up.'

'Yes, that's about it.'

'What did you say to him?'

'Not a lot. I made him hot chocolate and toast. Then his mother came to pick him up. I was left to consider my life so far. I can't help thinking that there are people with real jobs – policemen, brain surgeons, bus drivers for example. And there's me, a poet and an editor of a poetry magazine. I feel I could have done more. I could have had a proper responsible job.'

They were on a bench in Princes Street Gardens eating tomato sandwiches. It was something George always enjoyed. From not far away came the sounds of the city – traffic and voices and passing music pouring out of open car windows – but here it was calm, the air was fresh and the food basic. Basil or provolone cheese never occurred to Anna. She served buttered bread and sliced tomatoes. It worked. 'You wouldn't have made a brain surgeon and the police wouldn't have had you.'

'They might.'

'You're small. You never have stuck to wearing a uniform. You failed your driving test four times. You could never have watched and waited for a crook to come along. You'd have brought a book to a stake-out. And you are squeamish. If you'd had to attend a car crash, you'd have thrown up.'

'Okay. I'll give you all that. I've been doing this new job for a week and it's opened my eyes to the world. I let it in when I should have stayed in my comfort zone, playing Mozart and Joni Mitchell and reading. But I didn't and now I'm filled with doubt.'

'A child has done this to you?'

'No. A man.'

George nodded. 'Ah. The truth. A man.'

'I seem to be smitten,' Anna said. She told George about Richard. 'He isn't good looking. In fact, he's a bit ugly. But attractively so. He has a used face. I can see sorrow there, and intelligence, a bit of cruelty perhaps and tenderness. It is a face you want to stare at, only it would be rude.'

'And this is just his face. What about the rest of him?'

'Well, obviously his face is all I've seen. Except his hands. Good hands, big strong hands.' She told George about Richard's yard and the spice rack he was helping Marlon to make. She didn't mention the short-cut fiasco. There were some absurd doings you kept from your friends. 'I sit on an old car seat by a woodburning stove while the two work. I listen to them chat.'

'They don't talk to you, then?'

'I get some gentle mockery, mostly about being a poet. I don't think Richard sees them as being normal.'

'Perhaps he thinks you are an intellectual. They can be frightening.'

'Please don't tell me that. I want him to like me.'

'You are smitten.'

'I think I'm in love. This is new to me. I can't remember it happening. Is this what love is like? It comes to you uninvited. It grows within. It's like a disease spreading through you. You don't know how it got there or why. You don't know what to do about it. It makes you want to cry.' She looked suddenly hopeless. 'I am so happy to be miserable.'

George patted her arm. 'Maybe it's just a crush.'

'I've never had a crush before. Well, Lord Byron. But even I could see it wouldn't lead to anything. Not with him being dead.'

George stood up, dusted stray crumbs from her jumper. 'Let's get a cup of coffee. I would suggest alcohol but I'm driving. I had the most awful crush on Steven Parkin when we were at school. I went red if he came near me. I hugged my pillow in bed at night, dreaming it was him.'

Anna started tidying their picnic debris, shoving sandwich wrapping into her bag. 'I never knew. You and Steven Parkin.'

'No, just me. Steven Parkin liked older women. He was fourteen and lusted after Sheila Brown, who was sixteen. I hadn't a chance. But it was a trying time for me. In fact, I'd rather have had measles. God, I was in love.'

They made their way up to Princes Street and Starbucks.

'What do you imagine when you think of this man?' asked George.

'I think of us sitting on the sofa of an evening. Having a meal together, a bottle of wine and pasta perhaps. Chatting. Browsing a bookshop.'

'Not sex, then? Not his breath on your neck or his hands in your hair, his lips seeking yours?'

'No. I find that embarrassing with someone I've hardly spoken to. Not that I mind sex. I've had plenty of it in my day. Remember, I'm the woman who posed nude on the steps of the National Gallery.'

'Ah yes. I'd forgotten about that. Never saw the photos.'

'No. It was early March, three o'clock in the morning. We were hoping nobody would be about. And it was quite quiet. But chilly, very chilly. I stood with my arms spread, trying to look liberated and gloriously happy. Then some passing motorist called the police and they came and the photographer and his assistant ran away. I couldn't so much, on account of being naked.'

'The police caught you?'

'Yes, and they took me home to my parents. They weren't well pleased. Not with me being naked. And I'd left my clothes in a heap at the bottom of the steps. It wasn't a good time for me.'

'I remember. But the photos?'

'They were for a left-wing underground poetry magazine, *Down Dirty and Not Rhyming*. They never used them. I was in bed for a week with a chill.'

George worked at not smiling.

'I thought I was being brave and free,' said Anna. 'I can tell you, being taken home by the police stark naked and frozen isn't your finest hour. God, the look my mother gave me. But if you're asking about my sex life, it has had its moments. I have had lovers. Not as many as you. You have always been naughtier than me.'

'Have I?' George thought for a moment. 'I've probably had more lovers. I liked being in bed with someone. I loved that moment when you turned to one another. I felt wanted. But I've always been faithful to the one I had at the time.' They reached Starbucks and went in. 'Now I have Matthew and that's it for me.'

They ordered coffee and found an empty table. This was a small part of city life and George loved city life. Until recently she'd always lived near the centre but now that she was in the quiet of the outskirts she missed the rush and bustle of people and traffic.

She'd always walked to work. She noticed many things as she went – the way the seasons made their mark in gardens, a certain cat that watched the world from an upstairs window, breakfast bickering from a house on a corner, music that poured from another, people at bus queues. She'd had her winter heart lifted at the sight of primroses in a pot by a front door. Sometimes walking home after a gruelling day – perhaps she'd spent time with a dying patient or seen a horribly injured accident victim – she found solace in watching lives moving through the daily routines of buying food, chatting, raking leaves, hanging out clothes on the line.

'What happened to your clothes?' she said to Anna. 'You know, when the police caught you and took you home?'

'I don't know,' said Anna. 'I never saw them again. I had the loveliest velvet skirt. I missed that. The police wrapped me in a blanket. But they took it away when they delivered me.' She sipped her coffee, stared ahead and said, 'So there I was, standing in front of my mother stark naked and hair dyed bright green.'

'I don't remember you having green hair.'

'The hair I dyed was not the hair that is on general public view.'

'Ah,' said George.

'I did it for humanity, for freedom, for poetry, books, and to strike a blow for anarchy.'

'Well, if ever there was a reason to dye your pubic hair green, that was it.'

'My mother said I was a slut for leaving my husband and for cavorting in the street with no clothes on. I told her my husband left me because he was gay. So she said I was a stupid slut to have married a homosexual.'

George reached over and squeezed her arm.

'I was devastated. I felt utterly shattered. Stupid. Unwanted. Naïve. It all floored me. I crawled away emotionally. Went to work on the poetry magazine. In my little bubble mixing with writers and book people I had odd affairs but I stayed safe, no falling in love, no commitment, and now I think I missed a lot.'

'So what do you want to do about your teenage crush?'

'It's not a crush – it's an awakening. Something inside is coming back to life.' She stared into her coffee and sighed. 'There are so many things I haven't done. But mostly I regret small stuff. Sitting in comfortable silence with someone I love. Shared jokes. Meals. Planning holidays. I've shut myself away, afraid of relationships after my first absurdity and my mother's mockery. My marriage was a surprise to me. There was no sex, obviously. And we didn't get round to sharing other intimacies – underpants on the floor, sharing a bathroom, piles of washing up, bickering about radio stations. I don't know about them and I might like to. It's karma. It's what I get for being stupid.'

10

Home Is a Person

George was in the garden deadheading roses, yanking out weeds and thinking, working things out. This was something she did as she pottered in her flowerbeds. She'd wrestle with the vibrant growth that surrounded her and from the deep recesses of her brain revelations or solutions would appear and she'd toss a lump of unwanted grass into her canvas bag and shout, 'That's it. That's definitely it.'

She shouted it as she threw a dandelion into the bag and set off across the lawn to the back door. She was excited at the thought of sharing her latest insight with Matthew.

'It's not sex,' she told him. She clumped over the floor and sat at the table, giving him a gleeful stare. 'She's done that. Obviously. No, it's the small stuff of a relationship. You know, the trivial intimacies that come with living together.'

Matthew looked up from his newspaper and said, 'Huh?'

'I mean Anna. She's looking for a proper thing with a man. She's noticed that in marriages people bicker and it doesn't really matter because they know that they are safe. The other person, the one they're bickering with, isn't going to hit them or walk out.'

Matthew took off his glasses and stared at her.

'It's the business of liking as well as loving. We share a shower and I have never once complained that you use my expensive shampoo and have a strange habit of moving the showerhead as you get out. Often I turn it on first thing and get a blast of cold water. It's annoying. But I won't leave you over it. Then there's the underpants thing. I've known men who take off their boxers and toss them across the room before they jump into bed. Something like that can be off-putting. Anna wants to find out if she can be in a relationship that will survive such behaviour. Companionship, that's what she's after. What I'm saying is, she wants to be ordinary.'

Matthew said nothing.

'I'm ordinary. Husband, house, children, grandchildren, garden, ancient car. I'm so ordinary, it's boring. But Anna isn't. She dresses in an interesting way from charity shops, has far too much hair, stomps around and is so lost in her thoughts she forgets to speak to people. She used to be fearless. She is as a failed poet but not as a human being. That's what she wants to be, a human being.'

Matthew still said nothing. George headed back to the garden. But then came back.

'I wouldn't actually know, but I'm sure she would be good in bed. But what does good in bed mean? What do people who are good in bed do that people who aren't don't do? Are you good in bed? Am I?'

Matthew sniffed and took a sip of coffee from the mug in front of him.

George turned to go. Took a step, turned back. 'That's it, isn't it? I'm out there gardening, sifting through my thoughts and I come to a conclusion. I have a revelation and I come in to tell you about it. And I really annoy you. And you annoy me by being annoyed at me. But we're not going to divorce over it. That's human beings being married.'

Matthew said, 'I'm trying to do the crossword. Please go away.'

George said, 'I'll go away when you admit I'm right.'

'You're right. Go away.' Then he said, '"Meatier". Anagram.'

George stared ahead, wrestling with the letters in 'meatier'. She liked words, had favourites, but never was very good at puzzles involving them. She shrugged and said she was going back to her gardening. As she stepped outside it came to her.

She'd never before in her lift solved an anagram. The triumph was dazzling. 'Emirate,' she shouted. 'I'm on fire today. A revelation about marriage and an anagram solved. Eat your heart out, Matthew.'

He considered the grid. 'Bugger, you're right. I hate that.'

George had been working for another hour when Matthew joined her. He stood behind her, hands in pockets and said, 'You're doing a good job.'

'I know.' She looked up at him. 'I suppose you're not here to help?'

'Never did take to gardening. Too much earth. But I love being in a garden. Your garden.'

George smiled. 'So what do you want?'

'I was lonely.'

'Rubbish.'

'I was, a bit. Finished the crossword. Then I started to think about what you said about Anna.'

'She says she felt safe when she wrote poetry. She doesn't any more. She ground to a halt. I think she'd like a proper relationship.'

Matthew started to sit on the grass and got ticked off.

'It's damp,' George said. 'And you might get an embarrassing green stain on your bum.'

They moved over to the wooden bench under the pear tree.

'Anna had a good time a long time ago. She had lovers but they were all "sleep over a couple of nights a week, toast and coffee and off into the day" sort of men. They didn't linger. They certainly wouldn't have moved in. She was happy with that. She worked on her magazine. She went to parties and to the pub. She got into heated conversations about life and poetry and books. But it all just faded away. She got old. People died. She started to think she'd missed something. That's all.'

Mathew nodded. 'Not like you, then.'

'Not like me. It never crossed my mind to write a poem. It never crossed my mind not to marry or at least have a man in my life, in my bed. I like warming my feet on someone. Thing is – and it's a big thing – is that my mother loved me. I could be a shit, and I was, and still I was loved. Anna's mother regularly told her she didn't want her. Anna was scared to be a shit. Being shitty wasn't safe.'

Matthew nodded.

'She has fallen for a man who has a joinery business near her. She is smitten. I think it has knocked her for six.'

They sat for a moment enjoying the small touch of their thighs and her hand on his, soaking in the scents of the day – the earth, grass, perfume from some flower or other.

'You know,' Matthew said, 'I feel so blessed to be in this place and to have found you, George. Not a day passes that you don't surprise me and make me laugh.'

'Mhmm,' George said, not letting on her thoughts had drifted to tiramisu.

The phone in the kitchen rang and Matthew got up to answer it. Ten minutes later he came back. 'That was James.'

'*My* James?'

'Yes. The only James we know. He wants to come and stay for a while. He's having problems. He's lost his job. He wants to come home.'

George said, 'Fine, I suppose. Why not? Whatever's wrong, he'll sort himself out.' She tried not to think of any dreadful things that might have happened. Instead voiced a small protest. 'Actually, this isn't his home. The house I had with Frank was home to him. He was brought up there.'

Matthew said, 'You don't get it, do you?'

'What?'

'You're his mother. You're his home. You are home to Anna, who thinks the world of you and needs you. You are home to me. Where you are is my home. Home is a person.'

11

Swagger Boy and Lil

Anna regularly screamed and shouted in the shower. She'd raise her arms to the cascading water and curse herself. 'Stupid bitch.' Memories would crowd in on her. She'd scrub herself, chasing them away, yelling, 'Go away. Eff off.' Because it was never the golden moments that came to her. It was the embarrassments, the mistakes, the crazed lunacies – dancing naked with pubic hair dyed dazzling green on the steps of the National Gallery at three in the morning, for example. Briefly, though, moving through soft night air, arms spread and singing 'All You Need Is Love', it had felt wonderful.

Today, after a bout of cursing herself, she turned to song and rinsed off her soap with a rendition of 'Da Doo Ron Ron'. Exuberant sixties songs were excellent for an ageing morale.

Dressed in jeans and T-shirt, she went to the kitchen. She made coffee and toast and took stock of her food supplies. Today was a Marlon day, so she needed a tin of hot chocolate and a pack of the strange cheese spread he liked. She rather liked it herself. Marlon had introduced her to many new things – comic strip heroes, violent-flavoured yoghurts, twists on language, gadgets. She marvelled.

Things were improving. The child continued to dislike walking alongside her, but now kept himself to moving a few feet in front. This way it was possible to chat. Yesterday he'd asked once more if she was old.

'Yes,' she said. 'I am. I am officially old. No longer getting old. Just old.'

'What's it like?'

'Painful. Joints ache. I sometimes forget things. I sleep more. But I understand things. I do believe I am more tolerant. Or maybe I can't be bothered with people I disagree with so I ignore them.'

'Right,' he said.

She figured he had no idea what she was talking about, but couldn't be bothered asking for an explanation.

'I'm not old,' he said.

'Indeed you're not. You're new.'

He liked that. 'Yeah, new's best.'

'Not always. Being around for a long time means you have experience. I know stuff from experience.'

'What?' he wanted to know. He stamped ahead, not looking at her.

'Well, have you ever been married?' She loved that he took a long time to think about this.

Finally, he said, 'No. I've never been married. Have you?'

'Yes.'

'What was it like?'

'It had its moments,' she lied. 'Have you ever had a job?'

'No. Have you?'

'Yes, and I loved it.'

They reached the lane leading to Richard's yard. Marlon took off running. The conversation was over. So far there had been no eye contact and distance had been maintained. But questions had been asked and answered. They were beginning to get along.

Breakfast over, dishes washed, she set off for the corner shop. It was what she called an average British day. Not hot, not cold, clouds in the sky and a light wind. There was an assortment of weather, but nothing to trouble her. She hummed 'Da Doo Ron Ron' and let the beginnings of a poem drift through her mind. *On a cloudy day with a small wind/I met my love.*

Then what?, she thought.

She filled her basket with hot chocolate, cheesy spread, milk, chocolate fingers and potatoes, had a pleasant chat about the weather and headed home. She let 'Da Doo Ron Ron' hum in her head and two more lines of her poem popped up. *I was buying spread cheese/He was after frozen peas.*

Useless, she thought.

She stopped, hung her head in shame. 'Go away,' she told the lines, hoping they'd vanish, melt into the air. Someone was pulling at the handle of her shopping bag.

'Sorry,' he said. 'Just thought I'd help.'

She turned. Richard.

'Oh,' she said. 'I can manage. It's not that heavy.' She reddened. She realised she should let him take it. It was what women in love did. She let go the bag.

He was looking at her as if he might be thinking, *Oh, she's one of those feminist types. Doesn't want help.* He let go the basket too.

It crashed to the ground. A bit embarrassed and a bit guilty, they both looked at it. Anna snatched it up and continued her walk home. He fell into step with her. They didn't speak. She searched her head for some mutual subject. 'I've been buying some snacks for Marlon,' she said.

'That's nice,' he nodded.

'Do people feed their children different food from what they eat? It seems like they are a separate species these days.'

'Yes,' said Richard. They walked side-by-side, looking ahead. 'You get children's menus in restaurants and there's shelves and shelves of brightly coloured food in the supermarket.'

'Goodness,' said Anna. 'I rarely go to supermarkets. I fear I'd spend too much. I prefer the local shop, where there's not much I fancy.'

'Good plan,' said Richard. 'Of course, when I was a lad you got what was going and a slap on the side of your head if you didn't finish it. That or no pudding. I preferred the slap. My mother made excellent puddings.'

'Really?' said Anna. 'My mother was a diabolical cook. She didn't do puddings till Angel Delight came along.'

'Angel Delight?' Richard sounded interested.

'Yes. Butterscotch was my favourite. I don't know if they still make it.'

'I'll look out for it.'

They reached Anna's building. 'This is me,' she said.

He looked at the broken gate, the rough grass and weeds and said, 'Very nice.'

She could tell he didn't mean it. She nodded and strode briskly to the main door. Once inside, climbing to her flat, it crossed her mind that she should have invited him in for a cup of tea. *I would have got to know him*, she thought. *That's what women who know about men do.*

She took her shopping to the kitchen and dumped it on the table. She wished she'd bought a packet of Angel Delight. Perhaps Marlon would like it. Now she thought about it, she was amazed Richard hadn't heard of it. Perhaps he was a savoury person who never ate sweet things. She assumed he was a solitary sort. He didn't seem to need other people. But perhaps that was because he had a wife who gave him all the company he needed. She might make him huge satisfying puddings – crumbles, sponges, mousses, dumplings, and sticky toffee dishes – so there was no space for an instant packet in his life. *Oh my*, she thought, *all those puddings and Richard – I could die from longing.*

Back in the living room she stood at the window, watching the world out there. People coming and going. She had names for them all but had no real idea who they were. Neighbours. There was Swagger Boy with Lil, his girlfriend. She'd seen them often. He never walked, he strutted. He'd perfected a forward movement propelled by his shoulders. Lil was besotted with him. Anna wondered if one day she'd come to her senses. Still, Swagger Boy wasn't as tough as he appeared. Anna had seen him helping old Mrs Raincoat with her shopping. Mrs Raincoat lived above Mr and Mrs Orange, a dressy couple who had a posh car and looked like they spent a deal of time in a suntan parlour. The Normals seemed to have a busy life. There were four of them, two grown-ups and two children. They had a small green car and often looked glum. They reminded Anna of a family from a sitcom. Anna's favourite was Mother Dainty, who gardened all summer and had turned her piece of scrubland into a delight of flowers. These people had actual names. Anna had no idea what they were. Marlon would know. He'd know if Richard was married. She gave herself a talking to about her life, how she'd been so intent on following her dreams she hadn't taken time to get acquainted with the people who shared the neighbourhood.

At three she left the flat to meet Marlon at the school gates. She was now aware of the upmanship involved and made sure her T-shirt was ironed. She was contemplating putting on a smear of lipstick, but perhaps that was going too far. She was sure that only actual mothers did that.

Marlon was still among the last to come out of school. He slouched across the playground, stood in front of her, nodded and started heading for Richard's yard. This was an improvement. He no longer steamed past her, ignoring her. He trudged a couple of yards in front.

'I met Richard today,' Anna said.

Marlon said, 'Right.'

'We had an interesting conversation about puddings.'

'Good subject.'

'We thought so. He likes big puddings. You know, crumbles and pies. Sort of thing his wife would cook for him.'

'He hasn't got a wife. He said he didn't believe in having one. He cooks his own pies. Well, he buys them and heats them up.'

'Really?' said Anna.

Well, that was interesting. If Richard had been married, that would have been that. She'd have sought comfort in chocolate and might even have allowed herself a bottle of wine, now she had a bit extra cash. With the worry about Richard having a wife out of the way, she asked Marlon about the neighbours.

'Do you know the people who live near you?'

'The neighbours? Yeah. Why?'

'I just wondered about them.'

'They're the neighbours. That's all.'

'I see them coming and going and wonder about them. I have little names for them.'

They reached the lane that led to Richard's yard. Marlon stopped, looked at her and said, 'Well, they see you and they think . . .' His face reddened, a deep scarlet. He didn't finish his sentence. He fled.

For the hour that she sat on the car seat as Marlon worked on his spice rack, Anna tortured herself about what her neighbours thought of her. *Daft old woman*, she thought. *Fancies herself. Weirdo.* Oh God, it was all too terrible.

They walked home slowly. Marlon was enthused, talking about four little shelves he'd slotted into his spice rack and wondering if he should paint it or leave it as it was – 'just wooden'.

Anna listened, nodded and fretted inwardly about her reputation. As they approached her building she spotting Mother Dainty working in her garden, chipping at the ground with her hoe. Marlon waved to her. Mother Dainty waved back. 'Good day at school, Marlon?'

'Rubbish.'

Mother Dainty looked at Anna, who waved and in return got a stiff, awkward smile and an embarrassed hand movement – a wave that was a reluctant response to the wave that had been offered to her. Assessing that minuscule movement of hand and shy knowing smile, Anna thought, *Oh God, she knows about me. She knows about the naked night on the steps of the National Gallery and the green hair. And all the other stupid things I've done – the drunken nights, the shouting at politicians, the brief affairs, the dancing on tables, climbing into locked gardens, maybe even reading a poem about Tonto to the people on a bus. Oh no. Run and hide.*

12

The Don't-Be-Daft Count

'So,' said George, 'you're staying here.'

'For a while, till I get settled. I'll find a flat and I'll be off,' James told her.

'You won't be finding a new Sarah. I loved Sarah.'

'So did I. So do I. But it didn't work out.'

'Why?'

'Children.'

'She wanted them, you didn't?'

'Other way round. I want them. She doesn't. Not yet, anyway.'

'So wait.'

'She says I make her feel guilty.'

'Guilt,' said George. 'It's a curse. People feel guilty if they just think about eating a pie, far less actually doing it. She should accept that guilt will creep up on her about something. It's an emotional wart.'

George knew all about guilt. It was a dark shadow she lived with. There had been guilt after the birth of each of her children. Guilt about running away from her parents. Guilt about Alistair's death. Oh, the guilt about losing Willy. That guilt had been physical. It had hurt enough to feel like a stone lying on her heart. It had made her throw up. She'd wanted to tear her clothes off in the street, fall on her knees and wail.

'Don't talk to me about guilt. You and Sarah are amateurs at it.' She drank her whisky. 'You should go to Sarah, tell her you love her and you'll never let her go. That's what happens in love stories.'

'I'm living my life. It isn't a love story. I'll find a place. I won't stay long.'

'Stay as long as you like. I don't mind. But you should be with Sarah. She made you eat vegetables. She made you stop wearing hoodie tops and sweat pants. She liked reading and decent wine. How could you let her go?'

'I didn't let her go. She let me go.'

'Didn't it break your heart?'

'Yes. It did in a way.'

'Go get her.'

He sipped his whisky and smiled at her. 'I fear she doesn't want me to do that.'

It always surprised George to see her children drinking. She knew they'd done it for a good while before they did it in front of her. She knew they'd laugh if she offered them orange juice when she poured herself a glass of Pinot Noir or something stronger. But still it was a little hard to fully accept they'd grown up. They wouldn't ask for Jammy Dodgers and hot chocolate. They wanted booze.

James yawned. 'I'm tired. I have to go to bed.' He leaned over and kissed the top of George's head. 'Love you.'

'Don't be daft,' she said.

'But I do.'

'I brought you up. I thought you'd have better taste.'

'Nah. I love you.'

George tutted.

It was a game James and his sisters played. They told her they loved her so they could watch her lips tighten when she told them not to be daft. They'd clearly discussed this and none of them could understand it. It was like they'd agreed to tell her of their love every time they saw her, hoping one day she'd believe them. But in time telling George they loved her had become a game, a contest. They now vied over the don't-be-daft count. So far James was winning. She'd given him six in one conversation. She'd also given him a fierce look and told him he was being cheeky. 'I'm not being cheeky,' he'd said. 'I love you.' George had thrown a biscuit at him. Oh, how he and his sisters had laughed about that.

George always enjoyed having family around. Hearing them moving about in the house pleased her. But she knew the worry would return. It always did. When they were away from her they lived their lives. They came and went and she let them get on with it. When they slept under her roof she fretted about them. If any of them was out late she lay rigid in bed, eyes on the ceiling, waiting, listening for them to return. Then she relaxed. It was always there – the fear they would not come back to her.

She sat alone at her kitchen table, eyeing the whisky bottle. *Better not*, she decided. A second glass would keep her awake and being awake would lead to worrying or revisiting past moments that made her wince. Upstairs, James was running a bath. He always did bathe a lot. In his teenage years he'd light candles and take a radio into the bathroom with him so he could listen to music as he soaked. It still pleased her that her boy had pursued his pleasure so openly. Remembering him, the baby, the boy and the young man she'd known, she realised he'd always gone his own way. Never one to follow the crowd.

He'd been eight, George recalled, when she'd lost him in the supermarket. The panic, the wildly beating heart, the sweat and fluster as she steamed up and down the aisles thrusting her trolley in front of her as she searched for him. She was panting when she found him pressed against a display of tinned tuna, arms spread, preventing shoppers from picking a tin up. 'Don't buy this tuna,' he was shouting, 'dolphins get killed by the fishing nets. Save the dolphins.' He was succeeding. People were buying salmon instead. George had been embarrassed. She'd apologised to her fellow shoppers and trolley trundlers. 'He's passionate about animals,' she said. She'd lured James away with promises of ice cream. He'd followed her, walking backwards, keeping an eye on the rogue tuna tins. She'd scolded him for going missing. 'I was worried something had happened to you.' But he'd amazed her. She doubted she'd have stood up for dolphins as he had. 'You're brave,' she said. 'I am so proud of you.' She'd stroked his hair, kissed the top of his head. Pride made her tearful.

She put the whisky away, rinsed the glasses and climbed the stairs. Time for bed. Tomorrow was going to be busy. It was her day to take eighty-five-year-old Grace, who lived across the way, to the supermarket, the library and the hairdresser. She was going to be fully occupied hanging about as Grace selected her food, her books and her hairstyle.

In the end it all went smoothly. Grace always bought chicken, fish and a large selection of puddings, along with several bottles of red wine. In the library she chose several thrillers and a love story. When she was discussing hairstyles with Sylvia, her hairdresser, George went for a stroll.

It was a clear day, sun and a slight breeze. George had a coffee in a small café then bought cheese from a deli. After that she decided to have a look round a charity shop. You never knew what you'd find there. She had an illustrated copy of *Cider with Rosie*, two dark red mugs, a DVD of *Dances with Wolves* and a grey knitted throw she didn't know what to do with. Today might bring more treasures.

The shop was empty. George looked at the books and then shifted some jackets on a rail. The crockery today was boring, but a small print of a tulip in a glass jar caught her eye. As she went over to examine it, an assistant leaned over the counter and asked if she could help. George said she was just having a look round. The assistant said, 'Help yourself.'

There was something about her assertive tone that made George stop and look at her. She was oddly familiar. George stared and tried to place her. 'Have we met?'

'Yes,' the assistant told her.

George smiled. 'I am sorry. You seem so familiar but I can't place you.'

The assistant was tall, certainly taller than George. She was immaculately dressed. Everything she wore – neat grey skirt, white shirt, black cardigan – looked freshly ironed. Her make-up expertly applied. Eyebrows perfectly plucked. Her hair was a shiny neat bob, not a trace of grey. George envied that. The assistant's smile was frosty. It was putting George off the tulip print. In fact, the woman was so hostile George decided to leave.

Unexplained loathing was very disturbing, George thought, as she made her way back along the street. *Who was that woman? So familiar and so hard to place.* And then it came to her. She stopped. *Oh my God, Dorothy Pringle.* The nemesis of her childhood gang. The prissy girl whose downfall she and Anna had sought. *Bloody hell, bloody Dorothy Pringle.*

She returned to the shop to check. Didn't go in. Instead she looked at the woman through the glass pane on the door. The woman glared back. The hatred was so raw, so primal, so savage, so hot that had George held her hands before that rigid face she could have warmed them. Oh yes, it was Dorothy Pringle.

13

A Day Like Any Other Day

It was too exciting for a phone call and certainly too exciting to leave till she saw Anna in a couple of days' time. As soon as she dropped Grace with her shopping, her library books and her new hairdo, George drove to Anna's.

'You'll never guess who I saw,' she said as she puffed into the living room.

'Who?' Anna was intrigued.

'Dorothy Pringle.' George almost shouted it. She revelled in this wonderful moment of having extraordinary news to share.

Anna looked blank. 'Who?'

'You know, Dorothy Pringle.' This was said with more emphasis and even louder now. 'Dorothy Pringle. The Two Yellows plotted her downfall.'

'Oh my God. The prissy swot.'

'Yes.'

'She had a pencil case to die for and always did her homework and got to hand out the milk. I thought she was dead.'

'She lives. Works in a charity shop in Leith. You should have seen the look she gave me. Pure hatred.'

'We were horrible to her. You once threw a custard pie at her.'

'It wasn't a real custard pie. It was a mixture of flour, water and shaving foam. And anyway, I missed.'

'It was still horrible. Whatever possessed us?'

'We were kids,' said George. 'We didn't know any better. We should apologise.'

'You think?' Anna wasn't sure. 'Perhaps we should secretly atone. Do something good to her.'

'Yes. We plotted her downfall in secret. It was all subterfuge apart from the custard pie that wasn't a custard pie. That was because she sneaked on me. Told Mrs Watkins in Maths that I'd copied Susan Brown's homework. I had to write "I must always do my own homework and never deliberately copy the work of another and pass it off as mine" five hundred times. That pie was justified.'

'Absolutely,' said Anna. She added, 'Happy days.' She went to the kitchen to make coffee.

George wasn't so sure about happy days. She hadn't enjoyed school. But then she hadn't been enthralled with anything as much as Anna had been with English literature.

Anna boiled a kettle and laid out a couple of mugs. She had loved school. It had been a time of poetry and hope and music. She spooned coffee into each mug and hummed songs from her youth. Walking to school, bag of books heavy on her back, white ankle socks slipping down inside her brown Clark's sandals and 'Da Doo Ron Ron' humming in her head. Oh, how she'd loved that song. Though to this day she'd no idea what it meant.

'I loved Phil Spector's wall of sound,' she told George as she came back with the coffee. 'I remember walking across the living room at home and hearing it. Couldn't turn up the radio loud enough. Lying on the floor eating salt and vinegar crisps listening to "Da Doo Ron Ron" was heaven. When were you happiest?'

'Walking Willy to nursery. He'd hold my hand and we'd talk about manhole covers and if bears lived over the wall of Mr Mackie's garden. I knew I'd never have another child. I vowed to enjoy him. He was a little human being I savoured.'

'I know,' said Anna. She gave George a mug and patted her shoulder.

'I suppose I should think more about death,' said George. 'It's going to happen for sure. It's what's next. I've done everything else. Lost my virginity.'

'That's going back a while,' Anna said.

'Given birth. Had the menopause. I wonder what it will be like? What will the day I die be like?'

'A day like any other day,' said Anna. 'Only you might not be around for your tea.'

George could see this might be true. 'Well, now we know Dorothy Pringle is among the living we have to do something good to her.'

Anna looked out of the window. It was getting dark, a velvety gloaming. A time of day she loved. She heard a neighbour arriving home, slamming a car door. Didn't know who it was. But it wasn't Marla. This wasn't one of her working days.

She said, 'Marla from across the way. We could get her to go to the charity shop, play her a song and give her balloons and a cupcake.'

George was enthused. 'Excellent plan. Her being Dorothy, Marla could sing her selections from *Goodbye Yellow Brick Road*.'

They clinked coffee mugs in agreement.

*

In the early morning hours, Anna woke. First light shifted through the room. Her mind was clear. It wasn't that she was suddenly free of guilt and remorse; just that she knew what to do about her sins. She decided to do something good every day from now on, to make herself less ashamed of her naughty past. She would start by apologising to her mother. Not that her mother would know about it. She'd been dead for thirty years. But her demise hadn't dented Anna's shame.

It had started in this very flat where Anna lived now. Her mother had been visiting and had been in top insulting form. Anna was a disappointment, a girl that could have been a secretary to a proper businessman wasting her life to write poems. She never cleaned, couldn't cook and her clothes were an embarrassment. 'You're not like Lorna,' Mrs MacLean said.

Lorna had lived across the road from the MacLeans years ago. 'I met her mother last week. Lorna married a doctor. She has two beautiful children and a dishwasher. Her husband drives a Jaguar.' Anna hated Lorna. 'You,' her mother decreed, 'are a slut.'

Anna wondered where the slut accusation came from. It had been going on since she was sixteen. At first it had hurt enough to make her cry. She'd sobbed into her pillow, heaving and shuddering, working at breathing. As time passed it mattered less and less, but she always puzzled over it. She wasn't a slut.

The day after her mother's onslaught Anna had baked brownies. She laced them with hash. It had been a small cube that Michael, her then lover, had forgotten to take with him when he left her to go to Australia. They'd been together for over a year. Staying sometimes at his place, sometimes at hers. It had been an easy affair that she'd enjoyed. His leaving had been hard to get over, especially as he hadn't asked her to go with him. She wondered if he'd left the hash deliberately, thinking it might ease the pain, the loneliness. It hadn't. The pea incident had put her off drugs for ever. As a hoarder, she didn't know what to do with the hash. She'd wrapped it in cling film and shoved it to the back of her cutlery drawer.

Feeling marvellously naughty, she took the hash brownies in a blue plastic tub round to the house where she'd been brought up and where her parents still lived. Her father was away on a golfing weekend with old friends. He was often away. In fact, he was rarely home.

'Baked you brownies,' Anna said, putting them on a plate.

Her mother filled the kettle and looked at them. 'Didn't know you baked. They're a bit lumpy.'

'Yes,' Anna admitted. The brownies weren't visually appealing. 'That's the way of them. It's the nuts.'

Tea made and poured into neat pink cups, gold rimmed, Mrs MacLean sat at the kitchen table and took one. Ate it. 'Not bad. Bit of a strange aftertaste.' She took another. This was strange. She only ever ate one scone, or one biscuit, or one of anything really. She stopped after three and didn't notice Anna's abstinence. She smiled and looked dreamy. 'I always only wanted a puppy,' she said. 'But your father wanted children. So I got you.'

Anna said, 'Sorry.' She felt the gleeful mischief melt away. Oh no, drugs were going to make her mother even more painfully honest than she already was.

'Not your fault. Just me. I never liked children. Perhaps I should apologise.'

'No need.'

Her mother took another brownie. 'Oddly enough, these are making me feel cheerful and strangely relaxed. Perhaps it's that you took the trouble to make them.'

'I enjoyed it.'

'You were always so dreamy. Always reading or staring. You'd drift off into your own little world. What were you thinking about?'

'I daydreamed. I invented a world where I . . .' *Mattered*, she was about to say.

Her mother didn't notice the unfinished sentence. She'd drifted off and was looking at the floor. 'I never really liked this floor.'

Anna didn't know what to do. She drank her tea and waited.

After a while her mother said, 'I never liked being married. The whole thing took me by surprise. I was innocent. I didn't know. Nobody mentioned anything about men. You seem fine, though. Who told you?'

'George.'

Mrs MacLean laughed. She laughed and laughed. 'George, of course. I love George. A nurse and not a poet. George is lovely.' She laughed again, then settled to gaze at the sugar bowl. She seemed happy. 'Sugar bowl,' she said.

After an hour Anna decided to go home. She said, 'Goodbye.' Her mother had flickered her fingers at her and given her a lavish smile.

She threw back her duvet and got out of bed. It was not her fault. She wasn't a slut. Of course she wasn't. Her mother had hated sex, that was all. Once Anna had insisted she and George went to an art exhibition that was the talk of the Edinburgh Festival. There had been a statue of a naked man standing proud. 'Displaying his bits,' her mother would have said.

Anna had known nothing about men and her open-mouthed, red-faced shock when staring up at the statue had drawn more interest from other gallery-goers than the actual work of art. George had gently led Anna away and taken her to a coffee bar in Princes Street, bought her a Coke and settled her in a quiet corner where she'd told her the facts of life. Anna, amazed, had said, 'Well, I'll remember all this. But I'm never going to do it. Not ever.'

She pulled on a jumper over the T-shirt she wore in bed and went to the kitchen. At the table she opened her notebook. Her poeming book, she called it. The pages were full of half-finished verses, lines, thoughts and words she loved. It had crossed her mind that her father had from time to time wooed her mother with alcohol and promises.

She wrote: *Is it true that I was born/Of wine and powdered rhino horn.*

She stopped. Tapped her head with her pen. Sighed. She couldn't think of anything more.

Her poor mother had hated sex and had suspected her daughter loved it. *Too right, Ma*, Anna thought. *Sorry about that. And sorry about the brownies.* Tomorrow she'd buy flowers and place them on Mrs MacLean's grave. She hadn't been there in years.

*

She started early. At the supermarket she bought a large bunch of mixed flowers, mostly blues and purples. They were wrapped in cellophane with a gold ribbon round the stalks. She took the bus to Leith and before walking through the Links to the cemetery to lay her bouquet at her mother's grave, she walked to the charity shop where Dorothy Pringle worked. She wanted to get a look at the old enemy and enjoy imagining what Dorothy would make of getting a cupcake and a balloon and, perhaps, a song. She might wonder who had sent this treat. George and Anna would, however, savour their anonymity and know they had at least tried to atone for their childish insensitivity.

Clutching the flowers in one hand and holding herself upright with her stick in the other, Anna looked into the shop. There was Dorothy being unmistakeably Dorothy. She was neat as a pin, hair shiny, shoes polished, expression disapproving. She spotted Anna and came to the door to return the stare. She crossed her arms and glared. Finally she opened the door and stepped out.

'Ah, Anna MacLean, the poet,' she said. 'How interesting to see you. Flowers, I see.' She reached out and took them. 'Thank you. I appreciate the gesture, but really, I don't think they in any way make up for the misery you and George caused me.'

14

The Looking-After Rules

'I just went home. Had tomato soup,' said Anna.

'You didn't say that the flowers were for your mother?'

'No. She just grabbed them and stomped off. I was too stunned to speak.'

'So you didn't go to your mother's grave?'

'No, I didn't want to turn up empty-handed.'

'She wouldn't have noticed, on account of being dead.'

'Yes, in body. In mind, my mind, she is still around. Still criticising. I thought if I arrived to see her without bringing a gift, she'd rise up out of her grave and give me a stiff, unforgiving and scary lecture on how only a slut turns up anywhere without an offering.'

And George said, 'Oh Anna, what are we going to do with you? You're not a slut. Never have been. See you tomorrow.' She put down the phone.

In the living room Matthew was watching television. She sat beside him and looked at the screen. An American cop was chatting to a dog. 'Good film?' she asked.

'Yeah. It's easy. Makes me laugh.'

She touched his hand. 'Good.'

He asked if she'd had a busy day.

'Took old Dave Beverage to the hospital. He said he'd sprained his ankle but he'd broken it. They kept him in. He's eighty-four.'

'Good of you.'

'I try to do good every day. Pay for my sins.' She sniffed and gave a false laugh, trying to make this sound like a joke.

'It was a long time ago. After Lola was born. I was training as a nurse and I went a bit wild.'

'You've told me before. A lot of men?'

'Boys, really. Boys and booze. Did you sleep with a lot of women before me?'

'Some.' He didn't stop watching the movie. The cop and his dog were falling in love with a vet and her dog. It had its complications, George could see that, but they all seemed happy with the developments so far. She watched Matthew's fingers move. He was counting his loves. Four, she saw. She was winning there, then. She'd been a lot naughtier than him.

It had been a time of stifled rage and heated laughter. She remembered running and running through night-time streets. She had a green feather boa and used a cigarette holder though she didn't like smoking. Drinking vodka in pubs, dancing till she was sweaty and breathless in clubs, ears hot from the roar of music, whirling and flirting at parties in cellars and flats she didn't know. Laughing and laughing and then, sitting in strange lavatories weeping, sobbing almost hysterically with people banging at the door screaming to get in.

'Frank ended it?'

'My mother gave me a talking to. She knew. I don't think Frank would have understood. My ma did. She told me Lola needed a mum. Running about in a rage drinking and staying out nights and oh, you know, doing stuff to make me forget Alistair wasn't how a nurse and parent behaved. She wasn't polite about it. She was very angry with me. She was wonderful. We were in her car. She'd been driving up and down the High Street and Victoria Street looking for me. She yelled at me to get in the car. I was scared not to.'

Matthew said, 'Were you wearing your feather boa?'

'God, yes. And so much eye liner and mascara it was a wonder I could see.'

They sat awhile watching the cop and his dog. They were on a stake-out. The dog was enjoying it. The cop not so much.

'My mother said my child needed me. A child craves love and warmth and safety, and it was my duty to give it to her. I was so angry, I was neglecting the one I should love and who loved me totally and uncritically. Lola. And my mother told me I was young and didn't know the rules.'

'Rules?'

'Well, I had said that all I ever wanted was someone to look after me and she said the rules were that if you allowed someone to look after you, you had to look after them back.'

Matthew said he could agree with that. 'What about we drive down the coast tomorrow and find somewhere for lunch?'

'I'm seeing Anna.'

'Well, the next day then?'

'I probably have to pick up Dave from hospital and bring him home, and I have to meet Lola for coffee in the afternoon.'

'I had thought we'd spend time together. I planned for us to go on trips and walk about looking at stuff like couples in holiday adverts. Pointing and smiling and walking hand-in-hand. I thought we'd go on holiday to places like Barcelona or Paris or New York.'

'Holiday?' George was worried. 'I don't know about that.'

'You do all this stuff for other people. What about me? Don't I matter to you? What about us?'

She couldn't go on holiday. She needed to be here. She had to be safe and to keep everyone in her family safe. She knew in a small part of her brain that she refused to acknowledge that this was absurd. She imagined herself sitting in a hotel bar in Barcelona wearing beautiful shoes and sipping a cocktail and was scared. She'd be a dreadful companion; she'd be on edge, waiting for the terrible phone call.

'You went to Lucca,' said Matthew.

'I thought it would do me good. But I worried about my children. I loved the tiramisu, though.'

'So you won't go on holiday with me?'

She didn't reply.

In the movie a masked man was holding a gun to the cop. The dog attacked and the bad guy shot him.

Matthew got up and left the room. George heard him rattling about in the kitchen. Pots and crockery were being roughly handled.

She heard James come down the stairs. He stuck his head round the door. 'Going out. See you later.'

'Where are you going?' asked George.

'Pub. Couple of beers and watch the match.'

'I could come.'

'No, you couldn't. You're my mother. Blokes don't take their mothers to watch football at the pub.'

'Why not?'

'It's weird. Besides, you don't like beer and you don't like football. And . . .'

She stood, pointing at him. 'Don't you dare. Don't you say you love me. I know it's a game.'

He grinned. 'I was going to say you should go talk to your husband. He's clattering in the kitchen. When he does that, he's hurting. You need to talk to him. You need to look after him.'

James left and George went to the kitchen. She stood by the door watching Matthew furiously chop an onion then roughly put a pot on the cooker. She thought he hadn't noticed her but he said, 'I see you there.'

'I can't go on holiday,' she said. 'I can't go away. Someone here might die before I can get to them.'

15

A Strange Selection of Songs

Anna and George lunched in Leith. They ate at a fish restaurant by the shore. George had the seafood platter, Anna fish and chips. 'I am a woman of the people,' she said. 'This is proper working-class food.' The plate that was put in front of her did not meet her peasant food standards. It was classy. Chips placed upright in a white ceramic bowl and fish beside a layer of lemon slices with a flamboyant swirl of tartar sauce.

'What did you expect?' said George. 'This place is quite posh. It has tablecloths.'

As they ate, they spoke about mothers, love, the difficulty of thinking logically and life as it had been before gadgetry. Though the talk was laced with fond stories and reminiscences, Anna mentioned something new in her life. 'I've been noticing people around me. Things that were always there and I didn't see them.'

'Like?' said George.

'Like I look out of my window and there's Richard walking down the street. I never knew he did that. Then there's Mother Dainty and her garden. It's gorgeous. I stand and look at it. The colours. I swear foxgloves shine in the dark.'

She took a huge swig of her wine and grinned. 'Mother Dainty is so tiny and delicate and strong. I love her.'

'You have only noticed that garden now?' George couldn't believe it. That garden was extraordinary. Lush in a street of muddy areas and scrubby grass. Purples and reds and soft blues suddenly there amidst old cars and rubbish bins. It had always lifted George's heart.

'What's Mother Dainty's proper name?'

'I have no idea what she's called. Yes, I've noticed the garden. Who wouldn't? But it's like I have had something peeled from my eyes and now I really see it. It makes me smile. It takes my breath away.' She took another swig.

'You're getting drunk,' said George.

'I know. I'm happy. It's not a state of being I'm used to. But I find myself smiling a lot.'

George said, 'Maybe you're in love. Maybe Richard never walked up and down the street before he met you. Maybe he's in love, too. Maybe you should go out and ask him in for a cup of tea.'

'I couldn't do that. He might say no. He might look at me with surprise and embarrassment. I can't face rejection. I'd rather love from afar.'

George ate a prawn, sipped her water and waited for an explanation.

'So there's the garden across the road, Richard passing my window, the spice rack is coming along, and yesterday I walked to the shop for a tin of beans without my stick. I am happy. Not going to spoil it. Not going to risk a pain in my heart.'

'Good plan,' said George.

Anna dipped a chip in the sauce, took a bite. 'No, I've accepted my lot in life. This is who I am. This is all I want to be. This woman swigging wine and eating fish and chips.'

George thought, *Oh dear, this is not going to end well.*

Anna lifted her empty glass to the waiter, asking for a refill. Well, why not? She wasn't paying. 'What makes you happy?' she asked.

'Kitchens,' said George. She nodded at the refill. 'Enjoy.'

George never did get over the delight and awe she experienced when she'd crept into Alistair's kitchen on the first night of her runaway life. 'Kitchens can tell you a whole lot about people and the life they lead and the things they don't tell you. I first found that out about four miles and fifty years from here.'

'On a night when you were young and ran away because your mother called you George,' Anna joined in. This was one of her favourite stories.

'That kitchen was a wonder. A shining place in a grubby flat. It taught me a lot. You never know what people really are and what they long to be till they actually tell you. The man who rescued me loved cooking. I would never have guessed it. Now when I look at someone's kitchen I can see a slice of their life.'

'That's lovely,' Anna swigged. She'd swigged past tiddly and was headed for drunk. She didn't drink much – two large glasses would do it.

It sometimes bothered George that she so nearly had a different life. She imagined how it could have been. Perhaps she and Alistair would have opened a restaurant together. A bistro or crêpe shed somewhere that catered to a bohemian crowd. She pictured herself as a lusty soul, moving between tables laughing and making jokes and looking tenderly at her main man, the cook. *Later*, her longing glance would say.

She knew, of course, that this was absurd. She was not a lusty, jokey person. Waiting tables would have driven her insane. Still, at least three times a year she'd go and stand outside that flat looking up at the kitchen window. She usually kept back from the crowds by lurking in a doorway. She had been tempted to enter the building, climb the stairs, knock on the door and ask to see that room again. But no. Better not. Better leave it as it was when she first saw it and was entranced. Never go back, she told herself.

'Perhaps coffee and a stroll in the fresh air?' she suggested.

'Sober me up?' Anna knew the state she was in. 'And we can discuss cupcakes and songs of apology for Dorothy Pringle.'

'Yes, that,' said George. She leaned across the table to her friend. 'You know that by not approaching the object of your desire, by just letting things be, you are breaking your own heart.'

They passed restaurants, stood looking at the river and considered poking around shops but they weren't in the mood.

Anna said she was broke, but then she always was. 'How can you be so wise about my life and such a fool about your own?' she said.

'What do you mean?' asked George.

'You think when people go away they won't come back to you.'

George sighed. 'It's true. But it has happened and I got a pain in my heart.'

It being Marla's Minimart day when she worked mornings, she'd picked up Marlon from school and was already home when Anna and George arrived. She sat on the armchair opposite the sofa where George and Anna sat and took notes. Marlon was on the floor in front of the television. He turned down the volume, and after giving them a small smile settled to watch his programme, back turned to them.

'We don't really do apologies. Birthdays, anniversaries, congratulations and so on, but not apologies,' said Marla.

'Surely there's a call for it,' said Anna. 'People say sorry all the time.'

'I know. But we don't have an apology slot at Cupcakes, Balloons and a Song. Now, what flavour cupcake? Strawberry, chocolate or salted caramel?'

'Salted caramel,' Anna and George said together.

'Balloon? It'll be plain, since you don't want happy birthday or congratulations.'

'Plain dark red,' said George.

Marla handed them a list of available songs. There was a thick silence as they read. 'These are old,' said Anna. 'I mean "Little White Bull", "Lollipop", "Santa Baby"? This is a strange selection of songs.'

'It's the cost,' Marla explained. 'We have to download and play from a phone. There's copyright. We're starting out and being careful with money.'

'No Leonard Cohen, then?' said George.

'I love Leonard Cohen,' Anna said. She started to sing, swaying from side to side. 'Oooh,' she sang and launched into the first few lines of 'The Sisters Of Mercy'.

'Is she drunk?' Marla addressed George.

'A little,' said George. 'She was worse a while ago. She's coming down now. Wine. It doesn't take much.'

'"Volare"?' Anna wasn't impressed. Then she saw the perfect song. She whooped with joy. '"The Deadwood Stage". I love that song.'

'Please don't give us a rendition,' said George.

Anna sighed. Marlon also sighed, as if it was just dawning on him that Anna wasn't this strange, bookish, slightly aloof person he'd imagined she was. She was a woman and prone to sudden silliness like his mother. He was obviously uncomfortable with this.

'So, salted caramel, red plain balloon and "Deadwood Stage".' Marla wrote in her notebook. 'Do you want the morning cheap rate? You know, when nobody's about and people don't know what's happening? It goes up in the afternoon and it is expensive in the evening. We do workplaces, some bars and people's homes.'

'Morning, at her workplace,' said George. 'I want to be there at the shop when it happens. I want to see it. I'll be hiding, of course.'

'Me too,' said Anna.

Marla consulted her diary. 'We can do next Tuesday.'

16

A Salted Caramel Cupcake, a Red Balloon and 'The Deadwood Stage'

Years and years ago, when Anna and George had an adventure they'd go into their world holding hands. They held hands as they stood in line ready to go into school. They held hands as they watched the sky light up with whooshing colours on firework night. They might have held hands now, as they waited side-by-side in a doorway that gave a good view of the charity shop where Dorothy Pringle worked. But they'd stopped doing that long ago. Neither of them could pinpoint when. Still, they were hoping this would go well.

The weather was raw this Tuesday morning. A little annoying wind flapping round them and a merciless drizzle. They were remembering their private war against Dorothy Pringle. 'We weren't very nice,' said Anna.

'We were children and children can be horrible. We were horrible. But we've grown out of it now.' George said this adamantly but she was having doubts.

'The bike ride,' said Anna. 'We cheated.'

They'd agreed to let Dorothy join them on a bike ride. It was to be a short trip to the park and back. Dorothy had pedalled furiously, charging ahead, pigtails flying behind her. She never looked back. For a while Anna and George worked at keeping up with her. But it was sweaty and tiring and they fell behind. They preferred to cycle slowly, chatting as they went. They watched Dorothy speed ahead and disappear from view. 'Let's not bother,'

George had said. 'Let's just go home.' So they did. They turned round, pedalled home and left Dorothy to charge to the park alone. Home, they sat on George's front step with a glass of Vimto apiece, waiting for the cycling ace to turn up. When she did Anna said, 'Here you are. We got here ages ago. You must've been going really slowly.'

'No, I wasn't.' Dorothy was red-faced and angry. 'I was going fast. You two just came home and left me.' She wheeled her bike away from them. 'You're a pair of piggy farters.'

'Piggy farters,' said Anna, staring through the drizzle. 'That's a pretty good insult.'

'Yes,' said George. 'I used it a lot after she said it.'

'You put a worm in her shoe,' said Anna.

'You gave her laxative chocolate,' said George.

The wind rattled Anna's raincoat. A bus crawled past. A woman walking her dog beetled along the opposite pavement. The lights went on at the charity shop.

George sighed. 'God. We really were a pair of piggy farters.'

Marla's van appeared. It wasn't the van of Anna's imaginings. It was small and looked hand-painted. A line of black musical notes danced round the words 'celebrations' and 'joy'. A multi-coloured collection of balloons tied to the back doors jiggled about in the wind. Marla got out of the van, slammed the door and swept her hands over her uniform. It was yellow and dark navy-blue stripes. There was something of the Vatican Guard about her.

George said, 'Somehow I think this is not going to go well.'

Anna said, 'Yes. Who thought to do this?'

'You. I think alcohol was involved.'

Anna said, 'Stupid. Stupid, stupid.'

Marla took a small cake box and a large red balloon from the back of the van. People passing stopped to stare. It was an extraordinary sight. To her horror George noticed a few customers going into the charity shop. There would be witnesses.

Marla arrived at the shop, stood in the doorway and shouted, 'Dorothy Pringle, I bring you joy and apologies.' She pressed the play button on the phone in her top pocket and 'The Deadwood Stage' soared out.

'That's not Doris Day,' said Anna. 'That's a cheap cover version. It ought to be against the law for anybody other than Doris Day to sing that song.'

The famous words 'whip, crack away' rang out and Marla did a stiff knee-slap before bursting into the shop. The people inside turned, saw and froze open-mouthed. There was shock, bafflement and horror. George recognised the body language of people who didn't know what to do. Dorothy Pringle turned red; her hand flew to her mouth. The other hand was flapping Marla away. Marla was holding out the balloon and the cupcake and appeared to be delivering a speech. Dorothy swept past Marla, opened the shop door, pointed to the outside world and with a gesture invited Marla to join it. The cupcake was left on the counter; the balloon was refused. Marla stepped into the street, switched off the music and walked back to her van. Inside the shop Dorothy was spreading her hands to her customers, apologising. There were smiles as customers returned to browsing clothes and CDs. Dorothy came out into the drizzle and stared this way and that, looking for people to blame. Anna and George ducked deep into their doorway, hiding.

'That didn't go as planned,' said Anna.

'She kept the cupcake,' said George. 'I liked the balloon. It was a classy dark red.'

They set off through the damp air to find a coffee shop where they could sit and discuss their failure. They'd enjoy a flat white and wouldn't linger long talking about the Dorothy fiasco. They were both well acquainted with failure.

'It would have been the song. That's not an I'm-sorry song. It's jolly,' Anna said.

'I'd have liked "Into The Mystic". I love that.' George went misty remembering Van Morrison moments. 'Lying on the floor drinking wine and listening to that song. I was happy then.'

'Which floor?' Anna wanted to know. Details were important.

'Home. The home floor is the only floor for dreaming on. Away floors are populated by strange feet that can spoil things.'

'Michael and I used to sit on the floor of an evening, and he'd read his day's writing to me. We played Pink Floyd.'

'Didn't you read your writing to him?'

Anna shook her head, 'Nah. I wasn't writing much. I'd come home. Park the bike. He'd have cooked something. Veggie usually, with rice. We'd eat. Afterwards I'd sit on the floor and listen. I was happy then.'

'Happiness is a bitch. Slips away when you're not looking.'

Anna agreed. 'Michael just left. One day I went home and he told me he was off the next day just like that. I never saw him again. I was pregnant and I had an abortion.'

'I know.' George reached over and put her hand on Anna's.

'He never knew he was going to be a father. I was so angry and hurt. So angry.'

'I know.' George squeezed the hand under hers.

'It was awful. Man in a white coat saying he'd grant my termination. Then a week later doing it. I was guilty for years. Y'know, if I'd had a baby, been a mother, Marlon wouldn't be such a surprise.'

'You looked after mine when Willy died.'

'I know,' said Anna. 'But they were almost fully formed. You'd worked your magic on them.'

George said, 'They didn't need magic. They were wonderful anyway.' She sighed. 'I miss Willy.' She sighed once more. *Don't scream*, she thought. *Not now, not here. It's only life. One day you'll get the hang of it.* 'They do take you by storm sometimes. Odd, because I've had a few now and in fact I used to be one.'

'Me too. That's how I know the importance of being a mother. If I'd had a child, I'd have someone who loves me. Like you do.'

Don't be daft, George thought.

'My mother didn't love me. Didn't even like me very much. So she said, anyway. That goes to the very core of you. As much a part of you as needing to breathe. I always thought nobody would like or love me. I think my mother was shocked at my appearance. When we first met, I was a baby. I was toothless, bald and incontinent. I wasn't at my best.'

'That's a problem for us all,' said George.

'I just accepted my mother's rejection. I kept Michael at a distance, wouldn't commit. And he was happy not to commit. Two numpties destined to part. I'm a fool.'

George said, 'No, you're not. No more than me or anybody else.'

They drained their cups. George paid. Back on the street, they strolled. Two old ladies, one with a stick. They hummed the Van Morrison song. Than sang it. George gave a little twirl. They'd done a silly thing together, and now there was a song they loved to sing. They were a little bit happy. Just a little bit.

17

Mother Dainty and Old Dungarees

Anna took a delight in Mother Dainty's garden. Mornings, she stood at her living-room window and marvelled at it. Evenings, she drank a late cup of tea and marvelled once more. The garden glowed under the street lamps. She cursed herself for not having noticed it before.

She often watched Mother Dainty at work. She snipped and weeded. She worked at the soil and planted. She watered. People would stop at her gate and she would leave her work to join them for a chat. She walked slowly, smiling, head tilted to one side. She seemed to know everyone. There was laughter. Children lifted their toys to her, showing off their delights. Sometimes she'd reach out and touch someone's arm. She was gentle, kind, sweet and compassionate.

There goes Mother Dainty, Anna thought. She wished she'd had a mother like that. One who listened and would never insult her daughter. *If she'd been my mum, I wouldn't have had to daydream. I wouldn't have removed myself from the living room of my childhood to read about lamplighters and minarets and fantasise about Robert Louis Stevenson and Byron. I'd have been normal. I'd have been a bus driver or a marketing manager or a business consultant.* She knew this to be nonsense but indulged in a few moments imagining herself at the wheel of a double decker working her way through thick traffic, whistling.

Mother Dainty's husband wore light cotton trousers at the weekend. Weekdays, he wore dungarees over a pale blue shirt. Mostly he sat on a deckchair reading a newspaper as his wife busied herself at her plants. But once a week he brought out his ancient lawnmower and cut the grass. He'd mow round the edges then carefully cut the turf, going up and down creating stripes. Anna watched in wonder. There was a soft green Wimbledon lawn down there. He didn't stop to chat; he just nodded to anyone who stopped to watch. He was Old Dungarees. Anna loved them both.

She wrote them a poem:

It's raining and bells are ringing far away
Old Dungarees in the garden is making hay
Inside Mother Dainty lies making sleep seem simple
Within her head flowers dream, on her cheek a dimple

At that point she ran out of inspiration. The poem was absurd. Old Dungarees didn't make hay. He sat in his deckchair snoozing and reading the local paper. Mother Dainty did all the work. But Anna liked to think that when she slept, she lay under a floral eiderdown, head on a perfect pillow, sleeping the sleep of babies.

She was sleeping better herself these days. Sometimes she managed a full six hours before she woke and stared into the gloom, worrying about something that seemed trivial when daylight arrived.

*

Today wasn't the best of mornings; clouds overhead and it looked like rain. Anna made coffee and took her mug to the living room to consider the weather and enjoy Mother Dainty's garden. There was a small hostile crowd gathered on the pavement by the garden fence. There were angry voices. It took Anna a few minutes to realise what was going on.

The garden was in ruins. Plants had been ripped from the ground and tossed into the road. Delphiniums, pansies, lupins and more all lay in wilting piles on the tarmac. The lawn was trampled. Branches had been broken from the lilac in the corner and thrown to the ground. There was a wide and dreadful scattering of leaves and petals. The place looked post-apocalyptic. Anna moaned. 'No. No.'

She pulled on some clothes, took her stick from its place behind the front door and went to join the crowd.

Mother Dainty was in the middle of the group. She was looking round. 'The mess. The mess. I have to clean it all up.' She seemed to have shrunk. She looked about, obviously not seeing what she was looking at. Her face was pale, her eyes swollen and red. Old Dungarees was standing on his lawn, fists clenched. 'If I ever get hold of who did this . . .' Somebody led him to his deckchair. He was told to watch his blood pressure.

Anna stood and watched. She wasn't part of this. Nobody took any notice of her. Two people with large black plastic bags began picking up the debris. Somebody was sweeping the pavement. Someone else was replanting a few flowers that still had roots. Marla appeared and put her arms round Mother Dainty. 'Come on, Chrissy. You need to sit. A cup of sweet tea will help. That's what they say, anyway.' Of course, Anna thought. Mother Dainty was Chrissy. She had a proper name. And she heard someone talking to Old Dungarees. He was Ed.

She helped to pick up wilted plants and asked the man carrying the plastic bag if he knew what had happened. She knew him as Mr Beetle, on account of his car. His name, she discovered, was Pete. He told her the damage had been caused by vandals.

'But I heard nothing.'

'Silent vandals,' Pete offered.

Swagger Boy and Lil were in the crowd. They suggested that the culprits were in a gang. 'They'd have been on something. Cider and something else. Something stronger.' A woman Anna had up till now called Mrs Cauliflower Hair because of her tight perm slapped his shoulder and said, 'Don't you go mixing with them.'

He said, 'No, Ma.'

When the wilted plants were cleared away, and all the anger and disgust had been talked out, people drifted off. It was eight o'clock on a soft summer morning, already hot, but there were breakfasts to be prepared and jobs to go to. Marla led Mother Dainty inside. 'I'll get the kettle on,' she said. Anna went home.

She sat on her sofa and leaned back. She was shocked. She put her hand on her chest and quietly breathed. 'Awful. Awful,' she said. She shut her eyes and wondered what her neighbours had made of Mrs Stomper joining them.

She phoned George. 'They all have proper names. I knew they did, but actually hearing them surprised me.'

George said, 'Sorry?'

'I'd given my neighbours names like Swagger Boy and Lil and Mother Dainty and Old Dungarees. I'd written their lives and I didn't stop to actually consider they already had names and lives.'

'How poetic of you.'

'I know. I live on my own cloud,' said Anna. She told George about the destroyed garden. 'I want to do something. I should help. An unsaid apology for the names I've given them.'

'Money,' George told her. 'That's what people do when disaster strikes. They collect money and give it to the victims to help them get back to their lives. You might make Mother Dainty happy.'

'Of course. Thank you. You are clever.' Sometimes Anna was amazed at George's worldly wisdom. She always knew what to do.

*

At six in the evening the next day Anna set out on her collection mission. She carried her favourite box, a red and ochre floral thing that once held her writing pens, and tried to calm the nerves that stormed her stomach. She willed herself forward. She'd start, she decided, with Marla and Marlon. She rang their bell. Marla answered.

'I'm collecting for Chrissy and Ed,' said Anna. Chrissy and Ed? It was difficult to say the names. They'd always be Mother Dainty and Old Dungarees to her. 'I want to help them get their garden back together.'

'This is good of you.' Marla showed her into the living room. Marlon sat in front of the television. He turned and smiled to her. Marla took five pounds from her purse and put it in the box.

'Thank you,' said Anna. 'Very generous.'

'They're a lovely couple. I want to help.' She stepped back, folded her arms, sniffed. 'Your pal wasn't very happy.'

'No,' said Anna.

'She kept the cupcake, though. Everyone keeps the cupcake. Anyway, I have to thank you. The boss never thought of these old people. She thinks we'll get a whole load of new customers. Old people apologising.'

Anna nodded. 'Good plan.' She smiled to Marlon. 'I better get on.'

Marla crossed the room and hauled Marlon to his feet. 'Take him with you. He knows folk and folk know him. You'll do fine with Marlon.'

Anna said, 'I don't want to take him from his programmes.'

Marla pushed the boy to her. 'Take him. You need him. Nobody has a clue who you are. They'll think you are some sort of con merchant. You need Marlon.'

Outside, walking to the next house, Marlon took her hand. 'This is great. People will think I'm a hero and give me sweeties.'

He was right. They visited every home in the street and Anna was welcomed. She learned that Mr Beetle was a teacher, as was Mrs Beetle. Their home was filled with books, walls covered with prints of famous works of art. They each donated five pounds and Marlon got a Snickers bar. Mrs Cauliflower Hair was Mrs Thomson. She popped a pound into the box and insisted her son Swagger Boy did the same. Marlon got a packet of M&Ms. Anna had been invited into new living rooms, seen an assortment of wallpaper and sofas and television programmes. She'd smelled meals being prepared. Sometimes she wasn't invited in. Still, she observed hallways – some carpeted, some with shiny wooden floors. People had books and magazines and pictures of cafés or stags or woodland scenes on their walls.

At the end of her mission Anna had seventy-five pounds and Marlon's pockets bulged with goodies. 'It's all for Chrissy and Ed,' she told him. *Chrissy and Ed*, she thought. *Not the same.* They'd always be Mother Dainty and Old Dungarees to her.

18

Friendly Lessons

'That was kind of you.' Richard was making tea. He brought Anna a steaming mug. She was on her usual car seat and thanked him.

'It was exciting. People were so kind. I got money for a new garden and I saw people's living rooms and hallways. The things they have. Pictures on their walls, ornaments on shelves, magazines. I was taken aback.'

'What did you expect people to have?'

'Pictures on their walls, sofas, stuff and food cooking. But seeing it was thrilling. Life,' she grinned at him, 'is cheering sometimes.'

'Only sometimes?' asked Richard.

'Well, not when you've got a headache or the love of your life says he's off to the other side of the world and hasn't asked you to go with him or when the doctor says you've got . . . you've got . . .' She thought better of saying what the doctor might diagnose. 'Or when you've missed the bus and have to wait twenty minutes in the pouring rain or when you get thrown off the bus for reading a poem to your fellow passengers.'

He took a sip of his tea. Came to look at her. Considering how low the car seat was, he loomed over her. Across the work-shop Marlon had stopped working on his spice rack to take this speech in.

'And which of the things on your list are true?'

'Oh,' said Anna, 'the getting left when someone went to the other side of the world. He wasn't the love of my life, though.

But it hurt not to get invited to go with him. That, and the poem on the bus.'

Richard walked back to his bench. 'Oh good. I wouldn't want it to be the doctor thing. Wouldn't want you to be coming down with a hideous disease.' He was making a window frame. He measured strips of wood, keeping an eye on Marlon, and said, 'You read a poem to people on a bus?'

Anna wished she hadn't mentioned this. 'Yes. It was a long time ago. I was young, angry and full of myself.'

'Youth,' said Richard. 'What a time it was. Thank God we don't have to go through it twice. What was your poem about?'

'Tonto,' she told him.

'Tonto?'

'Yes. I got the notion, from the way he did all the dirty work and the Lone Ranger got all the hero worship, that Tonto was a woman. Well, an honorary woman. Tonto the feminist.'

Richard laughed. Oh, how he laughed. 'You,' he pointed to Anna, 'reading a poem about Tonto to surprised people on a bus. I love it.'

Anna shrugged. 'I was a kid. I was obsessed with poetry.'

Marlon asked, 'Who's Tonto?'

The afternoon drifted on. Richard and Marlon worked. Anna sat on the car seat, sipped tea and tried not to think of things she'd done in the past. 'We'll have to leave soon,' she said. 'We have to take the money to . . .' It was hard not to say Mother Dainty but after a deep breath she managed. 'Chrissy.'

She got up and gave Marlon a nod. 'Ready?'

He put away the tools he was using, picked up his bag and joined her at the door. Richard crossed the room to see them off. 'Don't suppose you'd like to come to a talk with me?'

Marlon said, 'Not really.'

'I think he meant me,' said Anna. She looked at Richard. 'Did you?'

He told her yes. 'It's about trees. We need more of them. So it'll be about that, but there will be poets reading poems. I didn't know there were poems about trees.'

'Oh yes. Robert Frost, Blake and others. In fact, there are poems about most things.'

'So you'll come? I was going to go alone. I don't know anybody who likes poems except you.'

Anna said, 'I . . .'

Marlon said, 'Is this a date? Are you asking her out?'

'It isn't a date,' Anna told him. 'It's a talk. Dates are more films and food.'

'You won't be kissing, then?'

'No,' said Anna. 'We'll be listening to a talk about trees.'

'Good,' said Richard. 'So you'll come. I'll pick you up at six tomorrow. I know where you live.'

Walking home, Anna felt confused. How had that happened? She'd been going to refuse Richard's invitation. She hadn't forgiven him for laughing at her Tonto confession. But somehow Marlon's intervention with the kissing comment had led to her accepting. Only she hadn't really accepted. She'd corrected Marlon's misconception. Then again, she was going out with the object of her desire. Not bad. Once upon a time, she'd have written a poem about that.

With Marlon, she collected the money from her flat and took it across to Mother Dainty. And now she had a new living room to enjoy. Here she marvelled at a red and yellow intricately patterned carpet, an extremely comfortable blue and gold striped sofa, a small bookcase stuffed with paperback thrillers, a sideboard with framed pictures of grandchildren and a large ginger cat snoozing on a leather armchair by the fire. It was a happy room. Mother Dainty brought a tray laden with mugs of tea and plates of biscuits and put it on the long coffee table in front of the sofa.

Anna thanked her. 'Lovely,' she said. She'd been hoping for warm scones fresh from the oven. That was what Mother Dainty would serve. Chrissy obviously didn't.

Anna handed over the money she and Marlon had collected.

'For your garden. Everyone in the street contributed. We are so sorry about what happened.'

Mother Dainty opened the envelope and stared at the wad of notes. 'I can't take this.'

'Yes you can,' said Marlon. 'Everyone wanted to give you something.' He put three spoons of sugar in his tea, lifted his cup and took a sip. He nodded approval then took a biscuit, dunked it and ate. 'This is very good.'

'You can start again with your garden,' said Anna. 'I know it's daunting. But you can't give up. You can't let a bunch of hooligans win.'

'It's the digging and bending. It's hard work.'

'She'll help,' said Marlon. 'She can dig.'

Anna wanted to say she couldn't. But she didn't. 'I could do a little,' she said. 'I could help.' She hadn't reckoned on this. She didn't want to help. 'You can decide what plants you want and get them from a garden centre.'

'Oh, the garden centre? Where is that?'

Anna didn't know. 'I'll find out.'

'And you'll take me? I'll need help bringing everything back.'

'I'm sure I can manage something. Leave it to me.' Anna stood. 'Thank you for the tea.'

Outside, Marlon said, 'That was good. I only had two biscuits, though.'

'Oh dear,' said Anna. 'You might die of starvation. Do you know you have somehow manipulated me to going to a talk about trees, taking someone to a garden centre and doing some serious digging?'

Marlon shoved his hands in his pockets, kicked a small stone and said, 'It's friendly. You should be friendly.'

It was a short walk home, just a few steps across the road, but they met Swagger Boy. He raised an arm, greeting Marlon. 'Yo, Marlon.'

'Yo,' Marlon replied.

Swagger Boy looked at Anna and made a nasal noise before moving on.

'Well, that's not friendly,' said Anna.

'Yes it is,' Marlon corrected her. 'For him, that's really friendly. Sometimes I think you should go back to school for friendly lessons. You're not very good at it.'

19

The Vanishing Kitchen

James told George he was bringing a new girlfriend home for dinner. 'Kate.'

'This hasn't taken long. You only split with Sarah minutes ago.'

'We actually split ages ago. We just kept on living in the same flat. It was easier than finding somewhere new for me. But she got a new bloke, so I moved out.'

'You didn't tell me this.' George was hurt.

'It's modern life,' he said. 'It's a money thing. I couldn't buy a new place till Sarah had enough to buy me out. Now she's got a new bloke, he'll buy in. I'll get enough to put down a deposit and we're fine.'

'You'll be moving out, then?'

'In time. I thought you'd be glad.'

'I am glad. But I like having you here. It's good knowing what you're up to.'

'Ma, I cant be living with you at my age. It's weird.'

'I suppose. So, Kate?'

'Three years younger than me. I think she's the one.'

'Does she know?'

'Haven't mentioned it to her.'

'Well, I won't either.'

'Does she know about your wanting children?'

'Yes. We've talked about that and it suits her. She already has one. A girl, Hannah.'

It was a small conversation that had taken place in the

kitchen as James drank coffee before leaving for his new job, but it had bothered George for the rest of the day. In bed, sitting propped by pillows, holding a book she wasn't going to read, she confessed her guilt to Matthew.

'I want him to be happy. I don't know why his meeting the one makes me feel sad, but it does. It has crept up on me.'

'You're sad because you are thinking you are losing your boy.'

'No. I didn't feel sad when he was with Sarah.'

Matthew gave up on his thriller. He shut the book, removed his glasses and put them on the bedside table. 'That's because Sarah, perfect though she was with her clothes, shiny hair, nails and so on, didn't want to get married. She didn't want her career and business life cluttered with children.'

'She was funny. I loved having her round for a meal.'

'Your boy is broody. It happens to men. He has fallen for a woman who will have a baby or babies with him. It's normal. He'll be a wonderful dad. A nappy-changing man. But he'll always love you.'

She didn't say don't be daft. She asked, 'Were you a nappy-changing man?'

'Hell, no. Nappy-changing man is a recent thing.' He slid down the bed, pulling the duvet over his shoulders. 'The master has spoken. Time to sleep.'

George poked him.

'What was that for?'

George said, 'For being right. I hate that.' She put aside her book and moved down to her sleeping position. Matthew turned to hold her. 'Sometimes I'm scared,' she told him.

'What of? Ghosts? Crocodiles under the bed?'

'Life. Just life.'

He kissed her. 'Just eat your five-a-day. Watch when you're crossing the road. Pay your taxes – and you'll be fine.'

They kissed once more. Almost more than sex, George had always loved deep, long kisses. They were full of love and promise.

James brought Kate to the house just after eight. She was tall, dark haired and attractive rather than James's usual stunningly beautiful. She smiled a lot. George liked her and gave herself a talking to for feeling slightly sad about that. Matthew made a rack of lamb and she did the pudding – a grape thing with caramelised sugar gleaming on top. It went down well. Candles flickered. There was laughter. The conversation was light and Kate was amusing about her little daughter. George didn't ask about the child's father. She'd be told about it soon enough. They drank three bottles of wine. Enough to be slightly silly and not overly sensible. James took her home by taxi and told George just to lock up, he wouldn't be back tonight.

In bed Matthew said, 'That went well. Kate's lovely, don't you think?'

'Yes,' George agreed. 'She loved my pudding. Anyone who loves my pudding is all right by me.'

'Well, she has taste.'

'Absolutely. She reminds me of someone. Can't think who. It will come to me.'

Matthew smiled. 'She reminded me of you.'

'I don't think so. She's attractive, well dressed, educated, articulate, funny. How does she manage that with a two-year-old?'

'Nursery, a helpful mother, and whatever else it takes.'

'I remember,' said George. 'I think I went through life with gritted teeth and face set in a fierce expression, eyes on the horizon. I was a don't-mess-with-me girl.'

'You still are,' Matthew told her.

'I was widowed and a mother with a baby. I was a mess. Grieving and angry. Training to be a nurse, I had a huge chip on my shoulder. I was a little bit wild. I barely recognise the person I was.'

'I still see her now and then. I like her. I wish I'd known her.'

'Now I'm old and confused, and the older I get the more

confused I am. I didn't have time for it back then.'

He kissed her. 'I love a confused girl. So easy to take advantage of.'

She took his hand and smiled. 'I'm not so furious these days. I don't mind being taken advantage of as long as it's you doing it.'

*

The next morning George decided it was time to get rid of her ghost. There was a kitchen she had to see one more time and say goodbye to it. It had haunted her for years now.

She stood in her usual doorway across from the flat looking up at the kitchen window. It had changed. *Well, it would*, she told herself. *It's been a while, years and years*. There was a wilting geranium on the sill inside and a blind pulled halfway down. The glass looked grubby. But then, it always was grubby. She didn't recall ever washing it. She was nervous. Nearly went home. *Go on*, she willed herself to cross the road. *Do it. Do it.*

Inside, the hallway was dark and cool. She took a deep breath. Once this place had smelled of garlic and slow stews simmering and now she realised that had been down to Alistair. He'd been very junior in the kitchen where he worked. He indulged in his passion at home. George thought he'd had a spectacular future ahead of him. His talent would have been recognised and songs of praise heard in his name.

She stood at the door of the flat. It was painted red. A poor job, she noticed. The brushstrokes were clearly marked. There was a postcard pinned close to the letterbox listing the names of the six people who lived there. *Used to be just me and him*, George thought. *Then me and him and Lola, then me and Lola*. She blinked away tears and knocked.

A young girl answered. She wore black leggings and a huge yellow T-shirt, no shoes. She was pale and thin with long black hair. She stared at George. 'Yes?'

George felt her face redden slightly, her mouth dried and she couldn't think what to say. She shouldn't have come here. She swallowed. 'I used to live here long, long ago. I was happy then.'

The girl stared at her blankly.

'The kitchen,' George said. 'I loved the kitchen. It had a huge effect on me. I'd never seen anything like it. My boyfriend, who became my husband, built it. I wonder, could you let me in to see it again?'

The girl said, 'Really? The kitchen?'

'Yes, the kitchen. Could I come in and look at it? I won't disturb you. I'll just be a minute.'

The girl stepped back, waved George in and pointed up the hall to the kitchen. George didn't need to be shown the way. She knew this place well. Saying thanks with every step, she bustled towards the door she longed to open. And there was the kitchen. She stopped. She stared, mouth open. Then stepped back into the hall.

'Where is the kitchen?'

The girl nodded to the room George had just entered.

'This isn't it,' said George. 'Is there another kitchen? Have I got it wrong?'

The girl shrugged. 'That's the kitchen.'

George went back into the room. 'What happened?' she said. 'This isn't the kitchen. It used to be fabulous. It shone. There were copper pots hanging from a rail and knives on a magnet thing on the wall and a row of pendant lights. The cooker was a huge range and there were worktops and rows of bottles of oils and vinegars and wines and herbs by the window over there. There was a long table with chairs and all sorts of exotic things in the cupboards. I'd never seen anything like it. I didn't know such a place could exist. It took my breath away when I first saw it. I didn't know someplace could be like that.'

The girl looked mildly interested. 'Well, this is it now.'

There was nothing to it. The fabulous kitchen was gone. The ceramic sink had been replaced by a stainless steel unit. A small free-standing cooker stood against one wall. There was a single worktop and a row of cupboards with stained yellow doors. A selection of breakfast cereals stood on the worktop alongside a bottle of milk and a bag of sugar. There was a small fridge with a collection of magnets on the door. A few pots were piled by the sink waiting to be washed. A kettle and a mug tree on a small plastic table.

'The kitchen that was here changed my life. It was everything. I have thought about it every day since I left here.'

The girl said, 'Wow. I didn't think a kitchen could do that.'

'I saw it and knew that things could be perfect. I was young and frightened and angry. I knew Alistair had built it. I didn't have the words to articulate it, but inside me I discovered that in life there are possibilities, hopes, a future. I started to think Alistair was a knight, a man who could do anything.'

The girl said, 'I think that's always wrong. Men are people, too.'

'I know that now,' said George. 'But I was young.' She looked round. 'Who did this? It's vandalism.'

The girl looked round. 'It was like this when I moved in. It's been like this for years. Years and years.'

'The food,' said George. 'You wouldn't believe the food. Steak in vodka, chicken in coconut with limes and coriander.'

'I love that,' said the girl.

'Pasta with clams and pine nuts and things I didn't know about. I was a kid. Straight from home. My mother didn't cook. She wasn't interested. Oh, she sang to me, told stories, gave me books, and we went to the movies. But food wasn't her thing. The cooking that went on here would amaze you. Alistair would shake pans over the flame and talk and sing and add things. He played rock and roll – the Stones, Grateful Dead. He put oil in a pan and heated it and added lemon zest. Have you ever smelled that? God. Then lamb chops.'

The girl said, 'That sounds amazing.'

'We had a baby,' said George. 'Then he bought a car. An MG soft top. I saw it from the window.' She crossed and looked down at the street. Summer in Edinburgh and it was heaving on the pavement. A tidal wave of people moving. 'It was red, the car. He took off in it. Whoosh. Top speed. And he never came back. He hit a tree and died. He couldn't even drive, the police told me. He hadn't passed a test. He just thought he could do it. He was like that. Doing over seventy when he hit that tree. And that was it for me. My kitchen days were over.'

The girl said, 'Blimey.' She was holding her phone. She looked like she was aching to tell her friends about the strange visit. George thanked her once more for allowing her in and left. She stumbled down the stairs, joined the mighty swim of tourists and headed away as swiftly as she could.

She made it to the Mound and then into Princes Street Gardens, where she found a bench. She sat open-mouthed, shocked, numb – unable to make sense of what she'd seen. *A kitchen*, she thought, *who would take out a fabulous kitchen and replace it with that collection of second-hand tat?* She crossed her arms and held herself. Perhaps it hadn't been true. Perhaps she'd imagined it. She'd wanted to make Alistair a god, a knight who'd rescued her, and it was a dream.

She fished her phone from her handbag and called Matthew. 'You have to come and get me. You have to take me home. Something awful has happened. You must come. I need you.'

He asked where she was.

'In Princes Street Gardens, just past the clock. Please, this is awful. I can hardly breathe.'

20

The World Needs Doors

Anna and Richard sat near the front, listening to the lecture on trees. She put her handbag at her feet, folded her hands on her knees and looked ahead at the platform. This was exciting. She was so close to Richard his leather jacket was touching her T-shirt. She hoped he couldn't hear her heart beating. It was behaving badly, thumping away, letting her down. She hadn't known hearts did that when they were as old as she was.

It had been a day. She'd fretted about what to wear. She wanted to look smart. She wanted to look like a woman who cared about how she looked, but not too much. She didn't want to look overdressed. This was a lecture, not a dinner date. In fact, it probably wasn't a date. It was a friendly outing. There would be no hand-holding.

She had phoned George several times for advice but she hadn't been picking up. In the end she'd asked Marla when she came to collect Marlon.

'A lecture?' Marla said.

'Yes,' Anna said. 'On trees. I'm not sure what to wear.'

'What have you got?'

'Well, I have a lovely silk shirt I put on over a scoop-neck camisole thing, I was thinking about that. And I have a good dark blue T-shirt that goes over a pinky-grey T-shirt so the pink one hangs down below the blue one and you can see a bit of it at the neck.'

Marla nodded. 'What's comfy?'

'The silk can get sweaty. The blue T-shirt is soft and very comfy.'

Marla looked wise. 'Well, the T-shirt it is. If it's a lecture, you'll be bored. If you wear the silk shirt, you'll be bored and sweaty and uncomfy. If you wear the T-shirt, you'll just be bored.'

Anna couldn't argue with that. The T-shirt it was. But she wasn't bored. She was enthralled. The lecturer, an ebullient middle-aged man with a lot of hair, in jeans and walking boots, spoke with passion. It seemed to Anna there was nothing he didn't know about trees. Behind him was a large screen on which forests, individual trees and thick tangled roots appeared. To one side stood a group of poets, straight and still as trees on a windless day. *A forest of poets*, Anna thought. *Or maybe a copse, there aren't many of them. But they speak, they pour out words like fruit. An orchard of poets. How lovely.*

She leaned towards Richard. 'An orchard of poets. Still as trees and fruiting words.'

He didn't take his eyes off the stage, but nodded.

'The oldest tree in the world is in California,' the lecturer told the audience. 'It's four thousand, eight hundred and fifty-one years old. It matters. Trees matter.'

Anna put her hand to her heart and said, 'Magic.' She was silent for the rest of the lecture.

Afterwards they went for a drink in a Spanish bar. Anna drank red wine and couldn't contain her joy at all her new tree information. 'They talk to one another. I never knew that. How exciting. What do you think they say? Good morning? Lovely day?'

Richard shook his head. 'Nah. They communicate. They don't discuss *Coronation Street* or politics. They defend. They feed. Their language is beyond primal. It is about survival. We are way past understanding it. We talk too much.'

'We speak when we don't need to speak.'

'Yes. What with mobile phones and reality television shows, we have given ourselves too much to say.'

'You may be right,' said Anna. 'Do you think they feel pain? Do they hurt when we cut them down?'

Richard said, 'I worry about that. I am always gentle with wood.'

And Anna loved him more.

He drove them home and parked outside Anna's building. They sat. Anna searched for something to say. 'That was lovely. I enjoyed myself. Thank you.'

'You're welcome.'

Silence again.

Then Richard said, 'A poet? You work with words?'

'Yes. I love words. Always have. But I'm not a good poet. Not like Sylvia Plath or Adrienne Rich or Byron or Leonard Cohen or any of them. I was never going to stop readers in their tracks.'

'Things you say sometimes, I think you're probably good.'

Anna shook her head. 'I daydreamed all the time when I was little. I read *A Child's Garden of Verse* and escaped the world. I think I've lived most of my life in my head.'

He smiled. 'Is it comfortable in there?'

This surprised her. Usually when she made this confession people would say, *Surely not?* She told him, 'Yes, it is very comfortable.'

'Well, I'd advise you to stay. It gets pretty miserable out here sometimes.' They were silent once more. But it wasn't awkward. In time Richard said, 'Me, I'm not creative. I make windows and bookcases and doors.'

Anna said, 'The world needs doors.'

He agreed. 'Indeed it does.'

Anna took a deep breath. 'I don't suppose. No, you wouldn't. I don't mind if you say no. It's all right. But I just wondered if you'd like to come round for a meal one night? Nothing much. I'm no cook. But the chat might be good.'

'Now why would I say no to that? I never refuse a meal. I'll bring wine.'

'Oh wonderful. What about Sunday? I'm taking the folks across the road to a garden centre on Saturday and I've no idea how long that will take.'

'Sunday's good.' He told her. 'Always a bit of a loose-end day for me.'

They agreed they'd both look forward to it.

Once back in her living room Anna tried again to phone George. But she still wasn't picking up. Anna left a message saying she'd had an excellent time at the tree lecture and Richard was a truly lovely person. 'See you soon,' she finished, before ringing off.

It was half-past ten. Anna heard the summer world outside – people exchanging small pleasantries, laughter, a dog barking, cars purring past, snatches of music pouring from their open windows. She thought life was splendid. Well, it was now. It hadn't always been.

Talking to Richard about her poet's life, small and narrow though it was, had brought back memories of what had been the beginnings of Anna. It had started with *A Child's Garden of Verse*. She'd lost herself in that book when she was still very young. She'd stroke the pages, touch the words. They'd fuelled her daydreams. She escaped when reading it to a safe place. The need to get away, even if it was only in her thoughts, had started after her mother had told her quite matter-of-factly that she didn't love her. Didn't even want her.

That had happened when her mother had been talking about wanting to go to see the pyramids one day. 'Only I have nobody to go with. I'd be afraid on my own.'

'I'll go with you,' seven-year-old Anna had offered. 'I'll keep bad men and outlaws away.'

'Oh dear, no,' her mother said. 'I wouldn't want you there. I'd need to be with someone I loved in such a precious place. I don't love you. I never wanted you. You were your father's idea.'

Somehow, and Anna didn't know how this worked, she'd forgotten about that. She'd put it away. Blocked it. It had hurt too much. She'd slipped into daydreams of being a prince who rescued his kingdom or a soldier who fought a cruel dictator or an Indian chief who rode out against the cavalry. These dreams were real to her. And so were Robert Louis Stevenson's verses. They were fabulous and exotic and gentle, and they came from the world Anna longed to live in.

One night after she'd exhausted herself trying to write a confessional poem about her state of being – *I got triple scabies, that's what I got* – she'd thrown down her pen, run her fingers through her hair and without warning that terrible moment had come back to her. She felt her blood freeze, her stomach churn. 'Oh God,' she'd cried. She wept for the child she'd been. Poor rejected soul.

That child had grown into the woman who'd sat alone in a cold flat waiting for the gay man she'd married to come home to her after he'd been out combing bars and dance halls for a man to hold and kiss. That child had grown into a woman who did favours for people she didn't really like, who had one-night stands with men she'd just met, who bought drinks for strangers and beat herself up trying to find friends. 'And I did it all. All the shameful things because I wanted to be liked,' she told the room. 'Not even loved. Liked. Loved would have healed a lot, though.'

George saved her. Of course George saved her. 'You've got to stop this,' she said. 'I don't fully know how all this relationship stuff works. Working at it myself. I know one thing, though. You've got to like yourself first. I'm trying that. I'm getting better at it. I won't ever be strutting my stuff, but my pain isn't so bad.'

Anna was still, after years, working on it. But she was also thinking, tonight, that the pain wasn't so bad. She'd have to tell George. Dialled her number. George still wasn't picking up. *I'll see her tomorrow*, Anna thought. And she went to bed.

21

A Couple of Old Biddies Crying

To celebrate her new happiness, Anna made crab sandwiches. She hummed favourite songs from her youth and did a small on-the-spot jig as she worked. She congratulated herself on doing something real and useful. *Nurturing a friend*, she thought, *this is what my life should be about*. She would ask George what to cook for Richard. George knew about such things.

They'd arranged to meet in Princes Street Gardens for a second time. This was unusual. They delighted in finding new places for outdoor eating when the weather allowed and small interesting restaurants when it didn't. Though when that happened, George had to pay.

Anna was early. She always was. She sat on a bench not far from the clock. That was how they met. One would start at the clock and walk along past all the benches till they came to the one where the other was sitting. Anna sat. She looked about at the other garden strollers and sunbathers and smiled. It was a beautiful day.

George was late. Well, she often was. Parking in Edinburgh in August was a nightmare. Anna didn't understand why she never used public transport. But it was now half-past one. That was a little disturbing.

Anna sat. She was hungry but didn't touch the food she'd brought. It was to be shared. She searched the passing crowd for that one familiar face. As time passed, she began to imagine what might be wrong. George had been delayed at home. Her house had gone on fire. Or there had been an accident on the way here. George's car would be lying on its side, bonnet crumpled.

George's broken body would have been cut from the wreckage and she'd be lying scarcely breathing in the back of an ambulance hurtling, siren wailing, towards hospital. Almost in tears Anna sat, hand on her Tupperware box, mourning her friend.

It was a surprise, then, to see George speeding towards her. Long linen coat flapping as she clutched her handbag. Her face was pale and anxious. She started apologising before she reached the bench where Anna sat. She sank down, patted her pounding heart and panted, 'Thank goodness you're still here. I thought you might have given up on me.'

Anna shook her head. 'No. I was getting worried. I imagined you in a terrible smash up in your car.'

'Matthew drove me today. He's off doing stuff. I'll meet him later.' She waved her phone. 'You should have one of these.'

'Who would I phone? Who would phone me?'

'I'd phone you to tell you I'm going to be late.'

'I can't afford a phone. Besides, I wouldn't want anything that would interfere with my daydreaming.'

She opened her plastic box and handed George a sandwich. 'Crab. A treat.'

'What are we celebrating?'

'My crush on Richard. He's coming for a meal and I need your advice on what to feed him.'

George took a bite of her sandwich, then raised it in recognition of its excellence. 'How should I know?'

'You know about men. You've married a few of them and produced others.'

'Roast chicken,' said George. 'Looks good when it arrives at the table. Smells good as it's cooking. Slap some butter on it. Shove a lemon inside and stick it in the oven.'

'Salt and pepper?'

'Obviously. Slivers of garlic slipped into the flesh. Tarragon, if you fancy.'

'Where do I get that?'

'Supermarket. Where do you think?'

Anna nodded. George ate her sandwich slowly, staring ahead, not speaking.

Anna asked, 'What's wrong?'

'Nothing.'

'Something's wrong. I know you. You are silently chewing instead of expounding your views on the passing crowd and the soggy state of my sandwich.'

George said the sandwich was excellent, then added, 'I had a shock yesterday. The kitchen was gone.'

Anna looked blank.

'It was replaced with a load of tat. It was dirty and neglected and horrible.'

Anna said nothing.

'That kitchen changed my life. I walked into it all those years ago and it was like walking into wonderland. I felt it. It was a physical thing. A thrill. I was in that flat feeling ashamed and lonely. I was going to go home in the morning and after I saw that room I knew I had to stay.'

Anna nodded. Said, 'Ah.' Now she understood.

'Alistair built that kitchen. He did it all. It took him a long time.' She marvelled at the memory of it. 'He made the units. Painted it all. One wall was covered in pictures of food – little crumbs on a plate or feasts all laid out. Cakes. Golden pies. Fruit bowls glistening. Oh, it was lovely.' She took a bite of her sandwich. 'We had a time of it. We went on adventures. Swimming at Portobello. We once thought to climb the rock up to Edinburgh Castle. But no, we decided against it. We walked all over Arthur's Seat. Kicked leaves in Corstorphine Woods. Mostly we just walked and talked. We had favourite shops – junk shops, bookshops, record shops and pubs where we drank beer and read to one another from our favourite books.'

'I didn't know that.'

'It was special. We had treasures, things we found. A blue stone, an old photograph of a grandmother outside a cottage with a basket of fish, a velvet waistcoat we took turns to wear.

We listened to the Stones, Sam Cooke and Marvin Gaye and Leonard Cohen and Neil Young. We danced in bed. Special lying down, kicking your legs and singing.' She turned to Anna. She was weeping now. 'We did Irish jigs the length of the High Street. He went down to Holyrood and I was at the Castle and we ran to one another. Singing Irish songs at the top of our voices. Him running uphill, me tanking downhill, when we met we'd whoop with joy and link arms and whirl round and round. Three o'clock in the morning, there weren't that many people about but sometimes people joined in. Oh, we laughed.'

'What fun,' said Anna. 'I never knew you did that.'

'Yes. He was my love. My soulmate. We were us. A pair. Then he bought that bloody car and crashed it and bloody died. I didn't know what to do. I remember walking about dazed and weeping and not accepting what had happened. Dreamless sleeps and lying staring at the ceiling, barely thinking. In fact not thinking, grief just sweeping through me. There are five stages of grief. Over forty years on, I'm still at anger.

'First Alistair dies. Then Willy dies. It's so, so painful. Physically painful. Effing death, it should be banned. Why can't I die instead of them?'

'Oh, George. No.' Anna wept.

'I need to see it. That room, that amazing kitchen. I'm starting to think I imagined it all. I made it up in my sorrow. I romanticised it. I'm gutted. I think maybe it didn't happen.'

'Of course it happened. There's Lola. She's real.'

'She's real. She's amazing. But the rest of it, perhaps I made it all up because I felt so guilty about running away? Perhaps it didn't happen? If I saw that room, I'd know.'

Anna reached over and took her friend's hand. 'I'll find it. I'll find that kitchen.' As she spoke she thought, *What am I saying? How the hell do you find a room from forty years ago?*

'How on earth could you do that?'

'Someone must know. You can't dismantle a room without

someone knowing about it. The tradesman. The neighbours. I'll track it down,' said Anna. But she thought, *I am insane*.

Side by side in the sunshine they wept. A couple of passing teenage girls in striped T-shirts and skinny jeans stopped to stare. As they continued walking one said, 'See that, a couple of old biddies crying.'

Anna told them, 'One day it will be you.'

22

A Recovering Poet

On Saturday afternoon, Anna and Mother Dainty went to the garden centre to buy new plants. Marla drove them, as Anna didn't want to bother George. She borrowed the van used for balloon, cupcake and celebration delivery, as she didn't trust her twenty-year-old car to transport four people to buy plants and bring them home again. 'It makes protesting rattles,' she said. 'I don't think it likes me.'

They set off just after three in the afternoon. Marla drove, Mother Dainty in the passenger seat and Anna and Marlon on the floor in the back of the van with several balloons. It wasn't a comfortable ride.

They bought delphiniums, lupins, pansies, hollyhocks and a lilac tree. There wasn't much room for people in the back on the way home. They sang the *Flintstones* theme as they travelled. Marla insisted this was a motoring song. Anna offered a version of 'Me and Bobby McGee', insisting it was what people on the road sang. She would regret throwing back her head and hollering the words for some time afterwards.

They stopped at a Tesco so Anna could buy a chicken to cook for Richard. Mother Dainty was shocked that Anna was also buying a ready-made pudding – apple crumble. 'That's nonsense. It takes minutes to make that.' She demonstrated peeling apples and making a crumble mixture.

Anna told her, 'That would take me hours. When it comes to food, I like eating it. Not good at making it.'

Marla agreed, but Mother Dainty loved cooking. 'Eating, not

so much,' she said.

The group wandered the aisles, marvelling at things such as the range of crisp flavours. 'Red wine and steak, who'd have thought it,' said Mother Dainty.

'It used to be salt and vinegar and nothing more. Happy days,' said Anna.

And they moved on.

*

The next morning she joined Mother Dainty in her garden to help plant the new flowers. She discovered that a woman with a recently replaced hip was not a lot of use for digging holes. But she could carry a half-filled watering can and soak the newly placed plant. She could also take part in the banter and listen to Mother Dainty's stories. 'You're fit,' she said, watching the old lady plunge a spade into the ground.

'Oh yes,' Mother Dainty agreed. 'Gardening will do that for you. Of course, when I was young I thought it was boring. I liked dancing and flirting with the boys. I was as stupid as they come.'

'Me too,' Anna agreed. 'I'd rather be stupid now I'm old. I'd know to enjoy it. But I'm not up to it. Too creaky.'

'In the days before I was creaky I ran everywhere. I had four children. All gone now. Canada, New York, London and one still here in Edinburgh. Busy times, everyone bickering and tripping over one another and playing music and coming and going. I'm surprised how much I miss it.'

Anna imagined a crowded household, warm and smelling of food being prepared. She thought Mother Dainty would have made a marvellous mother. She wouldn't call her child a slut. 'Did you work?'

'I taught sewing. Had a big classroom filled with young girls. Boys got woodwork. It was before feminism. It was a sunny room, girls chattered, and at least once a week one got a finger stabbed in the sewing machine. Some of us are not born to sew. Ed worked in a garage. He fixed cars. We came and we went and we had roast beef on Sundays.'

Anna felt a pang of jealousy. *What a fabulous life*, she thought. *A home filled with bickering and movement and music and roast beef in the oven.*

Mother Dainty leaned on her spade and smiled a small secret smile. To Anna, she looked like a woman who knew things she had never shared with anyone. But today the sun was shining, she was in her garden, her favourite place to be, and seemed to have a notion to reminisce. 'I left school at fourteen,' she said. 'Went to work in a small shop selling material for curtains and frocks.'

'A haberdashery?' asked Anna.

'That's the thing. Well, my boss had a brother who made soap, lavender bar soap. We had to use it in the toilets. It was new on the market. And my boss and his brother decided to market it. They produced hundreds of small bars and me and another girl had to deliver them to half the houses in Edinburgh. Can you imagine that?'

Anna shook her head. 'You were a kid. You shouldn't have been doing that.'

'I saw life. I saw things I have never forgotten. Poverty. Filthy, hungry children. Lovely, friendly homes. Huge dogs chased us. People gave us tea. A flat painted purple and a prostitute thanking us. A naked tattooed man standing flashing at a window. I know I shouldn't have been doing that. I have been a fighter and a marcher ever since. Of course, young ones like you are lucky you didn't have to put on your liberty bodice and get on with life.'

'You marched?' said Anna.

'Protested about the atom bomb and the Vietnam War. Marched against fighting in Iraq. I have marched and marched, and it was good. Every step was a step against violence and a step for the little girl who was sent round town with a huge, heavy box of soap and had her innocence ruined.'

'Gosh,' said Anna. 'You just never know about people, do you?'

'No. But now I am too old to carry a banner. I garden and I am happy.'

'I'm not young,' said Anna.

'You're young compared to me. You've got at least twenty years before you get to my age. All sorts of things can still happen to you. A mortgage?'

'No.'

'Marriage?'

'Doubt it.'

'You could get run over by a bus.'

'I absolutely could. God, I'd forgotten about liberty bodices.'

'Ghastly things – you wore them over your vest to keep you warm. And all those funny buttons. Went out of fashion when central heating came in. They'll probably come back, now folks are turning their dials down and wising up about fossil fuels. They'll be in bright colours and have a trendy name.'

'I think liberty bodice is quite good, actually.'

*

Back home, Anna cooked the chicken. It emerged from the oven golden, crisp on the surface, succulent within. Anna felt a strange jolt of optimism and quelled it. Optimism comes before a serious failure. But failure didn't happen. The food was good. They drank wine and Anna didn't get roaring drunk. She got pleasantly relaxed and then she got honest. Later, reviewing this honesty, she doubted herself.

'Ever been married?' Richard had asked. He'd already carved the chicken. Praised its goldenness and poured wine, then heaped parsley-speckled potatoes onto his plate and smiled.

'Yes, once,' Anna said. 'It wasn't successful.'

He raised his eyebrows, questioning why the marriage failed. His mouth was too full to speak.

'He was gay,' said Anna. 'So obviously the crucial part of the union didn't happen.' She drank her wine. 'No matter. I made up for it later.'

'Rock and roll,' he said.

'Oh yes. Have you been married?'

'No. I had a girlfriend. A love, really. We never got round to marrying. But we lived together five years. She died of cancer.'

'I am so sorry.'

'Broke my heart,' he told her. 'I lost myself for years, following music around. Smoking weed. Can hardly remember what I did.'

'When my husband divorced me, I sat in a bitterly cold room and wrote poems. They weren't very good.'

They exchanged a look of shared sorrow and regret. Later, as she dished up the apple crumble Anna said, 'I've done a really stupid thing.'

'Tell me.'

'I've promised my friend I'd find her kitchen.'

'Well, there're plenty of kitchens out there. All sorts.'

'No. A specific kitchen that was in a flat she shared with her first husband. Apparently it was beautiful and she wanted to see it again. But when she got there, it was gone.'

He opened the second bottle of wine. 'Tricky one.'

'I know.'

He filled their glasses. 'Where was the flat?'

'High Street. She moved in with him. The kitchen was already there.'

'So it was replaced by a new one?'

'No, it's a sparse, sort of rented-flat one now.'

'Do you think your friend and her husband didn't pay the rent? So when they moved away the kitchen was dismantled and sold off to cover the loss?'

'That could be true. They sounded to be a bit lost in love, looking for adventure and doing an Irish jig in the High Street.' She told him about the dance.

'They don't sound like dedicated rent-payers.'

'I don't think they were.'

'When was this?'

'Oh, years and years ago. When the world was young. The

summers always hot and endless. Mama Cass was still alive. Everybody smoked like chimneys and middle-aged men wore hats.'

'Right,' he said. 'I'll ask around. See if anyone remembers a beautiful kitchen in a High Street flat.'

He left at eleven o'clock. She wondered if he'd kiss her. Nothing wild and sexual, just a friendly peck on the cheek. But no. He hovered, hands in pockets, at the door and said he'd had a good time. 'I'll cook for you soon. I'm excellent at heating a pie.'

'I love pies,' Anna said. This wasn't true. But for him she'd try.

Back in her kitchen, she started to wash the dishes. Watching suds soak over plates she decided that today and yesterday something had happened. She'd joined in. She hadn't stood back and considered her situation, taking it in, analysing it and providing a narrative to her life as she lived it. She'd enjoyed each moment as it came along. *There's an amazing thing*, she told herself. *Perhaps I am a recovering poet. Or at least a recovering wannabe poet.*

23

We Were the Weather

George led a busy life. She swam at her local swimming pool twice a week. She met Anna for lunch. She visited the library. She sat on two committees and once a week she shopped at the supermarket with Matthew. And she fussed over her family.

They met every second Sunday for lunch in her large kitchen. It was considered a sin not to turn up. Absence was only excused if the missing person was ill, working, on holiday or in hospital having emergency surgery. Partners were welcome.

Emma brought Robbie. Lola brought her long-term partner Ben and, of course, her two children, Morgan and McKenzie. James decided not to bring his new love yet. Their relationship was recent and George guessed that so far he hadn't told her they were going to marry and have three children. In summer, if the weather allowed, the family sat in the garden and drank wine. In winter they gathered round the kitchen table, drank wine and looked out at where they'd sat in summer.

Matthew always cooked. But as James was still living with them, he helped. Today they'd served rack of lamb with roast potatoes and some green beans that George had grown. Pudding was a tarte tatin. They were inside, summer rain streaming down the windows and bouncing off the patio paving.

George watched it. She thought summer downpours romantic. Family sounds drifted past her. Emma was talking about some injustice at work. Lola was praising a film she'd seen. James was pouring wine. Matthew was listening to everyone, it seemed.

In the living room, the grandchildren were playing a game. Rain battered down.

Memories kept coming to George. Sometimes they crept up from nowhere and for no apparent reason. But this rain brought a new recollection from a distant time. Alistair had told her he wanted to make love in the rain. He enthused about this when she asked why. 'I want to experience everything. I want to know what it's like.'

She had agreed to it. Though outdoor sex never appealed to her. Knickerless in a field or on a beach was not a good state of dress. She didn't trust the sand, earth, grass or the insect life. There were places on her anatomy that she didn't want stung or bitten. But his eagerness was infectious. When he stood before her, put his hands on her shoulders and leaned into her, his face alive with the promise of rapture, she could see that sex in a rainstorm could be marvellous. But once alone, perhaps dusting the ancient sideboard or squirting Harpic under the rim of the lavatory, she doubted the venture. What was wrong with a bed? It was soft, warm and comfortable, and so convenient for a post-intercourse sleep. Alistair, meantime, was watching the weather, hoping for weekend precipitation.

He got lucky. A fierce summer storm was predicted for a Sunday in July. 'My God, perfect.' He was overcome with joy. Knowing George's worries, he bought a tartan rug. 'This will keep you safe.'

The storm was due to hit at four o'clock, so they started to climb Arthur's Seat at two. 'We want to be near the top and up to a bit of nookie before the weather turns.'

'Please,' said George, 'I hate that word. Nookie. I won't do it if you call it that.'

They started their walk to the top. The storm hit early and by the time they were near their goal the rain was pelting down. They were surprised to find they were not the only people who wanted to experience extreme weather. Though Alistair was sure they were the only ones who wanted to orgasm in the wind and rain.

They found a spot among some gorse bushes – a small, perfect patch of grass, soft and hidden from view. They spread out their blanket and kissed. The rain soaked them. Flattened their hair and beat the ground they lay on. They kissed and kissed and thunder clattered overhead. Lightning. And Alistair was right. There was at least a minute, maybe two, when they didn't notice the turbulence above them. A small slice of passionate time when George wasn't terrified.

'Beans, George.' Matthew handed her a bowl. 'Got butter and toasted almonds through them. They're good. Must be the gardener's touch.'

George said, 'Hmm?'

'You were miles away.' Lola was looking at her from across the table. 'What were you thinking?'

George thought, *I can't possibly tell you that.* 'Oh, nothing much,' she said.

'She's always doing that these days,' Matthew told them. 'Drifting off into her own little world.'

She sipped her wine, slipped a forkful of beans into her mouth and let his remark roll round her head. He was right. She was prone to drifting off these days. A new memory came to her. Afterwards, when they'd finished, Alistair had stood, raised his arms to the sky, shaken his soaked head and shouted, 'Wonderful! We were one with the universe! We *were* the weather!'

She'd sat up and said, 'We should have brought raincoats.'

There followed a long, damp trudge home.

She smiled. *What fools we were. How wonderful to have been a fool, though, for a little time anyway.*

These days she often thought about her husbands. How absurd to have had three of them. Frank had been a crush, almost adolescent in its intensity. He was good-looking, attentive, quick with a spot of flattery, keen to go out to dine or to party. He'd had affairs. She'd known at the time. She now thought he needed to constantly reassure himself that he still had whatever was needed to attract women. *Oh well*, she thought, *I wasn't exactly an angel myself.* Not that she'd had affairs. She'd been obsessed with work. Her life had been filled with keeping up to date with nursing and caring for her children. Busy with school runs and fish fingers and the correct procedure to drain renal abscesses and bed times and remembering which breakfast cereals to buy, she'd neglected her marriage. Her days were so hectic love and sex took a back seat. *But then*, she thought, *he might have helped.* He might have shown at least a little interest in their domestic affairs.

Husband number three, Matthew, was lovely. He cared. He brought her things she liked to eat. He'd actually learned to make tiramisu just for her. What a man. Though she suspected the pudding had gone commercial now. It was a passé pudding.

When they'd moved into this house she'd gritted her teeth, sweated and strained, vowing to be content. 'I deserve contentment,' she'd said. He'd agreed. They shopped together on Saturday mornings. She worked in the garden. He did crosswords and watched sport on television. They ate out. They drank Pinot Noir and talked about books they'd read and childhood days. They made sweet, undemanding but wonderful love that brought on easy sleep. They were content most of the time. 'As good as it gets,' he said.

Husband number one had been her love. He'd been her soulmate, her lover and her reason to live. Now, though, she had difficulty remembering his face. She didn't have a photograph. There hadn't been a camera in their flat. After he died, she'd left in such a hurry she didn't think to look through his things for something – a memento, a thing that had been his that she could hold on to and keep. All she had were memories and his favourite small kitchen knife.

After he'd died, when those men had turned up at the door asking for Alistair, she'd said she didn't know him. There had been a sense of menace about them. She sensed trouble. *The rent*, she thought. They want money. She realised Alistair never mentioned paying any rent. He just lived, went to work and spent every penny he earned. She had a tiny baby she had to protect. Penniless and scared, she'd gathered her things and fled.

That was how he was. He had passion. He had visions of himself. His first passion had been his kitchen. God, it was amazing. Then it was her. She hated to admit it, but she had been the centre of his life. He'd kept her to himself. Then it was cars. He'd wanted to experience speed like he wanted to be the weather. She sometimes wondered why her? But in time she knew it was because she never complained. She idolised him. He'd been a reader, a knight, an adventurer, a prince hurtling towards new experiences. Now she thought the only way forward for him had been to die young. But, oh, that kitchen had been fabulous.

She looked down at her food. The lamb was finished and now a slice of tarte tatin was in front of her. 'Ah,' she said. All eyes were on her.

'Miles away again,' said Matthew.

George nodded. 'Anna has said she'll find the kitchen.' She sighed. Now she would have to explain what she was talking about. 'The kitchen at the flat I shared with Alistair. I wanted to see it again. But it was gone.'

Everyone spoke at once. Questions. Questions. Questions. Why did she want to see the room again? Did she really expect it to be there? Was something wrong? Was she unhappy? Did she want a new kitchen?

She ate her pudding and said nothing.

James said, 'It was probably taken apart and sold off. It would be too grand and expensive for that flat.'

Lola said, 'Perhaps. But if it was so beautiful, someone might have fallen in love with it and taken it apart to put together somewhere else. They did that with Julia Child's kitchen. It might be out there.'

'You mean Anna might find it?' asked James.

Lola thought for a moment. 'Probably not.'

Even George agreed.

24

Absolutely and Definitely – Ace Detectives

Years and years ago, Anna's affair with Michael had started when he'd turned up at her door and said, 'I know what you need.'

'What?' She'd been surprised to see him. They'd met at a party and conversed for a while, drinking cheap red wine. She'd thought he was exciting and hoped she'd hidden this by being cool.

'Me,' he'd said. 'You want me in your bed. Sex is what you need.'

She let him in. He made it to her bed and was in her life for a while. He was handsome, articulate, messy and arrogant. He was what you got if you let someone see you were needy. She chastised herself regularly for this affair.

When Richard turned up on her doorstep and said, 'I know what you need,' Anna was ready with a reply.

'No, you don't.'

He'd lost the wine-induced confidence of their evening together and was awkward again. He didn't meet her eyes as he spoke. He shifted from foot to foot. He was nervous. But he stood his ground. 'I've been thinking of how to do it, and I think I know.'

'Really?'

He moved past her into the hall. 'Yes. Bookshelves all the way from the front door to the living room.' He turned to her. 'It would work. The hall is wide enough to take them. It would clear the floor. I've been thinking the book piles could be a hazard. You could trip.'

If she was honest, Anna was a little disappointed. But bookshelves would make a difference. 'Can't afford it.'

'I'd do it. I love a challenge and I'm not that busy these days. Odd door or window and a bit of panelling keep me going. But people buy flat-pack furniture these days.'

He pressed his hands to the wall. 'Good wall. It would take the weight. You know, of the books. Can't afford oak. But white shelving would lighten the hallway.'

Anna didn't know what to say. She too was awkward now. 'Bookshelves are excellent.'

'It would be a challenge,' said Richard. 'I love a challenge.'

'The floor would be cleared.'

'Exactly.'

She offered him a cup of tea. They sat at her kitchen table. 'I couldn't start for a week or two,' he said. 'Have to get the stuff. I need to measure up, too. I'll come back later.'

'Actually, I'm going to the library with Marlon. He's going to show me how to work a computer. I'll use it to find out who owned the flat George stayed at. Then I'll go and ask about the kitchen.'

He drank his tea, looking at her over the rim of his cup. 'I'll come with you for that. I don't trust landlords.'

They dipped into silence, awkward again. He shyly took a biscuit. They smiled to one another. She wondered if this was what love was like, no matter how old you were. She remembered having a painful crush on Brian Fraser when she was eleven. She'd gazed at him misty-eyed across the classroom and never ever said a word to him.

'There was word of a kitchen,' he said.

'Really?'

'Yes. Phoned around. People knew about it. Gas fitters, carpenters, plumbers. Word spread. Kitchen got dismantled and put back up. It was something, that kitchen. That's why it was spoken about.'

'Where did they take it?'

'I don't know. I just spoke to a couple of guys who took it down.'

'But you didn't work on it?'

'No, back then I was chasing the music. Went everywhere to hear "Love Minus Zero" or, later, Neil Young's "Helpless". Slept on sofas, slept on park benches, barely ate. Consumed by grief. Barely knew I was alive. My lost life.'

Her heart went out to him. She knew the songs and she felt a shiver of shame that she was jealous of the long lost woman who'd been loved enough to cause such misery.

*

After lunch she went to the library with Marlon to learn to go a computer, as she put it. Marlon wasn't often the knowing one in a situation. He took his position seriously.

He was known at the library and greeted warmly. 'Hey, Marlon. Who's this you've brought today?'

'Anna. She's my pal.'

She was delighted. Apart from George, there hadn't been any pals in her life. She hadn't often felt wanted.

The computing lesson didn't go well. Anna understood logging on. She liked Google. They put in the address of the flat and were rewarded with a map with a red flag thing showing where it was. 'Well, I knew that,' said Anna. She asked for a list of letting agents and was rewarded with a long list. 'Now what?' she asked.

Marlon had no idea. Letting agents were not part of his computing world. 'I just do games.'

'We'll go. We'll knock on doors and ask who owns the flats.'

The High Street was busy with tourists surging to and from the castle. Bagpipe music streamed out of shops. Overwhelmed by noise and movement, Marlon slipped his hand into Anna's. She squeezed it. A little hand in hers brought her comfort too.

The building was cool and quiet inside after the bustle of the street. Here on the ground floor were two doors opposite each other. One was peeling red paint, the other shiny blue. Marlon stood before the red door looking pale and unsure. He leaned towards Anna and whispered, 'We won't knock on this door. Bad men live in there.'

Anna agreed – though the poet in her thought it wrong to judge people by the state of their front door. They knocked on the blue one. It was safer.

A woman answered. She was in her fifties, wearing a long scarlet skirt and black T-shirt. There was yellow paint in her hair and on her hands. She was arty. She wiped her hands on the back of her skirt and said, 'Yes?'

'Ah,' said Anna, realising she hadn't prepared a story. 'We wondered if you could tell us about these flats?'

The woman said nothing.

'Only we'd love to live around here. Are the flats owned by the people who live in them or are they rented?'

'In this building, they're all rented. Willis and Cobb are the landlords, if you want to ask about getting a place. But nothing's available at the moment.'

'Thank you,' said Anna. 'So no flats here are privately owned?'

'No. We're not mortgage types.' She shut the door.

Anna and Marlon hit the street again.

'Ice cream time. We did it. We found out who owns the flat.' Anna was jubilant.

'You told a lie,' said Marlon. 'My mum and everyone says telling lies is wrong.'

'Yes, it's wrong. But the lie was only to find something out. It didn't matter. It didn't hurt anybody.'

'Why didn't you tell her the truth? You want to know who owns the flat so you can find out about the kitchen?'

'Now you mention it, I have no idea.'

They found an ice cream parlour. Ordered vanilla with salted caramel for Anna and chocolate and vanilla for Marlon with sprinkles for them both.

'Sprinkles are the best,' he told her.

'Absolutely,' she said. 'And we got the name of the landlord. Willis and Cobb.'

'Definitely,' he said. 'Even if you told a lie.'

'Detectives do that,' Anna said. 'Absolutely.'

'I suppose, Definitely,' said Marlon.

Anna raised her spoon in triumph. 'Absolutely and Definitely – ace detectives.'

25

Another Fine Mess

George woke, sat up in bed and said, 'I've just had a disturbing dream.'

Matthew stirred. He was a man with an enviable sleeping record. He went to bed, lay down, got comfortable, shut his eyes and opened them again seven or eight hours later. George wondered how he did that. 'A remarkable feat at your age,' she'd told him.

He turned to her and asked if she could remember what the dream was about. He never recalled his own dreams, or at least none that he shared with George. It was seven-thirty in the morning but he'd been asleep for seven and a half hours so was refreshed enough to be civil about being rudely awakened.

'I was sweeping a big corridor,' said George. 'Sweeping and sweeping. It was stone flags and covered with straw. I kept sweeping, and more and more straw kept appearing. You were in a lovely sunlit room just off the corridor and never came to see how I was doing. I could hear your voice speaking to someone. You didn't seem to care about what I was doing.'

'Sorry.'

'It was one of those hard bristle brushes. Very heavy.'

'Hard work, then. Good job you were sleeping at the time.'

'What does it mean? All that pointless sweeping?'

'Obviously it's about life. Life is one long, pointless corridor sweep. But there's ice cream and wine and espresso coffee to keep us going as we work our brushes.'

'And fish and chips and sex and Marvin Gaye singing "I Heard It Through The Grapevine".'

Matthew got up and went to the kitchen to make coffee. George lay back and let her dream roll through her before getting up and putting on her dressing gown to join him downstairs. They ate breakfast in the garden. George wondered if they'd started eating healthily too late in life. 'Might as well eat fried bacon and eggs and pop off early.' Death was on her mind these days. It was funeral time in her life. She'd been through wedding time, children's party time, empty nest time and this last one was inevitable, she supposed.

Today she planned to visit her youth. She wanted to see the places that had been part of her life when she'd been with Alistair. Had all the lunacy and adventures actually happened? The kitchen wasn't there. Perhaps it had never been there. She'd made it up. She'd put Alistair on a pedestal, made him into a hero he wasn't. A trip round their favourite places might trigger realistic memories.

She put on music of that distant time as she drove. She sang along to Creedence Clearwater Revival and she discovered the junk shop she and Alistair regularly visited had become a hairdresser. It was here they'd bought a turquoise parasol and a picture of a fishwife walking along a cobbled street, wicker basket on her back. The parasol had been parked in the hall. The picture had been put on the mantelpiece along with a blue stone, a perfect and delicately pink shell, a glass candlestick and an old clock that no longer worked. 'Best clocks just look good and forget the time,' Alistair said.

She joined Grace Slick, Simon & Garfunkel and Jimi Hendrix in song as she drove down the streets of her young days and found pubs, clubs, bookshops and old dusty junk shops gone or replaced by sports shops, wine shops, a baker's and a gym. She sang 'Visions Of Johanna' as she drove past what had been a second-hand record shop they'd once haunted, and was now a sandwich outlet. They'd found childhood treasures there – 'Sparky's Magic Piano' and 'Nellie The Elephant'. They'd danced round their living room to the latter. But after that they didn't play them much. They'd found old singles, songs they both loved – Del Shannon's 'Runaway', the Beatles' 'Love Me Do', Tina Turner's 'River Deep Mountain High'. This last they played so often, so loud, the neighbours complained.

Whenever they had to meet somewhere in town, their usual place was the top of the Scott Monument. An arduous climb but Alistair said he was keeping her fit. It had all been silliness. She had thought it wild and rebellious. They would never be tamed. They would never be dull, grey, boring nine-to-five people. She'd believed this passionately until inevitably doubts crept in.

She never minded that they had no money. But she began to wonder how they managed on what little they had. Then there was the Irish jig that went wrong. After many successful jigs there was a disaster. She had thrown herself down the High Street at three in the morning. It had been raining and the pavement was damp. But the air was cool. She sang. It was a tumble of silly words. She ran. A stitch forming in her side, her throat burning, she panted as her song came out. She stormed along and reached the end of the High Street without meeting Alistair. She started back up towards the flat, thinking she'd hurtled past him. She couldn't find him. Her mind flooded with imagined disasters. He'd been attacked, was lying bleeding down a filthy close. He was hiding from thugs. He had been whisked to hospital. She searched closes and side streets. She called his name. It started to get light and still no sign of him. She ached. Longed to lie down but fear and anxiety possessed her. Eventually at six o'clock, when the world was stirring again – cafés opening, first buses rattling past – she went home.

Alistair was in bed. His tousled head on their red-and-yellow pillow. 'You're here,' she shouted. 'I've been looking everywhere for you. I thought something had happened. I thought you were in hospital.'

He raised himself on his elbow and grinned. 'No. Just decided to come home.'

'You didn't tell me. I'm sore from walking and shouting.'

He said, 'Sorry.' Flopped back down on the pillow and shut his eyes.

Not a total hero, then, she thought as she drove.

Driving down Leith Walk she passed what once had been a junk shop where she and Alistair had bought a painting of a woman in a huge hat eating a plate of fish and chips. They'd carried it home in triumph and hung it in the hall by the kitchen door. They'd also found a signed copy of Hugh MacDiarmid's *Lucky Poet*. They bought it and sold it to a second-hand bookshop for ten pounds. A fortune back then. They'd squandered the cash on wine and steaks and a Bob Dylan album. You could buy quite a lot for a tenner in those days, she remembered. The shop no longer cowered under a layer of grime, its windows littered with a scattering of strange things – a stamp album, an oily wrench, two floral teacups and an umbrella stand. Now it was painted shiny green, its window shone, and there was a handwritten blackboard outside advertising a range of coffees. There was something unnerving about seeing the hot spots of her youth gone – though she knew she'd have been surprised if they'd survived the years. *Things move on*, she thought, and put on Joni Mitchell.

She'd thought that seeing an old favourite shop or club would bring back more memories. That it would be a comfort to know the things she remembered had actually happened as she thought they had and she hadn't turned them into a notion of an idyllically nonsensical time.

It was time to go and see Anna. She needed a familiar face.

*

Anna was wearing a pair of jogging pants – 'Not that I've ever jogged,' she said – and an ancient T-shirt with a heart on the front. She claimed she wasn't quite ready for the day yet. She'd been sitting at her kitchen table listening to Maria Callas on a cassette player even older than her T-shirt. She'd also been reading recipes in a cookbook she'd had for years. 'It's interesting,' she said. 'I'm thinking of getting into cooking. If only I didn't have to buy food.'

George said, 'There are always snags. You should stick to reading poetry.'

'I do sometimes read poetry. I haven't written a poem for over forty years. I used to be ashamed of this. But no more. Who needs a new bad poem?'

George sat down and glanced at the kettle. 'Coffee?'

Anna put on the kettle, took two mugs and a jar of Nescafé from the cupboard. 'I don't do posh like you,' she said. 'Why are you here, anyway?'

'Just felt like a chat. I've been touring my past.'

'Was it magical and mystical?'

'Depressing. Favourite places gone.'

'Along with your youth.' Anna put a steaming mug on the table in front of George. 'You didn't expect anything to still be there?'

'I hoped,' said George. 'I needed to find out if what we had was real or if I had made it up. Maybe I made it up.' She took her coffee mug in both hands. 'I've loved three men in my life – Alistair, Matthew and Paul Newman.'

'Good choice,' Anna congratulated her.

'Well, obviously I wasn't going to get anywhere with Paul. Not with him being in Hollywood and not knowing I existed. Matthew is lovely. I am lucky. I adore him. Frank was an extended infatuation. But Alistair – what was that about?'

Anna shrugged. 'I'm new to love. I've had relationships, but right now I am in love with Richard. He doesn't know about it. I have to say that while love is pleasurable, it is also inconvenient. I think about Richard when I'd rather be thinking of other things. Like what to have for tea and what is happening in the soap I watch or even if I might ever write another poem. I walk past the end of the lane several times a day, hoping to see him. I look out of the window wishing he'd be out there. I hate it. It's time consuming. So Paul Newman, I understand. He's so inaccessible your love can't hurt. Also he's dead, so no problems about him not getting in touch.'

George nodded. 'All true. But I am bothered by my time with Alistair. Where did our money come from? I knew his grandmother left him some, but he spent that doing the kitchen. I had nothing. How did we pay rent? *Did* we pay rent? We must have forked out for electricity and gas, otherwise we'd have been cut off. But food? We ate salmon and steak and, I remember, we had oysters. When I got home I found out that my parents had bought all the baby stuff. But who paid for everything else? Who paid? And clothes. He was cool. Jeans, boots, and he had new shirts every week. Where did he get them? He worked as a chef but that didn't pay much. D'you think he was a thief?'

'No,' said Anna. 'Maybe he just had a big wardrobe.'

'He came home with bags filled with stuff. I didn't think anything of it at the time. I was a kid. Things appeared – I never questioned where they came from.'

They drank their coffee and contemplated the absurdity of being naïve and trusting.

'There could be a massive debt for the rent,' said George.

'It would have been written off years ago,' Anna told her. 'The flat wasn't in your name. And if the clothes were stolen, you didn't steal them.' She leaned over, patted her friend's hand. 'You're in the clear, kid.'

George said, 'It was a lifetime ago. But still I think there's a lot I didn't know about the man who fathered my first child.'

'You want to find out about him?'

'What I don't know about him is everything. Fun was all it was, and when the fun stopped he died. It wasn't long after Lola came along. First few weeks with a first baby are not fun. He hated it.' She stood. 'I should go. I have to take Mrs Jackson to the chiropodist.'

'Why do you do all this taking-people-places community stuff?'

'Paying for my sins. I should have left Alistair after that first night on the sofa. I should have gone back to my parents. They must have been out of their minds with worry. I stayed because I fell in love with a kitchen. Shame on me.'

Anna offered a few words of comfort. 'You did go back. They always loved you.'

George sighed. 'I was selfish.'

She headed for the door. Anna followed. Feeling the need to breathe some fresh air, she walked with George to her car.

Stepping out was always a surprise to her. Air, fresher than the slightly warm stuff in her flat, would smooth over her face and fill her lungs. *I must come out more often*, she'd think. Today the air was cool and clear. She inhaled deeply. Looking around, she noted the street was empty. Mother Dainty's garden was growing – the new plants flourishing. A flush of wellbeing ran through her. For a moment she did not notice Marla hanging out of her upstairs window waving to her, calling her name. 'Hey, Anna. Wait there. I want you to do us a favour.'

George stopped rummaging in her pockets for her car keys and was obviously not going anywhere till she found out about the favour. 'Are you going to do it?' she asked.

'I don't know what she wants,' said Anna. 'But I'll probably agree. She's a person who is hard to refuse.'

George and Anna stood frozen with curiosity, staring across the road. Marla reappeared at her front door. She hesitated, looked up and down the street, then started to run towards them. She was wearing a tattered towelling dressing gown and fluffy pink slippers. She hurried over the road, moving with her arms folded under her breasts, and stopped a few feet from them. Her face was pale, her eyes puffed and her nose so red it looked painful. 'Flu,' she said. 'I'll not come near. Don't want to be giving it to you.'

George said, 'Thank you.' She took her hat off to someone with the confidence to appear in public dressed like that.

Marla came straight to the point. 'I need you to do a couple of deliveries for me tomorrow. I'm not well. Just the two – a happy birthday and a congratulations. I've got the tunes on my phone. I'll have the cupcakes and the balloons. Just pick them up and give them to the people and smile. That's all.'

Anna said, 'I can't drive.'

'She can.' Marla pointed at George.

'Why don't you just phone in sick?' George asked.

'You can phone in sick on your planet. On mine, you don't. Not if you want to keep your job.'

'It is against the law to sack people for being sick.'

'If you can prove you were employed in the first place perhaps.' Marla unfolded her arms and crossed them again forcefully.

George shrugged. 'Well, I could spare an hour or two.'

Anna said, 'I'm not wearing that uniform and I'm not singing. I never sing in public.'

Marla said, 'You don't have to wear the uniform. No singing. Just deliver the stuff, say happy birthday and congratulations, look happy and smile and come home. No problem. I owe you one.' Arms still crossed she ran back to her house and disappeared inside.

George opened her car and climbed behind the steering wheel. She shot Anna a disapproving look. 'Another fine mess you've gotten me into.'

26

The Hallelujah Chorus

'There are many things I do not want to do. Have root canal, go into labour, resit my driving test, sit final exams, kiss Billy Watson.' George shivered with distaste at this last memory. 'He stuck his tongue down my throat. I was thirteen and innocent. I'd no idea people did that. What a shock.'

'You lost your innocence to Billy Watson,' said Anna.

'Yes. Anyway, among the many things I do not want to do is this. Drive to a small office and congratulate someone I don't know with a cupcake, a balloon and a song.'

They were in George's car hurtling towards a small business park on the northern edge of the city. George was in a bad mood. 'I can't believe I agreed to this.'

There were balloons attached to the car. They bobbled in the wind as they hurtled. 'At least they are dark red,' said George. 'They look quite smart with the yellow paintwork.'

Marla had insisted on the balloons. She wanted the car to look festive and had tied some to the handles of the back passenger doors and the boot.

'Why would anyone want a festive car?' Anna had asked.

'To celebrate they can afford a car,' Marla told her. 'Not everybody can.'

'We live in doleful times,' Anna said.

George worried the whole thing was illegal. 'What sort of fine will I get if the police catch me?'

Cars slowed to stare as they drove. Mostly, though, people smiled and waved. Anna waved back. George pretended this wasn't happening. Their destination was a run-down and dusty collection of four single-storey buildings, each with a blue door (peeling paint) and a sign on the front. They were looking for Sea View Kilts. It was the last and smallest of the buildings. The wooden sign on the wall read *Kilt Maker To The Stars*. The two wondered which stars. But it was here Ewan Brown worked. Today was his lucky day.

Clutching their goodies, they entered. The place was tartan clad – walls and floor. Inside was busy. Three women worked sewing machines and a tall, very fat man with a huge beard stood at an ironing board smoothing out an expanse of Black Watch pleats. The ironer looked up. A ripple of shock ran round the room. The two intruders and the kilt workers stared at one another. The silence must have only lasted for a minute or two. But it felt like hours.

Anna broke the moment. 'Ewan!' she shouted, surprising herself. She was usually shy in new company. 'Congratulations. We bring joy and treats.'

Ewan put down his iron and stepped towards them, arms spread for a hug. 'I always love a treat.' Anna held up the cupcake. 'For you on this happy day.' She didn't want a hug. George pressed the button on the phone Marla had given her and an unfamiliar version of 'Oh What A Beautiful Morning' sang out. Ewan clapped and said, 'Almost my favourite song.' He took the nearest sewing machine woman by the arm, invited her to the floor and waltzed her round and round. He then cast her aside and took the next sewing machine lady waltzing. The music played. After a couple of laps he swept up the last sewing machine lady, held her in his arms and kissed her. The other two clapped. The room was filled with joy, love, morning song where the corn was high, and kilts. Anna almost wept.

'We have balloons.' George handed one to Ewan then hurried back to the car to get three more. 'A balloon for everyone.' She felt aglow with generosity. 'What are we celebrating?' she asked.

Ewan took her to the floor. She danced and repeated her question.

'I am marrying Wendy,' he said, and bowed to his wife-to-be. 'We've been together for twenty years and now she says yes. And we got a contract for a hundred kilts for staff in a new hotel. They'll be denim. Things are looking up.'

George thought it was all marvellous. But somehow a cupcake and a balloon didn't quite do it when it came to celebrating. 'There should be more.'

Ewan gripped her arm. 'This has made us smile. A smile is enough. That's my motto.'

She thought it an efficient and undemanding motto. 'It will do,' she said. 'Twenty years?'

He shrugged. 'It didn't seem so long as I was living it. I saw her – Wendy.' He pointed to the woman he'd kissed. 'And I loved. But I was married. And by the time I wasn't, she was married. So I waited. Waiting, longing and loving can be pleasant sometimes. Agonising at other times. It's life.'

George knew all about that.

*

Driving to their second appointment they were happy. 'What a job,' said George. 'You turn up, hand out stuff and make people jump for joy.'

'Who knew there was such a way to earn a living?' Anna agreed. 'No beating yourself up writing a poem.'

'No exams. No real routine. No rules. No seeing lovely people die. It's marvellous.'

'You don't even have to bake the cupcakes. Or choose the tunes. Just turn up, hand out treats, smile, and that's it.'

'A breeze,' said George. 'Where to next?'

'Leith. Lorna Simpson's birthday. Chocolate cupcake and the Hallelujah Chorus.'

'Big birthday, then.'

'Sounds like it,' said Anna. 'Fortieth maybe. Sixtieth. Or one of the ones you didn't think you'd get to.'

'Well, a hallelujah moment there then.'

Lorna Simpson worked in a small boutique called Lavender. The clothes were special and expensive – velvet jeans and skirts, silk shirts, linen jackets, multi-coloured scarves. 'Nice stuff,' George told Anna.

'I'd have to wait till someone decided they no longer liked it and put it in a charity shop,' said Anna.

She was wearing black jeans, black jacket, red T-shirt and white training shoes. She thought she was looking smart. George was in blue linen pants, white silk shirt and long grey linen cardigan. She knew she was looking smart, but didn't really care.

They entered the shop. It was quiet and smelled of lavender. There were three assistants. One was very young, one was thirty-ish and the third looked to be in her fifties. George and Anna decided she was the birthday girl. There was a long silent quizzical period when the shop women stared at the balloon-bearing intruders. At last the oldest assistant said, 'Yes? Can I help you?'

'We bring treats,' said Anna. But the silence had been heavy and her heart wasn't in it. She stepped past a rail of skirts, holding out the cupcake in a small box. 'Happy birthday.'

As the greeting came out the Hallelujah Chorus roared into the shop. George held the phone aloft.

The fiftyish woman shouted, 'Really? You're playing this? Really?'

'It's a special day. So a special piece of music,' said Anna. 'And we bring a cupcake.' She put the little box on the counter. 'And a balloon.'

'Who ordered this?' the fiftyish woman shouted.

George consulted the card Marla had given her. 'William.'

'My ex. My bloody ex. On my sixtieth birthday he sends the Hallelujah Chorus to humiliate me. He left me for a twenty-five-year-old.' She picked up the cupcake and threw it at George. 'Get out!'

'She told me she was fifty-three,' said one of the assistants.

The box burst open and the cake splattered into a rail of silk shirts.

'Look what you've done! These cost a fortune. Out,' shouted the birthday girl. 'Out. Turn that din off and get out.'

George turned and fled. Anna followed. They clattered into the street, George stabbing at the phone, trying to stop the music. As they bustled to their car the birthday girl came after them. 'Bugger off.'

Anna turned. 'We are doing our best. Buggering off isn't easy at our age. We were only trying to help a friend. She was meant to do this but she isn't well. We didn't mean any harm. I've left the balloon.'

She noticed to her horror, further down the street, Dorothy Pringle was standing outside her shop watching and shaking a disapproving head.

Inside the car George signalled and moved off. 'That woman is hurting,' she said. She drove round the corner and pulled over. 'I know her pain. My husband wasn't kind either. Not a happy time. Me working, looking after the kids, washing clothes, cooking, nagging about homework, and all the stuff – the sounds of their music and television programmes and me stumbling along, worrying. Frank just didn't think it wrong to sleep with other women. He just thought he should pay for things and leave everything else to me. The things we live through. Poor soul.'

'Love's shite,' said Anna. She didn't mention Dorothy Pringle.

27

I Know About Guilty Faces

Richard brought the finished bookcase. 'Not oak,' he reminded her. 'Can't afford oak. It's fake oak. But wood-coloured. I thought the white stuff wouldn't be right.'

Anna nodded. The bookcase seemed huge and filled her hall. Moving about was impossible, as along with the enormous bookcase there were three people. More than Anna could remember being in her flat at one time ever. Richard had brought Swagger Boy to help.

Swagger Boy looked at the piles of books against the wall reaching from the front door to the kitchen. 'Are they not a fire hazard, them books?'

Anna said, 'I hadn't thought of them in that way. Perhaps they are. But if they do go up in flames, I'll be happy to go with them.'

Richard said they'd better get on. 'Fit the case then put in the shelves. Takes two, though. Heavy.' He ran his palm over the wall and nodded. 'Good wall.'

Anna asked if they'd like a cup of tea before they started.

Richard said, 'Never say no to a cup of tea.'

Swagger Boy said, 'Do poets drink tea?'

Anna told him, 'Yes. What else would they drink?'

'Whisky? These funny teas with fruit and herbs that nobody likes?'

'No, poets drink ordinary tea. They dunk biscuits too. I do believe Auden was fond of a HobNob.' She bustled off to the kitchen to put on the kettle, smiling. She didn't like the notion of only drinking funny tea and whisky but was pleased to be classed in this absurd bias along with her hero poets. Though she knew she didn't deserve to be there.

Richard and Swagger Boy drank tea in the kitchen as Anna pretended to be doing something important at the sink. She was uncomfortable with having a couple of workmen in the flat. She sensed Richard shooting Swagger Boy silencing looks. Eventually she said how much she was looking forward to having somewhere proper to put her books. 'I should have had something like this years ago.'

Richard waved her thanks away. 'It's nothing. I've always liked doing bookcases.'

Silence again till Richard said, 'So what are you up to today?'

'I'm off to the landlords of the High Street flat to ask about the kitchen.'

'Who would they be?'

'Willis and Cobb.'

'I'm coming with you. This' – he waved to the bookcase in the hall – 'will take all morning. I'll pick you up after lunch.'

'I'm quite capable of going alone. I just need to ask about the kitchen.'

'What kitchen?' asked Swagger Boy.

'My friend lived in a flat in the High Street years ago. It had an amazing kitchen. She wants to know what happened to it.'

'What was it like?' he wanted to know.

'I never saw it,' Anna said. 'But I believe it was beautiful. There was a wall of pictures of food. Paintings and so on.'

'They'll have sold them. That's what they do. I'll come with you if you need someone to look a bit wild. I'm good at that.'

'I'll be fine,' Anna said.

'Willis and Cobb have a bit of a reputation. You be ready at two o'clock,' Richard told her. 'I'll come for you.'

She spent the rest of the morning in her living room reading. She secretly wanted to watch a rerun of *Brief Encounter* that was on but didn't want Richard to think she was the sort of person who watched television in the morning.

She ate a carton of yoghurt for lunch as she leaned against the sink wishing she hadn't arranged to go out. She'd fallen in love with her new bookcase and wanted to play with it. She'd put her reference books on the top because she rarely used them these days. Old-friend books would be near the bottom, where she could easily reach them, and favourite-friend books in the middle so she could say hello to them every time she passed on her way to the loo or bed.

At two, the car was parked outside waiting for her. She pulled on her jacket, hurried up the path and slid into the passenger seat. Swagger Boy was seated behind her.

'No need for you to come,' she said.

'Willis and Cobb, I think there is,' said Richard. 'They're not exactly . . .' He started the car, put it into gear and moved off. '. . . nice.'

'They're landlords, for heavens' sake. Not the Mafia. I'll be perfectly safe.'

'There are landlords and landlords,' said Richard. 'We're coming with you.'

She sighed. Told herself to relax. All she was going to do was ask about a kitchen from a distant time. 'I haven't told you the address,' she said.

Richard said, 'No need.'

He drove into Leith, skirted the docks and stopped in a small dusty backstreet. There were tenements and a row of three shops – a bookie's, a grocer's and Willis and Cobb. The window was covered with notices of flats for rent. None of them looked in any way desirable to Anna. *No bookcases*, she thought.

Inside was stuffy. The floor was green lino, the walls a grubby cream. There was a cheery holiday poster on the wall advertising a happy time in Marbella. A woman who looked to be in her thirties – blonde hair, scooped-neck black T-shirt and jeans – sat behind a chipped wooden desk tapping at a keyboard. She considered Anna. 'Yes?'

Anna didn't know what to say. She knew she should have a plan. She should have worked out in advance how to ask about a vanished kitchen. 'Um,' she said. 'I have a strange request.' At this point she worried about what Richard and Swagger Boy were doing. They could be standing behind her collars up, arms folded, legs apart looking menacing. Oh no. She turned. Richard was just behind her, hands in pockets, looking like a disinterested husband in a supermarket queue. Swagger boy was on a seat by the door, looking masterfully adolescent. His legs were stretched before him and he was staring at his trainers.

'I have a friend who lived in one of your flats in the High Street. It had a fabulous kitchen. She wonders what happened to it.'

The receptionist asked, 'When was this?'

'Quite a time ago,' Anna told her.

'If it was our flat, it was our kitchen and we can do what we like with it.'

'Yes,' said Anna. 'Only the tenant of the flat did the kitchen. My friend went back to see it and it's gone. What happened to it?' She gave the address.

The woman started tapping at her computer. 'Nope.' She went over to an ancient filing cabinet, opened a drawer and took out a file. She flicked through it, put it back and brought out another file. A man – small, stocky, wedged into a brown suit – appeared from a door behind the reception desk. He looked at Anna and took a seat under a glass panel.

'What's this?' said Anna. 'Is this some kind of heavy? A tough guy come to beat me up? I only asked about a kitchen.'

The woman said, 'There's nothing on file about a kitchen in the High Street. I think you must have the wrong letting agency.'

Anna said, 'No, I don't. You must keep records. 'Maybe you sold the kitchen off bit by bit. It had a lot of paintings. If I could trace one, I could give it to my friend.'

'You really expect us to have a record of what happened to a kitchen from years ago? You're off your head. Really. Go away.'

The man in the suit stood up and looked at Anna. She stepped back. Felt Richard's hand on her arm. 'I'm only making an enquiry. There's no need to get aggressive.'

Now Swagger Boy was on his feet, standing beside Richard. They gently pulled her to the door. She raised her stick. 'You're being rude. I am sick of rude people. Sick, do you hear? Who do you think you are? Ageist creep standing there with your files and your disinterested looks.'

Richard yanked her out into the street. She stood glaring at him. 'I will not be moved on the subject of my friend's fabulous kitchen.'

'Well, that's obvious,' said Richard. 'I don't know what they would have done in there. But I felt hostility. I don't think they knew about the kitchen.'

'The old guy did,' said Swagger Boy.

'What old guy?' Anna knew she sounded shrill but couldn't help it.

'The old guy who was watching from the glass panel behind the shouty woman. He was old. Really, really old. Older than you,' he nodded to Anna. 'I don't know about making bookcases, and I don't know about poems, but I fucking well do know about guilty faces. And he had one.'

'We should go and talk to him,' said Anna.

'Perhaps not,' said Richard. 'He'd have come forward, if he thought it was okay.'

'The atmosphere was a bit hostile,' said Anna. 'But that woman genuinely thought I was off my head. I'm sure she didn't know what I was talking about.'

They stood by Richard's car, looking across at the letting agent's office and wondering what to do. Not one of them had experience of this sort of situation and they were so intrigued by an old man with a guilty face that at first they didn't recognise that guilty man when he came out of the office, glanced at them and pointed to the pub at the end of the street. The three followed.

The pub pleased Anna. It was old-fashioned. The stained

glass on the door, ancient wooden bar and worn leather chairs reminded her of pubs she'd seen in films years ago. It was almost a surprise to see it all in colour and not black and white. The man with the guilty face was sitting at a table in the corner. He nodded to them. Richard nodded back and bought a round of drinks – three pints of beer for the men and a half pint for Anna. She didn't mention her feminism. She drank pints too.

'You want to know about that flat in the High Street?' the man with the guilty face asked.

Anna told him, 'Yes. I'm Anna.' She shook his hand.

'Gordon,' he told her. 'I was in that flat. Never seen anything like it. It was full of things – books, jewellery, clothes, pictures, wine, records. Amazing.' He turned to Anna. 'You'll know. The girl was your friend.'

Anna shook her head. 'She was my best friend. But at that time I was away at university. I never visited the flat.'

'She was learning to be a poet,' Swagger Boy said.

Gordon looked interested. 'I've never met a poet before. How many poems have you written?'

'I haven't written a poem for a while, years and years. What do you do?'

'I was an accountant before I retired. But I did inventories for Willis and Cobb. The receptionist there is my daughter. I was checking if she wanted me to babysit Saturday night. She does.'

Richard raised his glass. 'Good.'

Anna said, 'Inventories?'

'Yes. I did that flat. Went in and recorded every single item in there. Took me a long time. Never seen so much stuff. After I'd recorded it all, Willis got in experts. Some of it was rubbish. Some worth a fortune.'

Anna said, 'What about the kitchen?'

'Cobb took that. His wife was a cook. I mean, she was more than keen. She was fanatical about it. He brought her to see the kitchen and she wanted it. Didn't want it copied. She wanted the one she saw. They took it apart piece by piece and put it back together again in her house. Big mansion, back of Corstorphine Hill.'

'Do you think it's still there?'

Gordon shrugged. 'Who knows? It was special, though. I'd have loved to have a room like that. One wall was floor-to-ceiling pictures of food – plates of food and restaurants and cooks and steaming pies and tarts and slices of fruit with cheese. Then there was a huge oak table with candlesticks on and chairs round it and a long bar where the chopping and such went on. Pendant lights over it. Old sinks, one was dark green ceramic. Where had that come from? Huge range cooker and old American fridge. There was an American wall phone and drawers full of fancy knives, original Sabatier. Shelves of cookbooks and plates and other crockery. Copper pots hanging on hooks. And the whole place glittered. Shone. It smelled of classy cooking. You just wanted to sit at that table and eat.' He sank the last of his pint.

Richard went to the bar to buy him another. Anna asked, 'What happened to the rest of the stuff?'

Gordon said, 'You went into that flat and there were pictures all the way down the hall to the living room. There, the walls were crammed with pictures. Bookshelves at one end of the room full of books and records. Some of the books were rare first editions; there were small tables with things on them – little ceramic boxes with a pebble or a ring inside. In the bedroom were racks of suits and shirts, and she had velvet jeans and skirts and silks and satins. God knows how much Willis and Cobb made from it all. And everybody, absolutely everybody, took something. A mate of mine took a little picture, then a couple of years ago had it valued. It was worth three grand.'

'What did you take?' asked Anna.

'Nothing. It all felt wrong to me. I thought it was okay for the landlords to take enough to cover the unpaid rent. But they took everything.'

'Where did the couple get the money?' said Richard.

'I don't think they had money. I think the things were stolen.'

'My friend would not have done that. Never.'

Gordon shrugged and finished his beer. 'Well, my conscience is clear. It was a free-for-all. People dismantling the kitchen, people valuing things, me trying to catalogue it all, and over a week everything gone. I'd never seen anything like it and I always knew someday someone would come asking about it.' He stood up; it was time to go. 'I'll tell you one thing. Standing in that flat, surrounded by all the things, breathing in the atmosphere – it was like I was intruding on a love affair. I felt that a great romance had gone on and I was recording the remnants in a big ledger. 'Course he died, and she ran away with the baby and never came back to claim any of it. I never understood why.'

Anna said, 'For her, it was never about the stuff.'

28

Here's to Baby Lola

George took Anna to a posh restaurant for lunch. 'Wear something clean, since you don't have anything expensive,' she said. 'We're celebrating.'

'What?'

'Life. Romance. Yesterday I opened the fridge, looked in and remembered what I wanted. There's an amazing thing.'

'It's certainly something to celebrate. It's been a while since I've done that.'

'Top of Victoria Street one o'clock tomorrow, we're going to Ondine's.'

They ate lobster and drank Chablis. Anna wore her velvet pants and a dark blue top she'd found in a charity shop years ago and had rarely worn. 'It's too posh for ordinary.'

They clinked glasses, said cheers and sipped, this place being too refined for swigging.

'I have decided to relax,' said George. 'I'm not going to worry any more about anything. To hell with five-a-day and to hell with not drinking two days a week and to hell with walking fifteen million or whatever it is steps a day. I'm going to do what I want and when I die my last words will be "That was a blast!" and not "What was that all about?"'

Anna said she liked that.

'How's your love life going?' said George.

'Not a lot of progress. He made me a bookcase.'

'An act of love,' said George and refilled their glasses. 'You should reveal yourself to him. Tell him how you feel.'

Anna didn't think so. She amused herself briefly, imagining what she'd say. *Richard, I have to be honest with you. I have to say something I think is important. I love you. I dream about you. There is barely an hour in every day I live when I do not think about you.* She was sure his reaction would be to run. The panic and clumsiness of his speedy departure might be funny. But that would only last for a minute or so and then there she'd be with that old familiar pain in her heart. She was beginning to think that unrequited love was the best love. At least you knew where you were with it.

George sipped some more. 'I had a wonderful day yesterday. The successful visit to the fridge. So I thought I'd try and give you a wonderful day today. Sharing is my new creed.'

Anna said, 'Well, if you can afford it.'

'Obviously I can't. But Matthew can and he doesn't mind.'

Anna raised her glass. 'Thank you, Matthew.'

George leaned towards her and asked, 'Did you love Leonard Cohen?'

'Of course. Who didn't?' She quietly hummed a small 'Suzanne' solo.

'I cried when he died.'

'You always were a softie.'

'I went to see him here in town. It was lovely. A whole theatre enraptured and in love with him. Men and women, but mostly women.'

She remembered that evening well. She'd communed with strangers. She'd smiled and smiled. After the songs were sung, and the encore played and cheered, she'd gone to the loo. There was a queue. Of course there was a queue. Who would leave an auditorium when that man was wooing them with long-loved melodies? But what a queue this was. Someone in one of the cubicles started it. Entranced and probably dewy-eyed, she'd given a chorus of 'Hey, That's No Way To Say Goodbye'. The other cubicles and the queue had joined in. She'd found it magical and wished Leonard had been there to enjoy it. She was sure he would.

'What else happened in your wonderful day?' Anna asked.

'We went to visit a friend of Matthew's up a glen about three hours away. We stayed for supper so it was about nine or ten when we left to come home. But it was warm and the sunroof and windows were all open. It was a little narrow road, pine trees on one side, heather too. Matthew put on a music station and Leonard Cohen came on. Perfect on a summer night, "Sisters Of Mercy". It's lyrical. He stopped the car. Invited me out and we danced, waltzed in the heather by the road. Stars were out and a deer stopped to watch, ears pricked ready to run. And the music played. It's not a long song. But there was love.' She poured more wine. 'That's it. No need for a bucket list, I can die now.' She did a seated demonstration waltz and Anna laughed. Anna rarely danced. She was sure her brain and her feet didn't communicate, or at least her feet never did what her brain told them to do.

'What did you do yesterday?' George asked.

'I went to a pub with Richard and drank a half-pint. I didn't tell him I drank pints. Not that I don't want him to know that. I just accepted what he bought me and smiled. I'm growing up. I'm learning.'

She didn't mention the others present. It would have led to having to tell George why they were there, and what had happened to all the treasures collected in the High Street flat. Right now George was happy. Why break her heart with tales to ruin her memories?

'It was a good pub,' Anna said. 'Old-fashioned, like the ones that used to be in Rose Street. The first time I went to a pub it was in Rose Street. Later I went with a couple of poets. I was so excited. I thought we'd talk about life and literature and magical things. But they drank whisky and discussed why they loved Marks and Spencer apple pies. Talk about disappointing. Anyway, after the pub with Richard I went home and played with my new bookcase. I had fun.'

'Heroes often disappoint. I mean your apple-pie poets,' said George.

'Did yours?'

'Alistair was my hero. I wonder if he would have disappointed if he'd lived? Then again, I might have disappointed him. I am quite ordinary really.' Elbow on table, chin cupped in palm, she looked towards the window and wrestled a moment with this revelation. Watching her, Anna realised how beautiful she was. Not that this was a new observation. She'd always known George was stunning – the cheekbones, the full lips, the slightly hooded blue eyes – she just knew George so well, she forgot the face so familiar was also fabulous. But it was no wonder the woman attracted so many men.

Anna remembered when George was working in A&E she had gone to meet her at the end of her shift. They'd planned a few G&Ts before George had to go home to her children. Anna had been early and sat by the door waiting for George to finish. It was Saturday and busy. George appeared and everyone waiting to be seen looked up. 'Brian Peters,' George called. Nothing happened. Nobody moved. George called again. 'Brian Peters.' An old man in a battered raincoat and thick glasses shifted in his seat, gazing at her longingly. 'Is she calling me? Really?'

'Yes,' said George. 'Are you Brian Peters?'

'I think so.'

George had signalled him to follow her.

Beaming, he shuffled after her. 'Can't believe it. A woman like that calling me.'

A passing porter jerked his head at the scene. 'Happens all the time. They call her Nurse Stonker.'

Anna was pulled from her reverie by George touching her arm. 'You want pudding?'

'Of course,' said Anna. 'I never say no to a pudding. Did Alistair do puddings to die for in the fabulous kitchen?'

'Yes. I ate crème brûlée and gazed at our wall of pictures. They were fabulous pictures. It was a wonderful time. It was all about being young. Being young was our main preoccupation.

The affair started to fizzle out when Lola came along. I didn't know what to do about him. He hated not being the centre of my attention. But first baby wipes you out. Feeding, nappies, worrying. And the guilt – oh God, the guilt. Mother and guilt complex doing fine. He hated the kitchen being used to wash nappies and sterilise bottles. He hated nappies and baby clothes hanging up to dry. He hated the crying and me walking the floor with her. It took a while for me to get my figure back and I smelled milky and of vomit. Not sexy. A baby is a very effective contraceptive. You're too knackered to do anything in bed but sleep. What the hell were we thinking? I mean, all that sex we had, what did we think was going to happen?' She thanked the waitress for her double espresso. Lifted the cup. 'Here's to baby Lola. She made a woman of me. A smelly, sweaty, unsexy woman, but a woman.'

'Still,' said Anna, 'Alistair couldn't have totally minded Lola. He bought all the stuff – clothes, bottles, nappies and God knows what else.'

'Ah well,' George squirmed in her seat, 'I always thought that. He must *really* care, I thought. But no. My parents bought all the baby stuff – changing mat, yellow bath, nappies, bottles, carrying basket, cot. Everything. They had it delivered to the flat. They knew all along what was happening. I only found out about it later. I never properly thanked them.' She put her hand to her mouth, shook her head and looked at Anna. Her eyes glazed and fat tears ran down her cheeks. 'Shame on me. Shame on me.'

29

Love's Rubbish

It struck Anna that yesterday's lunch hadn't ended well. And it had been so jolly at the beginning. This was her fault. She should never have ruined a delightful lunch by asking questions about George's young life.

George had given in to full-face crumpling sobs. Anna had reached over and taken her hand. 'Oh, please don't cry.' She'd rummaged in her bag for a tissue. 'As you know, we sluts always have tissues.' Hoping to make her friend smile. People at tables nearby stopped eating and chatting to watch the goings-on. *Two old ladies causing a scene in a restaurant after one recalls a guilt too far*, she'd thought when she got home.

A waitress had come to their table and asked if anything was wrong. Had there been a problem with the meal? Dabbing her eyes on a napkin, George said that the meal had been delicious. 'I'm crying because I've had a memory rush and it wasn't very nice. I'm old. This happens sometimes.' They'd left soon after that and George had taken a taxi home. 'Guilt is getting to me. I need to lie down. Actually, I get tired a lot these days.'

This show of sorrow made Anna reluctant to pursue the kitchen. She imagined finding it and bringing George to see it and there being not just a fit of sobbing but a total breakdown. The past, she decided, was best behind us where we left it. So she spent the next day filling her new bookcase. She came across many old friends as she moved piles of books to their new home on the shelves. 'Oh, *Doctor Zhivago*, how are you? Haven't read you in years, and I do like a bit of poetry and revolution and snow in a book. I'll put you aside.' She delighted in coming across her pal Siegfried Sassoon. 'Why, hello. Let's burst out singing together.' Van Morrison was playing on her old turntable, so she danced Siegfried up and down the hall. *He'd have enjoyed that*, she thought.

*

Later she picked up Marlon from school and they dropped by Richard's workshop on the way home. Marlon thought his spice rack was ready, and magnificent. He wanted to take it home and present it to Marla. Richard thought not. 'It needs final touches. I like perfection.'

Anna enjoyed visiting the workshop these days. She sat in the car seat, drank tea and chatted about ordinary things – what she'd watch on television, her neighbours, the weather and what she might have for tea tonight. The weather was too warm for the wood stove to be on and Anna missed watching the flames.

'I'm a winter person,' she told Richard. 'I like open fires and wood stoves and thick jumpers. I hate to think what that says about me.'

'You like to keep warm? You like a layer of wool between you and the weather?'

'There's that. I just wondered if it said something about my personality that I prefer to be protected from the world by a cosy jumper.'

'See,' said Richard, 'that's the difference between you and me. I just put on a jumper. You analyse your chill and the need to fix it. That'll be the poet in you.' He handed her a mug of tea. 'Fancy some music on Friday?'

'Yes. What sort of music?'

'People playing in a small hall. A quartet. We could get a bite to eat after. Not before.'

'Yes, after is better. Though if we're hungry, rumbling stomachs might annoy audience members close by.'

'We'll wear thick jumpers to muffle the noise.'

Anna smiled. She was aware she did this often these days.

Richard glanced at Marlon, checking he wasn't listening. 'I've found the house,' he said, lowering his voice.

'What house?'

'The one where Cobb lived. Where he put the kitchen.'

'How did you do that?'

'Computer.'

'I failed at doing them.'

'I just started. Amazing and addictive. We'll talk about what to do on Friday.'

The rest of the visit was spent listening to Marlon complaining about not being allowed to take the spice rack home to his mother and Richard saying he expected perfection even in spice racks. Anna was glad to get away.

Walking home, Marlon continued to complain. 'I just want to give it to Mum. She won't mind if it isn't perfect.'

Anna said, 'That's the trouble with a master craftsman.'

Marlon walked slowly, scraping his shoes on the pavement. 'It's not fair.' He kicked a small stone. 'Richard used to say it was time to take the spice rack home. Then you started coming and then he said I had to make it perfect.' He stopped and stared at the ground, scowling. He was thinking. It was obviously hard. Wrestling with observations and opinions that were battering round his head. He looked, still scowling, at Anna. 'It's you. He bought a cushion for your seat and he bought a mug for your tea.'

'I'm sure he had more than one mug,' said Anna. She was aware of feeling uncomfortable about this conversation.

'He didn't have a nice one like he gives you. He only had cracked ones.' He resumed scowling. 'He doesn't want you to stop coming. That's why he won't let me finish.'

'Nonsense,' said Anna. But she was impressed by Marlon's reasoning.

Marlon's expression changed. His eyes lit up. The truth had

hit him. He pointed at Anna, arm at full stretch, finger with chewed nail rigid. 'Richard loves you. That's why he won't let me have the spice rack. He wants you to keep coming. He loves you.'

Anna more than reddened. Her face turned full-blush scarlet. 'Nonsense. Complete nonsense. I've never heard anything so silly in my life.'

Marlon strode away from her. 'This is crap. You and Richard are in love and I can't take my spice rack home.'

Anna bustled after him. 'You're wrong. We'll talk to Richard. He'll give you the spice rack to give to Marla. Then you and he can start making something new. A chair or something.'

Marlon strode on. 'I hate chairs. I don't want a chair.'

'Okay. But let's go home and talk about this. We'll put books on my new shelves and have hot chocolate and biscuits and everything will be fine.'

Marlon turned and glared. 'Love's rubbish.'

Anna's heart went out to him. Oh, the pain of thinking your hero prefers another. She put her hands on his shoulders and looked him in the eye. 'I so agree.'

*

On Friday Richard picked Anna up and together they went to the small community hall where a local quartet were playing Schubert. The seats were uncomfortable. They didn't complain. Anna was becoming used to discovering neighbourhood goings-on that she'd had no idea about. 'I always fancied being in a string quartet,' she told Richard. 'I loved the notion of meeting once a week in a beautiful living room with a piano and a luxurious sofa and bay windows. We'd sit in a friendly circle and play together.'

'What do you play?' asked Richard.

'Nothing. That's why I couldn't do it. It was wishful thinking.'

Richard said, 'Ah. Of course. Wishful thinking, I'd forgotten about that.'

The quartet clambered onto the little stage, took their seats and placed their music on the stands in front of them. Anna, Richard and the audience clapped. Two of the players gave a small friendly flicker of their fingers to Richard.

'You know them?' asked Anna.

'Oh yes. Violin and viola players have wonky doors, rattling windows and creaking floorboards like the rest of us.'

Afterwards he said, '"Death and the Maiden". Lovely. Sad he was ill at the time he wrote it but funny how sad music can cheer you up. Emotions are weird. Did you enjoy it?'

'Yes,' said Anna. In fact, she didn't really know. She hadn't been listening. She'd loved sitting next to Richard but her thoughts had been miles away. The music had made her reflective.

That morning, while moving books onto their new bookcase, she'd come across a book about motherhood she hadn't known she had. It had told her about women who'd had children because they'd thought that was what women did. They hadn't known how to cope with not wanting to be a mother. She'd been sitting reading this and had looked up. Sun was streaming in through the open door of her living room, dust motes dancing in the light. 'It wasn't that my mother didn't want me. She just didn't want to be a mother. Of course.' She cursed that she'd wasted a whack of her life recovering from her childhood. She should have put it behind her and forgotten it. Her mother was a woman who didn't want to be a mother; she'd wanted to be part of the world beyond the house. And why not?

Anna had gone into the kitchen, sat at the table, opened her notebook and written. *Don't blame your ma for your absurdities/ She probably only wanted to be a concert pianist like you do/ And aren't.*

Excellent. I'm getting better, she'd thought, and then went back to her bookcase.

'Do you like Schubert?' she asked as she and Richard walked round the corner to the Indian restaurant she hadn't known about till now.

'A bit. I prefer Bruce Springsteen. Music you can whistle and hum, and it's more working-class,' he said.

'Still, you bought the tickets. Supporting your local string quartet.'

'Actually, Lucy on the violin got locked out of her house and called me to open her door. I said I wouldn't charge so she paid me with the tickets. I thought you'd like to go. You being a poet, I thought Schubert might be your guy.'

'I, too, prefer Bruce Springsteen.'

'Good man.' He beamed approval and punched her lightly on the shoulder.

They drank beer with their curry. Richard accepted responsibility as Marlon's hero and agreed to let him take the spice rack home and start a new project. 'We could make a boat. I like boats.'

They ordered more beer. No matter if they drank too much. Richard wasn't driving.

'You want to talk about the kitchen?' he asked.

'Yes I do, and no, not really.'

'Like that?'

'Yes. I promised George I'd find the kitchen. Silly, but I needed to comfort her. Now you might have found it, I don't know what to do. Do I go to the door of the house and ask to see their kitchen? Or maybe I should wait till they're out and sneak round the back to look through the window. Then what? Tell George? And take her to go to the door and ask to see the kitchen?'

'Tricky,' said Richard.

The beer made Anna lightheaded. 'I love her. But now I see her slipping back into the place I've been for years, worrying about the past, while I am finally moving forward and making a way for myself. Caring for Marlon. Visiting you. Having neighbours I actually know. I am doing things ordinary normal people do.'

Richard patted her hand. Ordered more beer. 'It's hard.'

Anna nodded. 'She's not just my best friend. For years she

was my only friend. She listened to my woes. Encouraged me. Supported me when I read my poem to the people on the bus and walked home with me when we got thrown off for being a public menace. What a friend. I don't deserve her.'

30

You Will Stop Living the Life
You Imagine

'I have walked out on my home and family twice,' said George. 'I didn't know that.' Anna was surprised.

They were having lunch in George's garden. As it was her turn to provide the food, Anna had brought sandwiches, cake and a bottle of wine.

'Bagels,' said George. 'I didn't know you knew about bagels.' Now George was surprised. She hadn't been well recently and didn't feel like driving to any of Anna's sandwich spots.

'I knew about them. I didn't bother to try them till I looked up sandwiches in a cookbook I borrowed from the library. This sandwich is smoked mackerel mashed up with slices of pickled pepper and onion and cream cheese.'

'I can't believe it. You are moving on from a diet of beans, then?'

'Indeed,' said Anna. 'Richard suggested the wine. He knows about such things.'

George raised her glass. 'Thank you, Richard.'

'So you walked out twice. How cool you are. Tell me.'

'The first time doesn't really count. I was only gone ten minutes and nobody noticed.' She smiled. 'I'd just had enough. It was a this-is-not-what-I-planned moment, you know?'

In fact, Anna didn't know. Her whole life was not what she'd planned. It didn't come in moments.

'I was cooking supper. The television was on, music was

roaring from somewhere upstairs, the radio was blaring. Two children arguing. Frank paying no attention to anything, talking to a client on the phone. Me yelling for someone to set the table and nobody listening or caring. So I walked out wearing my apron and carrying the frying pan full of sausages. I stumped along the hall and out the front door, down the path and steamed along the street. I'd had enough.'

'Why did you take the frying pan?'

'I didn't really notice I had it in my hand till I got to the corner. I realised I'd no money, no coat, nothing, and turned round and came home. Nobody noticed I'd gone. Sausages were nicely done, though. Perhaps a furious walk in the middle of cooking does something for them.' She poured more wine.

'And the second time?'

'I got fed up of Frank and his affairs. I packed a case and stayed in a hotel. But I kept phoning home to check the children were cleaning their teeth and not living on crisps and Coke and Snickers bars. So I came home the next day to keep them on the healthy path.'

'Not good at dramatic exits?'

George said, 'No. Maybe one day I'll get it right.'

'I've never walked out on anyone. Nobody to walk out on.'

'Many would envy that.'

They ate in silence. Anna wanted to tell George about finding the house where the kitchen was taken but wanted to know if it was still there before she said anything. She didn't want George to be disappointed. She was also chasing a moment of glory in which she could show George the thing she longed to see again. Anna imagined the pair of them sweeping into the kitchen and her opening her arms – 'Look what I've found!' – and George swooning with joy. She wanted her friend's praise and adoration.

*

The day before, she'd gone to the house and stood outside staring at it for half an hour, willing herself to ring the doorbell and ask to be invited in. Richard had told her that the house hadn't changed hands since Cobb bought it more than sixty years ago. He was sure Cobb's daughter lived there now. Anna imagined a Miss Havisham creature wandering huge, cobweb-draped rooms staring hopelessly at layers of dust in an ancient wedding dress. It was too much to contemplate. She went home.

In the evening Richard had turned up and suggested he take her to the house. 'You can have a look at it. See if you want to go in.' She didn't like to say she'd already been to spy on it, so she sat in the passenger seat of his car and let him drive her back there. The house was still and silent. Three graceful storeys, with shuttered windows on the ground floor. There were trimmed bay trees either side of a glistening black door. Pot plants seethed to the ground in a small paved area and heavy black gates stood in front of a large double garage. 'Posh,' said Anna.

'Out of my league,' said Richard. 'You want to knock on the door?'

'There's a bell-pull but I'm too in awe to use it. I have to make a weird request. I'm not up to it. To tell the truth, I'm scared.'

'Understandable,' said Richard.

They continued to sit and stare. At nine o'clock a car drew up and parked outside the gates. A woman got out. She was thirty-ish, small with dark hair gathered into a bun at the back of her head. She wore a smart black business suit and a crisp white shirt.

'Not Miss Havisham, then,' said Anna.

'Too smartly dressed for that,' Richard agreed. 'Is that what you imagined?'

'I'd hoped for someone a bit deranged – so I wouldn't appear too deranged myself.'

The woman opened the gates. She brought a small remote control from her jacket pocket and used it to open the garage doors. Back in the car, she drove in, parked, and then walked out of the garage, pausing to shut the doors. When she was

closing the gates, she stopped and looked across at Anna and
Richard. For a fretful moment they thought she was going to
come across to them. But she didn't. She fished a key from her
bag, opened the front door and disappeared inside.

'You want to try now? You know there's somebody in.'

'No,' said Anna. 'She looks important and busy. I want to go
away and soothe myself with rock and roll and alcohol.'

*

George finished her sandwich, dusted crumbs from her shirt and
said, 'James has gone. I think he'll be the last. I don't see Lola or
Emma coming back.'

'Where has he gone?'

'He's got a house with three bedrooms and a garden. What
I hate is his leaving and me having to get used to it all over
again. Three times that man, my son, has done that to me. First
when he went to university. Second when he came home from
university and stayed with us for a couple of years till he earned
enough to pay for a place on his own. Then now. It's awful.' She
leaned back, stared at a hollyhock and added, 'He has become
a family man. He's gone all broody. His new partner has a child.
He wants more. I'm glad he seems to be settled. I can die now.'

'You're not going to, are you?'

'It isn't on my to-do list. But I won't mind if it happens.
My children are sorted. Emma is fine. Lola is Lola, and has always
known who she is and what she wants. And now James has come
to terms with being a grown-up. My work is done. Who knows,
I might see Willy again. My little love.' This thought seemed to
please her. 'My children don't really know me. Well, Lola perhaps
has seen my naughty side from time to time. But mostly children
only come along when you're settled. They're not aware of the
emotional turbulence and absurdity and alcohol and sly sex you
indulged in before they came along.' She laughed. 'You have to
smile when they look at you and accuse you of being boring.'

She poured another glass. 'I want Leonard Cohen played at my funeral and Nina Simone singing "Feelin' Good". And a party afterwards. I'd like to go to it but for obvious reasons that won't be possible.'

Anna said that she hadn't thought about her death. 'It doesn't matter really. When I'm dead, I'll be dead and I won't care about anything. I just hope I haven't paid a huge bill before it happens.' She looked about her at the garden. 'I wish I'd done something like this. It's amazing here. I'm in awe.'

It was beautiful. There was a small area of grass, complete with a table and chairs. This was under a pergola crammed with climbing blue and white clematis and roses. The rest was flowers. George planted them and gave them their orders. 'Grow. Grow. Grow.' And they did. They didn't dare not to. Blues, reds, scarlets, pinks and whites and yellows, all shoving and bustling towards the sky and flooding the air with scent.

'You've done all this. I can hardly believe it. I have done nothing really,' said Anna.

'Children. Oh God, I love them but I had to be safe and sane for them. I became a little mundane. I put my wildness into this.' She spread her arms and took a little bow. 'Here's my garden. But your time is coming. Some people blossom late. You will stop trying to have the life you imagine and start having the life you have, and you will be happy. How odd I have reached an end and you are just beginning.'

George's Kitchen

It took four visits to the Cobb house before Anna worked up the courage to pull the bell. Visiting up to this point had meant staring at the front door and imagining what was behind it. She had worked on a small speech she planned to give when she finally stood before whoever opened that door to her.

It was Grace Cobb, the woman she and Richard had watched the week before. She looked Anna over so critically that Anna forgot what she had to say.

'It's you,' Grace said. 'You've been hanging around here. What do you want?'

Anna opened her mouth but nothing came out.

'I was thinking of calling the police. I thought you might be planning a robbery.'

Anna shook her head. 'Me? Really?'

Grace looked her up and down, a slow scathing perusal. 'No. I suppose not.' She was dressed for relaxing – thin cotton wide-checked trousers and a T-shirt with LOVE printed on the front. Flip-flops on her feet. Yet somehow she looked stylish.

Some people just do, Anna thought. *Not me, though.*

'Could I look at your kitchen?' she asked.

Grace said, 'Huh?'

'I think your kitchen was designed by my friend's husband. I think it was dismantled from a flat in the High Street and brought here.'

Grace said nothing. Her face was without expression.

'Please,' said Anna. 'I promised my friend I'd find it. I think she needs to see it again.'

'They weren't paying the rent,' said Grace.

'My friend didn't know that. She was very young.' Anna met the critical glare. She thought, *So she knows. The kitchen is here.* 'Please,' she said again.

Grace stepped back and opened the door wide enough for Anna to step through. She pointed down the hall. 'First door on the right.'

The hall was lined with framed pictures floor-to-ceiling. Anna wished she could stop and look at them. The floor was highly polished old wood. The whole house smelled of scented candle. And Anna was nervous. She felt she had no right to be there.

The kitchen took her breath away. It wasn't just that it was beautiful; it was also that this room had marked the beginnings of George. This was where George had decided not to go home, because she'd found it too alluring to leave. This was where she'd spent time being loved and loving back. This was where she'd discovered who she was. For a moment Anna knew what it was like to be George, her best friend. It was almost too much information. She felt she had stepped into a place she wasn't meant to be.

'It's lovely,' she said.

Grace said, 'Yes. A good thing as I'm not allowed to change it. My grandfather left me this house on condition that the kitchen remained as it is.'

'Would you like to change it?'

'I like to make my mark. But I don't mind leaving this room as it is. I don't cook. My boyfriend does and he loves preparing meals in here.'

'Is this exactly how it was?' asked Anna.

Grace nodded. 'I've added a microwave and an espresso machine. Like I said, I don't cook so I heat stuff up and I love coffee. The original machine that's still here is too old to use.'

Looking round Anna saw that the pots and pans, china and

pictures enhanced the room. There was a large cooking range complete with deep-fat fryer along one wall. They were no-nonsense utility pieces that meant business. There was something pleasing and reassuring about them. In one corner was a floor-to-ceiling wine rack. Standing alone near it was a fifties-style American fridge. Three French-style pendant lights hung over the worktop opposite the cooking range. Either side of the lights hung rows of heavy copper pots.

'The knives in the drawer are all original Sabatier carbon steel. Some are Japanese too,' said Grace. She pointed to shelves. 'Books – not all cookbooks. Records and a turntable. They loved music.'

Anna said, 'I know.' Looking at the space between the table and the work unit, she noted there was room to dance. 'They'd have danced.'

On shelves beside the wine rack were a ceramic French coffee maker, white covered with blue flowers, a row of twenties soda syphons, an ancient coffee grinder, a nut cracker, a pottery stew pot and other antique kitchen gadgets. After taking them in, Anna turned to look at the pictures.

'So many pictures,' she said. They were all of food or people serving food. Aubrey Beardsley's *Garcons de Café* and below that a cheeky parody featuring three formidable fifties waitresses in full uniform, complete with little bonnets, standing looking like they disapproved of their customers. Pictures of picnics, pots of jam, hams, a Cecil Aldin print of a hunting party round a table at an inn, plates of pasta, glistening fruit, pies, people gathered at a table eating formally, seaside people laughing and holding piping hot fish and chips.

'It takes a while to really appreciate them. Some are valuable. Some are framed postcards. Actually, there's a *Mrs Beeton* first edition in the cookbooks,' said Grace.

Anna nodded.

'This room,' said Grace, 'is about them. The couple. There's food and eating and music and dancing and reading and wine.' She looked round and sighed for a life she'd never have. 'They must have lived in here more than any other room in the flat. Was she very beautiful?'

'Yes,' said Anna. 'She still is. Though she's older now. There's life and experience on her face. I think she suits it.'

Grace went to the wine rack. 'Red or white?'

'Red,' said Anna. Then, 'Oh look, a gramophone. Complete with horn. How absolutely lovely.' She crossed the room to examine it. 'It has a ragtime record on it.'

'Yes. I imagine they did the Charleston. I think my grandfather was smitten. He only saw her once. He said she was exquisite, made all the more beautiful by being pale and fraught with a tiny baby. I think he would have let her stay in the flat if she'd asked. Probably wouldn't have charged her much rent. But she was gone when he went back.' Grace put a glass of wine on the table and invited Anna to sit.

'She's happy now,' Anna said. 'I expect you know that he, Alistair, died. She married again then split with him after their son died. I thought she'd never get over that. I thought the grief would be the end of her. But she slowly got herself together. Started to breathe again. She met Matthew. Fell in love and almost stopped beating herself up.'

Grace smiled. 'A sort of happy ending, then. Or as near to happy as you might get.' She opened a drawer on the side of the table. 'Perhaps she'd like this. I think it was written for her.' She brought out a thick notebook with an elaborate dark green and red floral cover and handed it to Anna.

She opened it. *Eating With My Lovely One* was written in an exquisite hand in green ink on the first page. *Food For George* below that. Anna flicked through it. There were recipes, drawings of a sweaty cook, a couple beaming over heaped plates, the couple laughing and singing. And there were comments – *OK, so I won't wipe my hands on the seat of my trousers* and *Paella, eat it and weep, Georgie, baby* and more.

'Take it,' said Grace. 'It belongs to her. He wrote it for her. She ran away and didn't know it was there.'

Back home, Anna sat at her kitchen table and leafed through the book. She read one or two recipes for chicken and chocolate pudding and smiled at the margin notes.

She noticed the recipe headings and realised that they took her through the relationship from beginning to end. She knew she was going to read them. Even though they revealed her friend's private moments and even though she felt like a voyeur.

32

Fruit Pie for the Girl with Café Eyes

By midnight she was tired and bed beckoned. She wasn't taking in anything she read. She'd continue in the morning. At nine, she sat with a mug of coffee guiltily discovering a new truth about her friend's first love affair. She now knew Alistair had been obsessed with George. He'd seen her across a café and had fallen in love with her face. *Fabulous Face Milkshake* was one of the first recipes. The drink was milk, fresh strawberries and ice cream, and he'd drawn a chilled glass complete with straw below the heading. At the end of each recipe was a suggested piece of music to play while preparing the dish. The milkshake's song was 'I Saw Her Standing There'.

Anna sipped her coffee and brought to mind George's young face. *Beautiful indeed*, she thought. She remembered French classes in which boys abandoned all hope of learning the language. They lolled on their desks and gazed, almost panting with longing, at George.

Next recipe was *Fruit Pie for the Girl with Café Eyes*. It wasn't that intriguing. Just lattice pastry with apples. The song was Dusty Springfield: 'I Just Don't Know What To Do With Myself'. *Make better pies*, thought Anna.

And then she thought he had. The next recipe was *Tiny Onion Soup Keeps Café Girl Happy*. Anna thought it would. She fancied eating this soup. Tiny onions cooked till golden, add bacon then stock with tomato purée and pasta, and grated Parmesan on top. The song was 'Here Comes The Night'. *Good supper*, thought Anna. She pictured George and Alistair at that large table, eating this awkwardly and laughing. Van Morrison roaring out.

She envied them. 'I was probably struggling with Geography homework at the time.'

The doorbell rang. It was Marlon. He stepped into the hall as soon as Anna opened the door. 'My mum needs eggs. She wants to know if you've got any.'

'I do,' said Anna, following him to the kitchen. 'How many do you want?'

'Three. She's making a cake. She says she'll pay you back and I'm to say please and thank you.'

'I should think so,' said Anna. She put three eggs in a paper bag and handed it to Marlon.

He was looking at the book. 'What's that?'

'A book.'

'Doesn't look like a proper book.'

'It's a cookbook. It's full of recipes.'

Marlon considered this. 'Books are boring.'

'No they're not.'

'Yes they are. Phones are better. Computers are better. Books are boring.'

'Well,' said Anna, 'chocolate ice cream is boring.'

Marlon was shocked. 'No.'

'Chips with ketchup are boring.'

'No.' Marlon clearly couldn't believe this.

'Cakes are boring.' Anna was enjoying herself.

Marlon cottoned on. 'Poems are boring.'

'Games are boring,' Anna said.

Marlon started for the door. 'Bookcases are boring. Soup's boring. Eggs are boring.' He galloped down the hall. 'Shoes are boring. Hoodies are boring. Socks are boring.'

Anna heard him make his way back to Marla's kitchen. He was enjoying himself. 'School's boring. Cheese is boring. School dinners are boring.' He went into his house still chanting.

Anna laughed. She often got visitors these days. Mother Dainty came by yesterday with four blueberry muffins to eat with a cup of tea and a gossip. Swagger Boy knocked on her door to tell her he was sitting his driving test. 'I'll fail. Always do.'

'Don't wear your baseball cap. Especially don't wear your baseball cap backwards. Not a good look for a driving test,' Anna had advised. 'Put on an actual shirt. Try to look responsible and not like a boy racer.' She pointed to his CRASH & BURN T-shirt.

'I am a boy racer,' he admitted. 'My car doesn't go fast, but I love speed.'

'Just for an hour when you're sitting your test try not to look like one. The test bloke might approve of you if he doesn't think you're going to go roaring about.'

'Okay,' the boy agreed.

'And,' Anna poked him gently in the chest, 'you shouldn't whizz about all over the place. Every time you get the urge to tank along, you should think about having a pint of beer or sex. Yes, sex. Because if you crash, you might die or injure yourself so badly you'll never stand at a bar drinking or have fantastic sex again. You'd miss it.'

'Okay,' he'd agreed again. Though she could tell he didn't think she'd ever had sex in her life and didn't know what she was talking about.

This was all new to Anna. She'd never had many visitors before and wasn't sure what to do with them. She'd sit them at the kitchen table, make them a cup of tea and listen. At first she was baffled that people could chat about things and people they knew little about. But soon she found herself interested to find that Mrs Mackay three doors down had been taken to hospital after tripping over the back doorstep. And, to her surprise, she found she had opinions about television shows and new biscuits on the market. 'It would appear,' she told herself out loud, 'that I'm only an ordinary human after all. This is a relief.'

George in the book was eating well. Alistair had melted a

Mars Bar and poured it over ice cream. *Dream Girl Food*. There was a drawing of a longhaired girl in late teenage raptures licking a spoon. Van Morrison's 'Cleaning Windows' had been playing. Perhaps this was a reward for some housework. Well, she'd given that up. There was a week of curries and Miles Davis. Later, a celebration of some acquisitions – a brass microscope, a square copper kettle and an ancient coffee grinder – with a frozen grape pudding that followed an escalope. They'd danced to an old recording of 'The Blue Danube'. Anna imagined they'd played this on the horn gramophone they'd got some days before – drawing of George with her ear to the horn, recipe for garlicky roast chicken and Jelly Roll Morton.

How did they get that food? And, Anna wondered, *how did George stay so thin?* Well, she was lucky that way and she'd walked everywhere. Anna remembered George returning to school and being hailed as a hero by her fellow pupils. Her mother had forbidden her to talk to her old friend, but Anna ignored that. She'd given George her pocket money to pay bus fares. It was a hike from the High Street to Leith and it wouldn't be pleasant in winter. They'd exchanged secrets. Vowed teenage love for John Lennon and shared lunchtime buns. But George had gone home to her magical, carefree bohemian life. Anna, to a mother she hated.

Later, when they'd left school, Anna had gone to university, strived to become a poet and excelled at being young and stupid. George, before Lola came along, had slipped into a life of playing music and wandering Edinburgh with her love. They had almost lost touch. This was the time that interested Anna.

At two o'clock she was still reading the book when Marla turned up. She'd brought a slice of her cake on a cracked green floral plate and leaned on the kitchen unit holding it. 'I'm not much of a baker but this is so good I thought you'd like some.'

Anna thanked her.

'Would you like a cup of coffee?' asked Marla as she filled Anna's kettle and switched it on.

'I'd love a cup, thank you. The mugs are in the cupboard behind you.'

Marla brought two out. Examined them and declared them to be cool. 'Where d'you get your stuff?'

'I'm the queen of the charity shops,' said Anna.

The kettle boiled. Marla spooned coffee into the mugs, poured in water and fetched milk from the fridge.

'Make yourself at home,' said Anna.

'I will. I need to talk to you about telling Marlon all these things are boring.'

'It was a joke. He knew that. He enjoyed it. He doesn't think chocolate and chips are boring. Or books, come to that. But he was a bit bored and he let loose and shouted. It was good for him. We all need to shout sometimes. He's a little boy. He likes to feel mighty.'

'Don't we all,' said Marla. 'What's that you're reading?'

'A recipe book.' She pushed it across the table.

Marla thumbed through it. 'It's got music to cook to and eat to. I like that. And drawings. Here's a recipe for gaining strength for an Irish jig.'

Anna pulled the book back. 'Oh my. Irish stew and Guinness. I could have guessed. They'd have been stuffed full.'

'Then they did a jig? Who would do that?'

'My friend and her boyfriend used to do Irish jigs in the High Street.'

'Really? Why?'

'They were young and stupid and it seemed like a good idea at the time. Weren't you young and stupid once?'

'Yeah.' Marla reached over and took the cake from the unit. She picked off some icing and ate it. 'Still am stupid. Not young, though. My husband left me, y'know.'

'Why?'

'Sleeping around.'

'It's hard being alone at home knowing he's out there with someone else.'

'Maybe you'd know about that. I don't. I was the creep that slept around. I didn't deserve him.'

Anna said, 'Ah.' And thought, *How surprising things are sometimes*.

Marla stopped picking at the icing of the cake and took a proper bite. 'Was your friend ever stupid?'

Well, thought Anna, *she ran away from home on account of her name. I rather think her first husband was a rogue of some kind. She did Irish jigs in the street at three in the morning . . .* 'Yes.'

'Were you?' Taking huge bites of the cake now.

I married a gay man who said he'd make me a famous poet. I died my pubic hair green. She covered her face with her hands. 'Oh God. Oh God. Oh God.'

Marla said, 'That's a yes, then.'

33

The Truth About George

The next day was Sunday. Anna was still leafing through the book, still feeling like a voyeur and unable to do anything about that. The book was too fascinating. She would give it to George next time she saw her. Right now, she was reading about George's sex life. Afternoon treats while chicken marinated. Anna thought this fun. Lovely naughty George. Lola would follow. In her own life, Anna had moved away from home and was living in a draughty flat with a gay guy who'd promised to make her famous. She cooked for him and cleaned for him and sat at home worriedly working on poems while he cruised bars, picked up boys, drank and had a lively old time. She'd been a fool. Perhaps George had been too. But George had been warm, fed and loved. And that meant everything.

It had been a time of giving herself up to love and finding she wasn't loved back. Yesterday Marla had complained of suffering the same painful thing. 'It happens,' she said.

'Was that Marlon's father?' Anna asked.

Marla shook her head. 'No. Before him. I was just crazy for this bloke and he wasn't crazy for me. I thought about him all the time. I think I went a little bit insane. I punished myself for not being good enough. I shaved my head.'

'Goodness. Were you living at home? What did your mother say?'

'Nothing. She fainted. She saw this strange bald woman coming into the kitchen and wham – she hit the floor. It felt good at first. Cool air round my head. Then I realised what I'd done and

I cried and cried and wouldn't go out for days.' By now she'd finished the cake and was dabbing the plate with her finger, picking up crumbs. 'Thank goodness for hats.'

Anna agreed.

Marla looked at the empty plate on the table. 'I seem to have eaten your cake.'

'It's okay,' said Anna. 'Embarrassing memories can make you do such things.'

When Marla left, Anna returned to the book. Not being much of a cook, the recipes didn't really interest her. They were full of instructions like *sear the meat, marinate overnight, put in hot oven for twenty minutes then reduce heat, finely slice onions, peel garlic.* She had no intention of doing such things and classed them along with bungee jumping, motor racing and marathon running. They were not for her. The margin notes amused her – *after eating this leave dishes till morning, cook for length of Sad Eyed Lady of the Lowlands, put in pan, listen to sizzle and tango with your love for two minutes.* There was a list of ingredients that usually included a sketch – an onion perhaps, a chicken, a row of olives dancing.

The pair enjoyed a honeymoon time of Champagne breakfasts and long evening dinners. There were recipes for slow-cooked food while the pair walked hand-in-hand through the city's ancient streets and down narrow wynds and cobbled lanes. They sang Bob Dylan songs and discussed his lyrics. *Love Minus Zero* pasta spicy with clams and tomato sauce was a favourite dish. Then Alistair lost his job. After *Unemployed Boy Tuna Bake* the food got more and more austere. Anna was well acquainted with cheap food. George and Alistair were dining on potatoes, rice, carrot soup and homemade bread. Anna suspected that George didn't know or care. There were sketches of her dancing to music on the horn gramophone and looking joyful at a plate of spaghetti and smashing chocolate cake into Alistair's face. There was food for after polishing a junk shop kettle, food for recovering from a late night swim, food for rock and roll on the radio. Food for every occasion.

Anna shut the book. Stared ahead. Pages and pages and no friends were mentioned. Every recipe was *for two in love*. The pair had never entertained. They were lost in their world of food, sex and music. Anna remembered herself at that age. She had friends she sat with in the pub making a pint of beer last all evening. There had been flats she visited where she'd sat on the floor, talked about her dreams and ambitions and given critical opinions of films she hadn't seen and books she hadn't read while listening to Joan Baez.

Things were intense for the lovebirds. Anna knew what would happen next. A baby. Tiny, noisy, demanding, messy, milky, incontinent and with no concept of an eight-hour night's sleep. The end was nigh.

It came slowly. Their finances healed and Alistair showed off his cooking skills with *Jiving to Fish Peppered Halibut with Lemon and Caper Mash*. Music played – 'Downtown', Satie's *Gymnopédie*, the Rolling Stones' 'Get Off Of My Cloud'. This last was played to *All Hail Ma and Pa Flambe Steak*, which made Anna wonder if the injection of cash had come from George's parents.

She wasn't prepared for the final entry. *Goodbye Sweet Times Roast Monkfish* followed by *Kissing Café Girl Adieu Intense Chocolate Pudding*. He played 'Hey, That's No Way To Say Goodbye' and drank Chablis. *Café Girl isn't drinking*, he wrote, *finished the bottle by myself. No wine for Lola, then. Little bit of cognac for me, though. Lola doesn't mind. Café Girl isn't smiling any more*.

Anna read and re-read this. It seemed like this was Alistair's farewell. She assumed George didn't know at the time, but did she know now? Had she known Alistair spent her parents' money on luxury food? *I mean*, she thought, *if you give somebody money for food, you're thinking maybe a bacon sandwich or some chips. You don't think fillet steak, monkfish and Chablis.*

Remembering how George had been when they had lunch,

waltzing in her chair one minute, in tears the next, she wondered if she should give the book to her. The memories might be unbearable.

So she had a cup of tea and watched a brain-numbing game show on television. It was what she always did when she was bothered and wanted to avoid her thoughts. She went to bed early, wondering what to do.

George had always been loved. Her parents loved her, Alistair, Frank, Matthew and her children. So much love, and George had denied it. She hadn't thought herself worthy. 'Me,' Anna said, 'I've never really known love. The unloved child gives herself to anybody, just wanting a little bit comfort. I think I used to smile too much.'

If she was really honest, she had to admit she wouldn't have liked the sort of relationship George had had with Alistair. He'd loved too much. Kept George to himself, maybe even needed her to make him feel important. 'A somebody,' Anna said. He'd wined and dined his love then, drunk, he'd crashed and died.

George had been suddenly alone; broke, friendless and a mother of a tiny child. How scary was that? She'd gone home. She'd have been relieved and ashamed and probably so entangled in her emotions she wouldn't have known what to say. Her mother would have held her close, patted her back and said, 'Never mind.' How lovely to be told not to mind. Of course, it didn't work. George had minded. Oh, how she minded.

Up till that time George had led a glistening life. Anna was sure her friend had never known self-doubt, self-loathing or even loneliness. Head on her blue pillow and not at all sleepy, Anna said, 'Me now, I am self-doubter, self-loather of the universe. Gold-star worrier, me.' Talking to herself was a long-held habit. Part of living alone. She provided a voice to break the silence. It didn't matter what she said. She could be profound, ridiculous or silly – who cared? She could sing absurd songs like 'I'm off to fry an egg' to the tune of 'We're Off To See The Wizard'. It was one of the joys of the single life.

'Of course,' she told the ceiling, 'George would be welcomed home. She was always loved. I wasn't. But I didn't realise this till I was a lot older and could look back with what little wisdom I had.'

She recalled times when she'd catch her mother looking at her with a disturbing who-are-you? expression and sometimes it morphed into a what-was-I-thinking-to-have-you? look. 'I wasn't that bad,' she said. 'I was a kid who wanted to be famous for writing poems. These days people just want to be famous for fame's sake.'

Her mother had been demanding. Anna remembered being ostracised for not coming up to standard. Her mother stiffened and turned her back when she entered a room. Usually she didn't know what she'd done, and as her mother wasn't talking to her she never discovered her sins. Her father didn't help. He was a quiet man, afraid of his own opinions. He turned being non-committal into a fine art. 'Hitler,' he once said, 'didn't really mean it.'

'Yes, he bloody did!' Anna had shouted. She'd been cold-shouldered for a fortnight after that. Not for her opinion, though. It was the *bloody* that did it.

Her father had been an immaculate man. Hair well-oiled, moustache trimmed, he'd mowed the lawn in a shirt and tie. He was a warehouse manager and kept perfect hours. Anna had written him a poem. It was one of her first. She'd been twelve or thirteen at the time.

Here comes Jack
In his cap and mac.
He says good morning every day
And then bye bye when he goes away.

Even then she'd known better than to show it to her mother.

The night rolled on. Sounds dimmed. She yawned. She knew what she'd do about the book. She'd ask the opinion of the one person she knew who was close to his emotions. He was, after all, experiencing some of them for the first time. Marlon.

34

The Pain of Being Me

They were strolling the short distance between school and Richard's yard. Marlon no longer took her hand. This hadn't been discussed, Anna just knew he considered himself grown up and needed to walk alone. She understood but missed the contact. Late August and the first sniff of autumn in the air. Mellow days on the way. This gladdened Anna's heart as she preferred colder weather. She could put on a jumper and have a layer of wool between herself and the world.

They were talking about names.

'Were you always called Anna?' Marlon asked.

'Yes. It's the name I was given when I was born. Were you always called Marlon?'

'I'm the only Marlon I know. There are two Jasons in my class and two Beaus and one Marlon. Me. My mum wanted to call me Luke. But she wasn't well on the day my dad got me registered and didn't go with him. So he called me Marlon after his favourite film star.'

'What did your mother say?'

'She wasn't happy. But now she thinks I'm Marlon and I look like her Marlon and she thinks "There's Marlon" every time she sees me. So I'm Marlon.'

'I've always thought the way Native Americans give names is best. They wait till you've grown up a bit and they can see what you're like. I'd call myself Finally Thinks Before She Speaks.'

Marlon didn't think much of this. They strolled in silence for a while.

'I'd be Runs Fast In His Underpants,' he said.

'What an excellent name. Do you?'

'Yes. I run fast but I am even faster if I only have on my underpants. Mum can't catch me to put me in the bath. But then she always does and then I get dumped in with the underpants on.'

Anna laughed. 'Can I ask you something?'

'Is this something you've thought about before you speak?'

'Yes. If you had a best friend, someone you'd known for years and years and loved, and you found out something that might hurt them – would you tell them?'

Marlon stared at her, puzzled. He stopped walking and looked at the ground, frowning. 'Huh?' He started walking again. 'I can't say. I don't really have a best friend. You're my best friend. I'd like one who was the same as me, 'cos you're old and I'm new. But you'll have to do for the moment.'

'Never mind,' said Anna. They walked on. 'That's the nicest thing anyone's ever said to me,' she told him, and decided she'd ask Richard.

*

Today was the big day. Marlon was at last allowed to take his spice rack home. He laid it on the workbench, ready to pick up when it was time to go. Meantime he and Richard discussed the boat they were going to make. Richard fancied a Mississippi paddle steamer. Marlon wanted to build a raft. 'The sort you use to escape from a desert island.' Anna suggested an ordinary boat with two funnels and an anchor hanging over the side. 'A dirty British coaster with a salt-caked smoke stack sort of thing,' she said. 'It would be butting up the Channel.'

Richard gave her a long look. 'That's an actual poem, isn't it?'

Anna confessed it was. 'But I think the coaster would be easier than Quinquireme of Nineveh.'

'And easier than a Mississippi paddle steamer,' he agreed.

The rest of the visit was spent drawing a plan. The boat would be yellow. The funnels black. Anna sat in her car seat sipping tea, listening to the plans and wondering what George was doing now. *Bossing the flowers in her garden*, she thought. *Or maybe she's on her patio drinking wine. Then again, she's probably taking someone to the optician's or the hairdresser. She's quite the saint these days.* After that thought, Anna napped. Her favourite thing to do these days.

When it was time to leave, Anna asked Richard if he would drop in to see her this evening. 'I've something to show you.' Then she added, 'A book.' In case he thought she was doing a Mae West thing.

She carried Marlon's school bag as they walked the last part of the way home. Marlon carried the spice rack, holding it aloft with two hands. He couldn't really see where he was going, so from time to time Anna had to reach out and guide him to safety after he'd stepped off the kerb. A warm wave of responsibility and nurture swept through her when she did this. She welcomed it, enjoyed it. And knew that at one time she would have run from it, or howled at the moon resenting it. How odd to have never wanted to mother a child and then find they were quite nice after all. Still, she reckoned she'd have been a dreadful parent.

Marla was early coming to pick up Marlon. He was at Anna's kitchen table with his usual hot chocolate when she arrived. He slid off his chair, fetched his spice rack from across the room where it leaned against the wall and presented it to her. She took it and held it before her and said nothing.

'It's a spice rack,' said Marlon. 'I made it for you.'

Marla still held the gift and still said nothing.

'Well, Richard helped,' said Marlon.

Marla took a breath. 'It's beautiful. The wood is lovely, the colour of honey and so smooth. You did this?'

Marlon nodded. 'I sanded the wood and everything.'

'There's a little shelf for the spices and little sticky-out bits to hang the bottles. Amazing.'

There was a happy silence. The all grinned at one another.

Marla said, 'We'll have to get spices.'

'We got you some.' Anna brought out a small cardboard box. 'There's cumin, turmeric, mustard seeds, garam masala, nutmeg, ginger. Oh, lots. We've been collecting them.'

Marla stared into the box. 'Cumin? Celery salt, I understand that. Turmeric? I'll have to get a cookbook.' She glanced at the book on Anna's table.

'That's not so much a cookbook as a collection of recipes of a life. It's not mine.'

Marla lowered her voice. 'I have no idea about spices. I do fish fingers and that sort of thing.'

Anna whispered back, 'I'll find you a cookbook with spice things in. I'll look in the charity shop.'

Marla nodded. She brought an envelope out of her bag. 'Your money.'

'Now,' said Anna. 'I have to tell you Marlon and I have been discussing things. Apparently I'm his best friend. Well, I am till he finds someone more suitable, he tells me. So I'll still collect him till he doesn't need collecting. But you can't take cash for babysitting your best friend.'

Marla said, 'I think you can.'

'Nonsense. Buy me a present from time to time. Wine will do. I'm getting fond of that. I see your son has left the building and is heading home. I think he's keen to put the spices in the rack. We can both assume he'll get more of a kick out of it than you will.'

'You'll find a book,' said Marla. 'Then I'll do one of the things in it and you can come to tea.'

'Exactly.'

'And I'll buy wine and you can come to my house to drink it and chat about the stupid things you did when you were young.'

'I was very good at being stupid. So why not?'

After Marla left, Anna realised that this was an offer of friendship and she had almost refused it. She hadn't, in fact, recognised it. 'That's what's become of me living alone and mostly thinking about the pain of being me.'

*

Richard knocked on her door at half-past six. 'You had something to show me?'

'A book,' she told him again. She led him to the kitchen and offered him a cup of tea. 'Or would you rather have a glass of wine? I have some. Red.'

He nodded. 'It's a good time for a drink.'

She pointed to the book on the table and fetched the wine from across the room. She got two glasses and poured. 'What do you think?'

'It's a cookbook. Lovely handwriting.'

'It's my friend's life through the recipes her first love cooked for her.'

'Romantic.' He read and smiled. 'He adored her.'

'I know.'

'I'm getting that she was beautiful.'

'Oh yes. Very. Still is. Though older.'

He raised his glass. Sipped. 'So what's the problem?'

'Well, it's not mine. It was given to me to give to my friend, but I'm not sure I should do that. If you look at the last recipe, it's a goodbye meal. I think he was leaving her. They'd had a baby and he felt neglected. He wanted to be her only love. I don't think she knew he was going.'

Richard said, 'Hmm.' He took a second sip. 'Maybe he knew the landlord was coming to throw them out. Probably he couldn't face what was about to happen.'

'So he left her?'

Richard said, 'It's likely. Where did you get the book?'

'From the woman in the house we looked at. I asked if I could see the kitchen. It was amazing. I'm jealous of George spending time in it. Eating in it. Dancing, and all the things they did.'

209

'Well, give it to her.'

'I think it might break her heart. She doesn't know he was leaving her.'

They sat considering this. Then Richard said, 'All his clothes were in the flat. The bloke in the pub mentioned them. If he left his clothes, he must have been planning to come back. Perhaps he wasn't saying goodbye to her. He was saying goodbye to the life they'd had and the people they'd been.'

'How romantic.'

They sat. She looked at his hands – one holding his wine glass and the other on the open pages of the book. She thought them wonderful. Strong hands, she could see that. She wondered what they had built and who they had touched. Her own hands were plain. A few brown spots on their backs and nails kept to a practical length. She considered the people these hands had touched. Some people she'd loved and some who'd been lovers for a night. They'd brought brief comfort. That had been all she wanted. She'd never considered marrying again. She'd come to the conclusion that a husband would be a distraction. He'd want to chat when she wanted to read. Or he'd occupy the bathroom when she needed to get in. Or he'd just be there, a presence when she needed to be alone. But this man was different. She loved having him here. He wore a navy polo shirt open at the neck and a brown tweed jacket. His life was on his face. Lines round his eyes and lips. He'd known pain. She thought him beautiful.

'You're not going to give it to her,' he said.

'No. I'm not. I don't know why. I just have a feeling I should keep it for the moment.'

'The recipes have made me hungry. You want to go eat?'

'I don't have much money.'

'I know that. I'm asking you if you want to eat.'

'Yes.'

'Well, let's go.'

They walked to the end of the street then stopped at the

kerb, checking it was safe to cross the road. There was no traffic. Yet to keep Anna safe on the tiny hike to the opposite pavement, Richard put his hand on the small of her back. She thought it the most thrilling thing that had ever happened to her.

35

The Room Stopped. I Went On

'So,' said George, 'how is your great romance going?'

They were in George's kitchen. It was her turn to provide a meal. It was raining. A teeming downpour battering against the window.

'It's not a romance really. It's more about food than sex. We've had meals together.'

'You don't think eating together is sexy? Because it bloody well is.'

Anna remembered the book. Of course it was.

Their meal had been prepared by Matthew – a crab quiche with salad and a bottle of chilled white to sip with it. George was not in a sipping mood, though. She was feeling hearty. She drank.

'Right, best sexy meals. Peaches and ham and Gorgonzola in a hotel in Florence with wine a long time ago. Juice ran all over the sheets, though. But lovely. Windows open. Breeze and sounds from the street. You?'

Anna slipped a forkful of quiche into her mouth. The pastry was crisp and cheese-flavoured. God, Matthew could cook. She mentally flicked through sexy meals she was prepared to discuss openly. 'A sausage sandwich in a shared bath with a man who was writing an epic poem about Elvis.'

'Didn't it get soggy?'

'I am very careful and particular with sausage sandwiches. No, it didn't.'

'Fish and chips in a seaside B&B on Mull when it was

chucking down rain outside. Propped against pillows and feeling warm and safe.'

'Cheese and chutney and apple and pork pie in a holiday chalet with beer and a man who fixed my bike on holiday. We never exchanged names. But he looked like Robert Redford.'

'What more could you want? Dark chocolate, Marie biscuits and rosé wine in a sleeping bag on a beach in the South of France.'

'Hot toddies in a freezing flat in Dundee. Not sexy, though. Just trying to keep warm.'

George pointed across the table. Suddenly very excited at an unearthed memory. A magical meal from a time when she could jump on the bed and wildness was wonderful. 'Smoked trout and new potatoes with fizz in a rented cottage on Skye. Log fire burning. Joni Mitchell on the hi-fi.'

'Cheese on toast with whisky in a flat with his landlady banging on the door shouting, "Have you got a woman in there?"' Anna snorted. 'Your sexy meals are sexier than my sexy meals.'

'I'm a sexier eater,' said George. 'I take dietary risks.'

Anna said, 'I know that.' She considered her plate. Forked a tiny baby potato finely covered with chopped parsley then said, 'I've found it.'

George raised an eyebrow.

'Your kitchen,' said Anna. 'I found it.'

George put down her fork. 'It still exists?'

'Yes. It's in a huge posh house out Corstorphine way.' She ate the potato. 'The landlord of the flat saw it and fell in love with it. So when you left he went in with some workmen and they took it apart and put it together again in his house.'

'I find that hard to believe.'

'Apparently the rent hadn't been paid for some time. So he took it instead of the money.'

'I suppose he took all the other stuff too,' said George.

'Probably.' Anna didn't want to mention the emptying of the flat.

'I want to see it,' said George. 'Take me there.'

'I need to say we're coming. There won't be anyone in at the moment.'

George fetched her phone from the kitchen unit and handed it to Anna. 'Did she give you her number? Phone her. Tell her we're coming.'

Anna took the number from her pocket and put it into the phone. Grace answered.

'Hello,' said Anna. 'It's me. I'm the woman who wanted to see your kitchen.'

'And now your friend wants to see it?' said Grace.

'Yes.'

Grace sighed. 'Okay. Let's do it. Tonight? Seven o'clock?'

'Excellent.'

They ended the call.

'She's Grace,' Anna told George. 'She's your old landlord's granddaughter. He left her the house on condition that she didn't change the kitchen. She'll let you see it tonight, seven o'clock.'

'Is she annoyed?'

Anna shook her head. 'She knew I'd get in touch.'

'What's it like? Is it the same as it was in the flat?'

'I never saw it in the flat. But I think so. There's an old horn gramophone. And a turntable. Lots of pictures. Cookery stuff. A coffee machine with a long handle.'

'Yes,' said George. 'Yes. That's it.' She took up the phone. Got Matthew. 'Anna has found the kitchen. We have to go see it.'

'When?' Anna could hear him clearly. There was wind in the background.

'He's playing golf,' George told her.

'When?' Matthew asked again.

'Tonight at seven o'clock.'

'Sweetheart, that's five hours away. I'll be home about four. Plenty time.'

'You will be here? I have to go. You won't be late?' George was nervous. 'I can't miss this.'

'I'll be there. There's margarita ice cream in the freezer. Relax.'

'Margarita ice cream,' George said to Anna, as she ended the call. 'I never knew there was such a thing.' She swigged more wine. 'We might get drunk.'

'You seem a little agitated,' said Anna. 'A little light tipsiness might be in order.'

*

Matthew drove them to the kitchen house. 'You're not driving,' he said to George. 'State you're in, all nerves and wine. You'd crash the car.'

They arrived outside the house at a quarter to seven, parked and sat staring at the gates.

'I've got butterflies,' said George. 'I was really just a kid when I first saw this room. I'd gone home with Alistair and didn't know what to expect. He showed me to his sofa, which was filthy to be honest. Then I needed a pee in the middle of the night, as you do. I found my way to the bathroom but couldn't find my way back to the sofa. Which door? I didn't know. I opened the wrong one. There it was. The kitchen. I was bedazzled, overwhelmed. I'd never seen anything like it. I'd intended to go back to my mum and dad next day but when I saw that kitchen I decided to stay. I wanted to be in there, to sit and eat at the table. I thought it would make me sophisticated.'

'Did it?' asked Matthew.

'You know it didn't. But there's nothing like feeling sophisticated when you're a kid. Drinking your first espresso with too much sugar in and thinking you're Elizabeth Taylor.'

At seven exactly the three left the car and went to the front door of the house. Grace was waiting for them. She ushered them inside and pointed the way to George. She beetled ahead. 'I want to see this alone.'

They heard a gasp as she walked through the door. 'Oh my

God.' She reappeared in the hall. 'It's exactly as it was. I've got old and wrinkled but it's as young as ever.' She went back inside.

They waited twenty minutes, thinking they'd be summoned when George had recovered from her slap of nostalgia. But nothing happened. They stood, not even making small talk, waiting to be given the okay to join George. When it didn't come, Anna peered round the kitchen door.

George was sitting at the table, hands neatly folded in her lap as she stared round at the room. 'This is where I sat,' she said. 'Alistair was over there, facing me. We didn't do an end each. That would've made us too far apart.' She smiled. 'Pasta, risotto, stir fries, curries, stews, tarts, all sorts of puddings I discovered at this table.'

She got up, walked to the wide area between the kitchen unit and the table. 'We danced here. Charleston to old records on the horn gramophone, jived to Bobby Vee singles, waltzed to Tchaikovsky's *Nutcracker* and "The Blue Danube". We impersonated Bob Dylan and John and Yoko. We'd eat and sing and dance. And the coffee from that machine,' she pointed to the Italian espresso machine, 'was to die for. You don't think that magic like this is going to happen to you when you're a kid in the suburbs, living on egg and chips and beans on toast.'

Anna agreed.

'And you don't think it's going to end,' said George. 'You just live and think nothing of it really.' She returned to the table.

Matthew and Grace joined her.

'The smell is missing,' said George. 'It used to smell of coffee or garlic and onions in here.'

'I don't cook,' Grace told her.

Matthew took in the pictures. He smiled to note a drawing of Desperate Dan's cow pie next to a painting of a bowl of cherries done in heavy oils. 'I like it,' he said. Then, 'Where did he get the money?'

'An inheritance from his grandmother.'

'Is that what you lived on?'

'Alistair had a job. He was a chef. He went off in the morning and came home again late afternoon.'

Matthew said, 'Ah.' He nodded. 'So what did you do?'

'I went back to school. And after I left, I cleaned and waited for him. I was young and not in love. I was besotted.' She sighed. 'Just words. They don't describe the truth. I cleaned. The place was filthy when I arrived there. Except for this room, of course. I slaved. I scrubbed. I sweated. There was a lot of bleach involved. Being besotted makes you do absurd things.' She turned to Anna. Her eyes brightly glazed, tears coming. 'It's most peculiar to sit here in the place where I was young. It is proof that all the things I thought happened did happen. It was the beginning of me, this room. Alistair was already the man he was destined to be – stubborn, funny, a perfectionist, and in love with me. This room stopped. I've moved on.'

She got up. Moved to behind the unit and stroked the Italian coffee machine, placed her hand on the horn gramophone, ran a finger down the pile of albums, remembering each one. 'Classics all,' she said. She looked at the copper pots hanging from the ceiling and at the row of books on the shelf beside an old manual coffee grinder. 'There,' she said. 'I've touched my lost friends and told them all goodbye. Time to go.'

She kissed Grace on the cheek. 'Thank you for letting me see this. It means a lot. I was once very happy in this room.' She looked at Anna and Matthew. 'C'mon, chaps. We'll take Anna home.'

*

They parked outside Anna's building. Matthew got out of the car to walk Anna to her door. 'Because I'm a gent,' he said.

George leaned out of the window. 'Come by soon. Eat food that isn't good for you. We'll drink wine, play old songs and be happy.'

Anna waved and said it sounded like a plan.

Matthew took her arm. 'There's something odd about Alistair

217

driving off like he did. Did he keep her away from people? Did he want her for himself?'

'I think so,' Anna said. 'I think that after Lola came along, he knew she'd give him less attention. He knew he'd lose her. I think he wasn't one to share.'

Matthew said, 'Probably. You know, I am ashamed of how jealous of him I am. The times they had. The fierceness of their love. I want it to have been me.'

Anna said, 'I'm jealous too. What a time she had. I wish it had been me.'

36

The Awkward Age

Anna went to the library, returned her books and took out two more. After that she shopped for food. These days her list included more than baking potatoes and tins of beans. She got goodies for Marlon – chocolate fingers, little oranges and tuna for his sandwiches. Today she also bought a remote control jeep for Marlon's birthday on Saturday. This excited her, as did the hideous orange wrapping paper. She knew he'd love it. She thought one of the best things about being a child was you didn't have to bother about good taste. You went for bright colours and gaudy design.

Shopping done, she went into Jessie's café for a flat white and a Danish. She'd been coming here for years. Long before anyone knew what a flat white was. Back then, she just drank coffee. When Jessie had installed a huge industrial espresso machine behind her counter Anna had loved the place more than ever. It was the booths that had originally won her heart. She loved slipping into a high-backed wooden booth. It was so like being in a fifties American movie.

Sitting with her coffee in front of her, admiring the wrapped gift in her bag on the seat beside her, Anna felt a glow of belonging. She was so known here, she was brought her usual without having to order.

Someone slipped into the booth opposite her. She only looked up to see who it was when the person said, 'Been shopping?'

Dorothy Pringle sat looking at her. She didn't seem friendly. But then, she never did.

Dorothy Pringle, thought Anna, noticing that it was always 'Dorothy Pringle' and never just 'Dorothy', even though they'd been at school together. 'Yes,' she said. 'Got a birthday present for a little boy I know.'

Dorothy nodded. 'I saw you coming in here and thought it an opportunity for a chat.' She looked at the counter and ordered tea.

Anna smiled and said, 'Indeed it is.'

'Where's your pal?'

'George? She's at home. Well, I think she is. She's often out doing good works. Taking people with mobility issues to hospital or the hairdresser or wherever.'

'Atoning for her sins?'

Anna agreed. 'Aren't we all?'

'You two were horrible to me for years. I was very hurt and upset.'

'Yes, I know,' said Anna. She shrugged. 'We were kids.'

'You lost me on a cycle run. You played tricks on me. You called me names.'

Anna nodded. 'I know. We are very sorry. It was a long time ago.'

Dorothy Pringle's tea arrived – a single small teapot, a cup and saucer and a small jug of milk. She thanked the waitress and returned to her theme. 'I never fully recovered from the treatment, you know.'

Anna picked a piece from her pastry and ate it. 'I know. But we were awfully young,' she said.

And you were a complete stuck-up arse, she didn't say.

'I cycled mile after mile on my own in tears, and I was afraid. I thought I was lost and you two had just gone on without me. Or you'd turned back and hadn't told me. Terrible thing to do. Then there were the names. People sniggered when I passed them in the corridor at school. You were horrible.'

'I'm sorry,' said Anna. She was sure the names and subsequent sniggering had nothing to do with her or George. Dorothy Pringle must have had other enemies.

'Pokey Face,' said Dorothy. 'Pointy Nose. Really, really not nice.'

Anna agreed.

'Of course, I blame George. She always led you astray.'

'No.' Anna shook her head. 'We were buddies. We did everything together.' She was bored now. Accusations always made her slip away inside herself. They had since she'd been a teenager blocking her mother's tirades. Back then, she'd made things worse by yawning. She resisted the urge to do that now.

'But you didn't run away. You didn't shack up with a man. You didn't drive your parents insane with worry.'

'Well, no. But George's parents knew where she was.'

'Yes, they knew. And they were paying that rogue she was with money to keep her fed and well.'

'How do you know that?'

'They told my parents. They were friends with them. I'm sure George didn't know about her parents giving Alistair money. They had all the baby stuff waiting for her when she went home to them.'

Anna was shocked. 'But she didn't know about them giving Alistair money. She has never forgiven herself for what she did. Alistair adored her. And she suffered when he died.'

Dorothy took a sip of her tea. 'He committed suicide.'

'He crashed his car into a tree.'

'He deliberately crashed his car into a tree. He killed himself. The police were after him for theft. He'd been shoplifting for years. He knew they'd arrest him and he'd get put in jail.'

Anna said, 'Why doesn't George know this?'

'Her parents kept it from her. It was in the newspapers but they didn't let her see them. There was mention of a woman living with him, but nobody knew it was her. And by the time the police got to their flat, it had been ransacked.'

Anna said, 'He killed himself? He just drove into a tree?'

'Yes. He couldn't face what was coming.'

'He wouldn't have wanted George to know the truth. He was obsessed with her.'

Dorothy said, 'Yes, she was always beautiful. But a bit silly.'

'She became a very good and respected nurse. She brought up her children. She has a beautiful garden. She's my friend.'

'I know. And I saw the pair of you giving out balloons and cupcakes as celebrations.'

'A favour for a friend.' Anna played with her Danish. She'd gone off eating it. 'You won't tell her, will you?'

'You don't think she should know the truth?'

'It was all a long time ago. Why upset her?'

Dorothy sighed. 'She is at that awkward age.'

'She's a bit older than that. We all are.'

'Nonsense.' Dorothy finished her tea. 'The first awkward age, the teenage thing, is only a short, blushing, difficult time. A rehearsal for the real awkward age when you're this age – old. You forget people's names. You walk into rooms and can't think why you are there. You are stiff and groan when you get out of a chair. You pray you don't run out of money before you die. You know who and what you are but can't be proud because you remember all the mistakes you made and they keep slipping into your mind when you're not expecting them. Sometimes you even cry out, "Oh God".'

Anna continued playing with her Danish. Her coffee got cold. She'd married a gay man when he'd said he'd make her famous. Never mind love or companionship. Fame was the spur. Oh God. She'd died her pubic hair green. Oh God. She'd been thrown off a bus for loudly trying to perform one of her poems to the upper deck. Oh God. She'd sat in her freezing flat, wearing two jumpers, woolly hat and fingerless gloves, trying to write a poem about everything that was happening in the world at that moment – people paddling canoes up the Amazon, a woman in Ohio hanging out her washing, a couple making love in Glasgow, armies on the move at enemy borders, children in schools, buses crawling through traffic, ships being built.

There had been too much to put in. She'd cried and thrown her pen across the room.

Where are you, little world?

Where I marched all day with my flag unfurled?

It had started. Then:

Where are you, little zoo?

Something something something that rhymed with zoo. She couldn't remember. Oh God.

Meantime George had been shacking up with a rogue who shoplifted and hadn't told her about her parents' love and financial help. Oh God.

'Yes,' she said. 'The awkward age. I think it lasts a lifetime. I have to tell you, George and I never called you Pokey Face. But I will if you ever dare tell George about Alistair.'

37

Everybody Loves George

August gave way to September, evenings got darker, leaves turned gold then brown. Autumn slipped in. Soon the first frosts would come and Anna could wear thick jumpers, a woolly layer between her and the world. And still the book lay on her kitchen table. She didn't know what to do with it. She had no intention of keeping it, yet she was reluctant to hand it over to George. Memories might be sweet or poignant, but they were also painful and the last entry could cause a lot of upset.

She phoned Lola and asked her to drop by one evening. 'I've got something for you.' She thought Lola would know what to do.

She knew when Lola's convertible parked outside her building that her neighbours would be wondering who she was. She knew too that they would ask about her. 'Who was that in the fancy car?' Lola did not disappoint. She wore a perfect business suit – crisp black linen. Her shirt was indigo and pink floral, her shoes were fringed moccasins. She never was one to conform. She ran a small fashion business and had resisted offers to expand because she needed to stay in charge. She said she hated the thought of having to design and promote something she didn't approve of.

She breezed into Anna's kitchen. 'So, what do you have for me?'

'A book,' Anna told her. 'It's a sort of memoir about your mother.' She shoved it across the table.

Lola flicked it open. 'This is full of recipes. My mother's life is recorded in a cookbook?'

'What better book? It's spattered with ingredients, grease marks of the times she lived through. It has the food she ate and the music she loved. It has margin notes to die for. Your mother was to die for.'

'I know. She was gorgeous, wasn't she?'

Anna nodded.

Lola looked through the book. 'She did an Irish jig in the High Street?'

'Yes. Sometimes, in the middle of the night, different times – there was more than one jig. He, your father, went to one end, she went up to the Castle and they hurtled towards one another. When they met, they linked arms and whirled and whirled. You couldn't do that now. Too many tourists.'

Lola smiled. 'Fabulously silly. Did you ever meet my father?'

'No. I was away at uni. I now think he didn't want to meet any of her friends. I think he wanted to keep George for himself.'

'Yes. I think so. Where did you get this?'

Anna told Lola about finding the kitchen. 'It was dismantled and put back together again in a house in Corstorphine. It's amazing. Anyway, the woman who owns the house gave it to me to give to George.'

'So why didn't you give it to her?'

'The last meal,' Anna told her.

Lola read it. 'He was saying goodbye.'

'George didn't know that. She still thinks his death was an accident. She thought he was coming back to her.'

Lola stared at her. 'What are you saying?'

Anna took a deep breath. 'Alistair killed himself. He'd been stealing, and the police were after him. He couldn't face what was happening.'

Lola stared at the book. 'My father?'

'Yes.'

For a long time, Lola didn't speak. She touched the book. She took this in. At last, she said, 'You can't tell her. That heart has been broken twice. When Alistair died and then when Willy went. She went deep into a grieving place. Let her be. She's happy right now.'

'I think I love George more than I've ever loved anybody,' Anna said.

'I know. Everybody loves George. She's something. She's been beating herself up about these few years most of her life. I think she became a nurse so she could give herself to people. If a patient was seriously sick, she'd stay with them after her shift was over, just holding their hand and chatting.'

She picked up her handbag and pulled out a photograph. 'Here's my mother and father strolling through the High Street.'

There was George, fresh-faced and smiling, hand-in-hand with an absurdly handsome young man. They were dressed in silks and satins, beads and scarves. George's hair was long and had a flower tied in at the side. He had a drooping moustache. George's skirt was skimpy. They were beautiful.

'They were a well-known couple about town. Probably the clothes. They went to clubs and gigs. People looked out for them. I get the impression people wanted to know them but they hid away. I don't think they actually had anybody round for drinks. They had each other.'

Lola smiled.

Oh my, thought Anna, *there goes my friend, marching through her little world with her flag unfurled.*

Lola stood up. Held the book close. Stroked it. 'Thanks for this. It's a treasure.'

Walking to the front door, Lola said, 'I am the result of a love affair. I always keep that in mind. It was wild and probably foolish. But I comfort myself by thinking of George and Alistair dancing and singing and tucked away from the world, living only for themselves. I love that.'

Anna opened the front door. 'It's a good way to look at it.'

Lola kissed her cheek. 'She's tired these days. Sleeps a lot.'

Anna said, 'So do I. I used to hate sleeping during the day. Now I love it. I've learned to relax at last.'

*

It had been a pleasant day. Autumnal and just right for a large warm polo neck jumper. Anna was happy. She'd met Marlon from school, and walking to Richard's they'd chatted.

'What do you think is the meaning of life?' Anna asked. She wondered what someone Marlon's age, starting out on the voyage to adulthood, work, mortgage and other bothersome things, would think.

Marlon paused briefly. 'It's when two of the boys at school are picking their football team and you get left out and you don't cry. You just pretend you don't care. That's the meaning of life. Pretending you don't care.'

Anna was impressed. 'Excellent answer.'

She'd sat on her car seat in Richard's workshop drinking tea, listening to music on his radio and rejoicing that it was now chilly enough for the log burner to be lit. Life was splendid.

Once home, she made hot chocolate and a tuna sandwich for Marlon and read her library book as he watched television. Now Marlon had been collected by his mother and Anna was alone. She was debating what to cook for tea. A boiled egg? A bacon roll?

The phone rang.

It was Lola. 'She's gone.'

'Sorry?' said Anna. 'Who's gone?'

'George. My mother. She's gone. She went for a nap this afternoon and didn't wake up. She's left us. I don't know what to do. But I had to tell you. You have to know.' She was panicked, desperate and weeping.

Anna went cold. She felt the blood rush from her face. 'George? She died? But I spoke to her yesterday. She was fine.'

'No, she wasn't. She hasn't been fine for some time. But she didn't tell us. I think she gave herself permission to leave us all after she'd seen the kitchen. But she was a nurse. She knew what was coming.'

'She died? She actually *died*?'

'Yes,' said Lola. 'I'm sorry. We are all devastated here. Just staring at one another. Don't know what to say. Emma's in bits, sobbing. We're just walking up and down, struck dumb.'

After that she had to go.

'I can't speak any longer. I'm finding it hard to breathe.'

Anna put down the phone. She sat on her sofa staring ahead and not seeing anything. Outside the world carried on. In this room, it stopped. It was seven o'clock in the evening and it was getting cold. But Anna sat. At midnight she was still sitting, still staring. She hadn't moved and she was cold, though she didn't really notice. She waited for truth and grief to take her.

*

The funeral was on a Friday. Anna calculated it would have been George's turn to provide a meal. It would have been special. On the way to the crematorium she amused herself by thinking that George had gone pretty far to avoid picking up the bill. George would have laughed. She knew that.

The place was crowded. Anna couldn't believe it. How many people had come to say goodbye? *Over a hundred*, she thought. Richard had come with her. 'Funerals can make you feel lonely,' he'd said. 'When you're saying goodbye to someone special, it's good to have a friend to see you through the day.' There was the clattering rumble of many voices and she looked around her, hoping for a familiar face. She wore her best linen trousers and black jacket over a pale blue shirt and had a large dark blue silk scarf draped round her neck. She leaned on her stick. This was going to be dreadful. She was going to weep and wail in public. She was going to call on George to come back to her. She felt lost. Richard took her hand.

Lola was at her side and guided her to the front row. 'You're one of the family. We want you to say a few words. You've known her longer than anybody here.'

'I don't think I can.'

'Please,' said Lola. 'Just a little something. George would want that.'

So Anna agreed and sat for most of the ceremony worrying and dreading the moment when her name would be called. There were no hymns. But 'Into The Mystic' hummed out. Lola stepped up and said something about a wonderful, wise mother who laughed and sang and cared. 'Who knows, she might be with her beloved Willy as I speak. Hope so. She'll be happy.' James said his ma was a one-off and could fleece him at poker. Emma couldn't speak. There were nods and voices of agreement. Lola told the crowd that George's oldest and best friend had a few words to say.

It had crossed Anna's mind to talk about the Two Yellows and the encouragement George had given her to read a poem on a bus. She thought to mention their meals and how George had waltzed in her seat in a posh restaurant and how she'd furiously insisted that her garden grow. But instead she said, 'I am so privileged to have had such a friend. What a friend. She told me to drink wine, play old songs and be happy. I'll try. But without her it will be hard.'

Nina Simone sang 'Feelin' Good'. But, right then, nobody did.

There was a gathering afterwards. People milled about, talking, reminiscing. Wine was poured and downed. Anna sat on the sidelines, looking on. In the end she went outside and sat on a bench in the grounds, holding her empty glass and staring as she had stared on the night she'd been told of George's death.

Richard found her. Gently took the glass and put it on the bench. 'I'll drive you home.'

It was a quick journey through back streets. Anna looked out of the window and felt loneliness and grief coming for her. She said nothing.

'Will you be all right?' asked Richard.

'No,' said Anna. 'But I'll try. I don't think I really know how to be all right. How do you go on without your friend?'

38

There's an Amazing Thing

The year moved on. The winter was cruel. Anna and Marlon walked the short distance from the school to Richard's workshop bent against stinging rain, wind curling wildly round them. It snowed and their feet froze. Their faces were nipped by icy blasts. Marlon stepped ahead and led the way.

The boat he and Richard were building got bigger. In time they'd take it to the pond and sail it. 'A trip,' said Richard. 'We'll take supplies. Crisps and biscuits.'

Anna taught Marlon silly poems and took him to the cinema. They shared popcorn and loved the warmth and the dark and the unfolding story on the screen in front of them.

The walks to and from school strengthened Anna's hip. She could manage without her stick but took it everywhere just in case she needed it. She noted she was doing well. And when spring came she forced herself to go out without her favourite woolly layer between herself and the world.

Richard came by for tea and conversation. Sometimes she cooked him a meal, sometimes he cooked her a meal and sometimes they ate out. They shared jokes and songs.

Anna missed her friend. There were times when she'd think of George and clutch her stomach, bend double and say, 'Oh.' There were days when she did not want to leave the flat. She needed to sit still, stare ahead and mourn. She knew George would disapprove.

But today she went out into the sunshine and walked down the street. She noticed she'd said hello many times before she got to the corner. She'd greeted Mother Dainty, Mrs Raincoat, and a new couple who looked interesting. The woman had blue hair and the man a ponytail. Anna called them Mr and Mrs Vegan. She greeted Swagger Boy and Lil. He'd passed his driving test. She was pregnant.

Anna congratulated herself on living like a normal human being and not someone who hid from the world and dreamed. *Well*, she thought, *things change. Things shift and move on. As if anything lasts for ever*.

She said hello again. Old Dungarees was shuffling up his drive, pulling his bin. He grunted a return greeting. 'Just going to get a few things from the shop,' she told him. He grunted again.

Then she saw Richard walking towards her. He waved and speeded up. She smiled wildly and waved back. And there it was, a sudden spark of happiness. She thought, *There's an amazing thing*.